AS

BELOW

LYNZEE SCHOTT

1

200 Bicentennial Bash!

Leave it to the citizens in Foxtrot to design such a terrible banner. The two is crooked, arguably a z. One of the zeros is torn, the other sharing a mystery splotch in the center. It's wrinkled, worn, and downright redundant. Judging by the stellar decorations, it's supposed to be quirky, but it's more of an eyesore. Considering I won't be around in the next ninety-nine years, I'll go ahead and name the next one the *300 Tricentennial Tombstone!*

The bicentennial is a few weeks away, and it'll be my first and last time witnessing this milestone—if it's worth celebrating at all. Humankind might've been better off extinct with everything else on the surface. Our meddling with Mother Nature seems to have brought with it a curse of complacency.

Two centuries on the seafloor, wow. Without the tens of thousands of us living in this underwater city, Foxtrot would cease to exist. What a *shame* that would be. Why, yes! I'll join in on the festivities with a room-temperature beverage. I'd love a second helping of overcooked noodles and factory-made meat, thanks for asking. Let's dance and sing as if we aren't marking another century at the bottom of the Atlantic Ocean. Oh, is that a party horn? If I blow with all my might, it'll drown the dread ringing in my ears. This historical event is enough to make me want to twist a knife through my—

"Samara, you seem tense."

Past my clearing tunnel vision, Mason steps into view, palming his crew cut fade with a shit-eating grin on his face. I give him one right back. "For the love of the Atlantic, why did you cut off all your hair? Here I was thinking you couldn't be more hideous."

Raising his right hand to his brow, fingers extended and palm facing down in the salute, he straightens his posture. "At least now you know what you'd look like if you shaved most of your hair."

"Unlike you, I could pull it off." I run my palms across his prickly temples, catching a glimpse of a folded piece of paper in his saluting hand. "What's that?" He shrugs, a coy gleam shining in his eyes. I advance a step, reaching to grab hold of the paper. "What are you hiding in your hand?"

He steps back, clasping his hands together like the maddening, younger-by-three-minute brother he is. Unfolding the paper, he clears his throat. "Dear Mason Quinn, this correspondence serves as confirmation that you've been satisfactory in the training program. Your hard work and eagerness to protect all sectors have been apparent. Report to Watchman Perry in two shifts at 0800, and all remaining shifts after that. He will brief you on your first assignment. We welcome you, Watchman."

Caught in a limbo of rolling my eyes to the back of my head or stealing the paper from him and ripping it to shreds, I hide my disapproval and swallow a retort, indulging him with an embrace. "You're officially a Watchman. Congratulations, shithead."

He's been training in the academy these last six months, hoping to become a Watchman and take after our adopted father Jerald, but I haven't given any real thought to whether he'd be accepted. Mason may be tall, slender, and somewhat awkward, but he's pleasant to be around. He's not a well-built machine willing to take commands like a single-celled organism. Jerald had been the exception to that putrid standard, and I suppose now Mason is too.

We may be cut from the same cloth, but the duality of being a twin is that we're opposite sides of the same coin. Mason has earned the *heads* side of the coin since he leans toward responsibility, while I've adopted the *tails* side simply because being enigmatic is much more fun than being pragmatic.

"Sam, why are you here?" He cuts the hug short, motioning to the outskirts of the Husk I was moments away from entering until he found me.

Trading hub, market, Husk—it's all the same word, and the only trading section in the entire facility. Some long-ago Warden tried banning it once, but there was pushback. To remind everyone who was in charge since he couldn't have his way, he renamed it the *Husk*, declaring it to be a dried-out, worthless, outer layer of Sector Four. I'm sure he meant for it to be demeaning, but the citizens have coined the slander as a term of endearment. Need anything at all? Food, recycled clothing, spices, gadgets, outlawed items, secrets, and anything in between? Go to the Husk.

"The better question is, how did you know I was here?" I fire back, rerouting the conversation to think of a lie to offer him. Damn that banner. If I hadn't been gawking at it, I would've disappeared into the crowd. My steps were careful, my path to get here planned out. I deviated from our usual route by cutting behind residential buildings and the library. Mason isn't supposed to be here.

"I was waiting for you out front of the school to show you my acceptance letter, but you did your *I'm on a mission* walk, so I followed you. And here we are. What's going on?"

"Care to demonstrate?" I turn away from him and the Husk with exaggerated steps to lead us away, but his familiar presence at my side is absent. I sigh. "I needed to clear my head, so I went on a walk." My half-truth spins me on my heels. He's staring at me, his head cocked. I can tell from his eyes, the same mahoganies flecked with the same shades of green we share, that he knows I'm evading. "I'm going to trade something," I confess, forfeiting the bottle of homemade nail polish to his open palm.

Pressing his lips together with knitted eyebrows, he examines the glistening blue liquid. "And what would you be trading this for?"

I take the nail polish from him, internally shaking off the unwanted anxiety. "Listen, shithead. I don't have to explain myself to you. Since I can't snap my fingers to make you disappear, I'm trading this for *lady items* if you must know." A deflected white lie, but a harmless one.

Dropping eye contact to fidget with the middle finger on his right hand, he absentmindedly massages it with his thumb and pointer finger from his left. He's thinking. His nervous tell is minimal and over within a millisecond, but I've memorized it. "Lady items?"

He believes what I'm saying. I don't have time to overthink before blurting out, "The good news about being a man is you don't have to worry about lady items."

With a final attempt at a stare-down, he relents, beckoning me to enter the Husk with him. I wasn't planning on the company; this task would be simpler if I were alone. But if I change course, he'll question it, and I can't afford to have him questioning me right now. Reinforcing the ruse, I fall into step beside him.

Closest to the windows, a merchant with blankets and quilts for trade stands behind a new booth. Foxtrot is coldest next to the windows, near the dark, empty water. Other stations have blinked offline over the decades, but hopefully, there are some left out there. But maybe Alpha through Zulu weren't meant to survive underwater this long.

My fingers run through the deep purples and forest greens woven together in the soft, recycled blanket. "These are beautiful." The onyx quilt with splatters of bumblebee-yellow is especially wonderful, but I doubt she cares what a bumblebee was. "What will you trade for this one?"

Leaning over the stand, the woman gestures to the blanket. Her lips part in anticipation of a response, but the man seated behind her stands up, grabs her by the waist, and pulls her away. She flashes me a careful smile, playfully trying to wriggle free from his grasp. His forearms glide across her collarbone, tugging against her pull enough to wrinkle the skin on her chest. He whispers something into her ear, and the light in her eyes dim.

Her arms fall to her sides, a cluster of bruises dappling her wrists—too many for an accident—before her long sleeves conceal them. She shakes her head, flicking her palm outward at me.

"Get out of here," the man warns me.

Mason appears at my side. "What's going on?"

"I'd love to trade for one of these quilts," I tread, directing my comment to the woman. "What sort of currency do you take? I have batteries, ration cards, and nail polish. Would you like to see what colors I have?"

Not waiting for *his* response, I set my backpack on the table and unzip it, sifting through it.

"I told you to get out of here," the man repeats. "We have the right to refuse service to anyone."

Men like him are too common in Foxtrot. A superiority complex where men are strong, women are weak, woman do what man say. I stopped listening to them long ago. "I don't believe I was speaking to you sir, but I'm curious—do you refuse the right to serve anyone, or women in particular?" I hold his stare for as long as he holds mine. When he breaks it, I ask the woman, "What's your favorite color? I might have polish already made."

She turns to face the man, her head bowed, shoulders hunched. "Am I allowed to—"

"—Hurry up and get her out of here. I don't have time for this shit," he huffs, retreating to the seat behind her. "Don't touch a quilt, girl," he says to me from the shadows. "You're not a customer."

"Orange," she whispers to me.

"Orange? Fantastic choice. I have three here." I put them on the table. "Which one do you like best?"

Her fingertips hover over the three options in front of her, narrowing the decision down to two. She picks up the neon, holding it close to her face to examine the shimmer, then sets it back down, mimicking the same with the blood-orange.

"You don't have to pick one," I tell her. "You can have them both." I place them in her palm. Her smile meets mine, genuine and wholesome.

The man's footsteps are silent until he's beside her. Until she's shoved to the ground, her knees knocking against the floor.

"I don't need your charity," he seethes. "I don't need you giving her extra things and I end up owing you back later. I'm doing fine. She gets *one* of these polishes." He slams the neon to the ground, oil, pigments, and wax exploding onto the woman and her quilts. "Now get lost, or I'll get a Watchman and see to it you sink."

Growing up in the system, I've learned a few things about life. Like how to not take shit and how to not give a shit. Living in a nest of vipers from infancy until the age of nine was a jarring experience, full of mental and physical abuse. Hands were allowed on bodies that were not theirs to touch, and I fought back. With nails, teeth, and anything within reach, because people need to keep their unwanted hands to themselves. People like him get away with it, and those bruises on her arms are my invitation.

I've picked up enough to know this man is a brute. His hands go on her body to discipline and shame her. He believes she is his, and she doesn't get a voice. If there is anything in Foxtrot I despise more than living in this god-forsaken facility, is when men take possession and claim women to be *theirs*.

My knuckles crush against his nose—once, twice. He lets out a yelp, his head snapping back. I sweep his awkward movement with my right leg. He lands hard on his tailbone, and I kick him in the groin for good measure.

The woman stands, her attention flashing between me and the man, electricity gathering behind her eyes. "Please, go. I will handle this." She hands me the quilt.

Shoving it into my backpack, I place the blood-orange polish back into her palms. "Nobody gets to touch you. You matter." She nods and nods, the man stumbling to stand.

"You matter," I repeat.

"Sam, let's go," Mason says, tugging me to follow him past booths. He holds back a nervous laugh in his chest. "Please tell me what the hell you were thinking."

I shake off the pain in my wrist, glancing back to the merchant's booth. To the man cupping his bloody nose and the woman yelling something fierce at him and storming off. "Assholes don't get to be assholes without getting punched in the face now and again."

"You can't go around assaulting people."

"Why not? He does."

"You don't *know* that, Sam."

"I do know."

"What if someone reports this to a Watchman? Do you have a depth-wish?"

Such a logical thing to say. Will he ever learn that it's more entertaining to be unpredictable? "Oh no, a woman with raven-black hair punched a merchant in the nose, she went that way." I point to all the women in the line of sight with dark hair. "You know as well as I do that Watchmen hardly patrol this area. Besides, the Husk has a few hundred people in it at any given time. I know how to get lost in the crowd."

"You're not lying to me about why we're here, are you? You need to get some lady items and nothing else?" he asks, passing the stand for spirits.

I stop at the booth, examining the green liquid inside the jar. Flagging down the merchant's attention, I make a twisting motion with my hands and point to my nose. He approves with a friendly nod. It's citrusy with a hint of cream—and mint?

"Yes, Mason." I sigh, setting down the jar. "I'm here for lady items, nothing else."

Is it considered a lie if it's safer not to admit something? Mason would argue that's manipulative, but I'm protecting him. A newly established Watchman doesn't need to be swept into my mess. There's a difference between a lie and a well-planted truth.

The section of the Husk dedicated to women is a section Mason has clearly never stepped foot in, considering he's pretending to be interested in a jar of dried beans at the adjacent stand. He picks up a jar, turns it upside down, then right-side up. I discreetly meander to the booth for women's needs.

"Maeve," I whisper to the merchant.

Maeve pulls me in for a hug from across the booth, her long dread-locked hair whipping my shoulder with the sudden movement. "Samara, please tell me you were able to make me a blue one." I dig through my backpack and retrieve it for her. Her energy fills the booth with a feeling of warm syrup. "It's too wonderful. Thank you so much."

I glance back at Mason picking up a jar of dried cranberries, silently thanking the Atlantic he's distracted, and level my voice to a whisper. "Something else came up. Can you help me with one more thing?"

Mason's still at the dried foods stand studying dehydrated carrots. He sets the jar down with a heavy hand, nearly knocking over the others on the table, then taps the top of the lid. "Are we leaving now?" He doesn't bother to turn around.

I wave the clean, sanitary napkins I didn't need in his face to lighten his mood. His cheeks flush red, and I slip them into my backpack, mentally noting he bought the distraction. Half-truth, partial truth, planted truth, it's all the same.

I didn't *lie* to Mason.

I do need lady items—eventually. And I did come here to trade with Maeve. It so happened I also needed proof of lady items because of him, and an upcycled ring was all I had left to offer. I adored that ring and wore it every shift, but Mason didn't *need* to know I came here to trade nail polish for a name.

I change the subject before he asks any more questions. "We have a couple more hours to burn before it's lights-out. What do you want to do?"

Considering my question, he cracks his knuckles. "Do you want to stop by the library?"

I shake my head. "Sort of in a reading slump."

"What about the commissary?"

"Do we have enough ration cards? I'll be getting mine in a few shifts."

He shakes his head, hands sliding into his pockets. "What about the museum?"

"The museum? I haven't been there since I was a girl. Do you think Warden Calum Gryme's portrait has been added yet? Or does he have to die first before it makes it in there?" He doesn't meet my shit-eating grin. The museum. Not like any of the displays have been swapped out. There are only so many natural disasters to portray. "Earthquake simulator," I say in a spooky voice, wiggling my fingers in the air. "Volcanic eruptions and wildfires!"

"Then what's your great idea?"

"It's not that it's a bad idea, Mason. But if you've seen it once, you've seen it a thousand times. I'll take my second-graders there soon. How does that sound?"

"Sounds like we're back to figuring out what we're doing before lights-out."

Ah, the monotony of Foxtrot. Go to work, go home, go to sleep. Wake up and do it all again. Grab something to eat if you have enough ration cards in your pocket or head to the library to read the same books over and over. Don't forget to visit the museum, where you can be reminded of everything that almost killed humankind. Feeling extra existential? Stop by the Arboretum and look through the glass at everything you're not allowed to experience firsthand.

This bunker had a simple beauty to it when I was younger—when I didn't see it through adult eyes. Back then, this facility made sense because I didn't know there was an alternative. Now it's a constant, dull reminder.

Despite the starfish-inspired layout, the massive tunnels make the fuzzy feeling of confinement only a *little* claustrophobic. The relentless hum of fluorescent lights *can* be cozy and not unbearable if you learn to tune them out. And the windows framing the inky expanse aren't *always* ominous, so long as you don't stare out them too long.

Turning down Sec-Five, I crane my head back, taking in the buildings. "Are you still afraid of heights, or did training at the academy make you numb to it?" I give him a playful elbow.

He puts on a show of stumbling around, elbowing me back. "That is not going to happen. Besides, we haven't been up there in years."

He hasn't been up there in years. I sneak to the top of our apartment complex whenever I can't sleep. It's quiet up there. It makes me feel small, somehow. All my worries go silent. It's comforting.

Guess we're watching reruns until lights-out. Again.

2

I enjoy children, but having any of my own is far from appealing. It's selfish to bring a child into this glorified steel coffin, full of circulated oxygen and the stagnant decay of hope. Still, I've dedicated my life to teaching our youth to be educated, express themselves, and chase their dreams. Well, so long as their goals and dreams follow the Warden's constrained standards.

"Miss Samara, how come we can only see the Arboretum through the glass? Why can't we go inside?" my new second-grade student asks with a raised hand.

Three shifts ago, the Sector Two Watchmen found her screaming on her doorstep. Authorities said her mother succumbed to an unforeseen Indicator, dying from self-inflicted wounds. With the elementary school in Sec-Two at capacity and no living relatives, she's been placed in the foster program pending adoption, and temporarily assigned to my class.

"That is an excellent question, Wren. Who can help me answer why we aren't allowed inside the Arboretum?" I ask the class.

"It's because we don't have beepers," a student yells from the back of the class.

"No, it's because we're not s'posed to," another says.

I cut in before the bickering starts. "You're both correct! But we are lucky to be able to see the Arboretum through the glass from the main corridor. Who can remind me where the main corridor is?"

"In the middle!" the students yell in unison.

"In the middle? Middle of what?" I plant a hand on my hip, the other tapping my chin.

"Of all the sectors!"

"Of course, of course. How silly of me." I cross my arms, blowing wisps of hair from my face. "And remind me again, how many sectors do we have in total?"

"Five, five, five!" Little giggles slip out in between their chant.

"You all are too smart. You must have a good teacher. Let's settle down and open our Foxtrot Studies. Turn to page—"

"—How come I'm not important enough to go inside?" Wren crosses her arms, her brows wrinkled. "I see people inside sometimes, they're wearing those funny yellow suits. How come I can't get a suit and go inside like them? Why can't I stomp on the leaves or pick the berries? How come I can't listen to the creek or lay in the grass?"

"To answer your question," I begin, but pause to think. She's too young to understand, but questioning anything outside of the *norm* is a depth-wish. Everything is what it is without further explanation. It is because of what happened to the surface, and the Warden makes the rules how he sees fit. End of discussion.

Though only a fear, it feels as if Warden Calum Gryme's piercing eyes are on me through the surveillance camera in the classroom, waiting to see if I answer the classroom-approved way. As much as I'd like to entertain her curiosity, I have no desire to be placed in the Vat, awaiting the deep.

"Warden Gryme is in charge of who can go inside the Arboretum. The ones who enter it have to have special permission first, but only certain adults can go in to take care of all the trees and plants." I fumble through my response for teacher-appropriate answers.

"When you grow up, maybe you can be a part of that team, too. Trust me when I say this Wren, you *are* important. Even if you're not wearing a funny yellow banana suit." I smile, but her eye roll is her only response as the end of the school-shift bell rings.

"Remember, next shift, we're going on a field trip to the museum in Sector One. Have your parents sign your permission slips," I call out to the kids while they gather their backpacks, but I doubt they heard me.

Through all the movement, Wren stands awkwardly at her desk, holding what little possessions she has in her arms, patiently waiting to leave as the kids rush past her.

Emptying the contents from my satchel onto my desk, I approach her with an honest smile. "You can borrow it until your new pack gets here."

She brushes my offer aside with a wave of her hand, tears filling her eyes. "My mom made a knapsack for me. She *made* it for me. She sewed it together with my favorite colors. But it's in my room, at my home where my mom died. The Watchmen said I don't live there anymore, and I can't go back to get it. They told me no one can get it for me because it's *off limits.* All my things are there. I've lived there my whole life, so how come I can't go back? I don't know anything else. I don't have anything of mine anymore. I don't have *anyone.* Guess I can't go on the field trip since I don't have any parents to sign the permission slip." Her copper ponytail is lost in the crowd of students before I can dislodge the lump in my throat.

Placing my personal items back into my satchel, the pain that Wren is feeling resonates deep in my bones. The heartache that comes with longing for a stable home is a harsh, muted hope. It's a numbing pain that whispers eternal solitude.

My hurt cauterized when a couple gained custody of Mason and me and saved us from the system. Ruth and Jerald adopted us and opened their hearts to us as if we were their own. They recognized how damaged we both were and still had enough patience to help us through our self-destructive ways and soothed us after a drift.

Ask anyone in Foxtrot what *drifting* is, and they'll say it happens during a sleep shift and that it's the opposite of dreaming. That dreaming is wonderful and full of magic, but drifting is insidious and full of terror.

Night and *day* became foreign to everyone in Foxtrot; how could we understand the words behind descriptions we'd never seen? How could the sensation of sourness be described to someone who has only ever had sweetness?

Nightmares were renamed to *drifts* to erase the strange word from history, but after Jerald told me its origin, I enjoyed the word so much that I kept it for myself.

Nightmares are the creative monsters who live deep inside my frontal lobe. I've yet to discover a remedy for remaining at rest instead of jolting awake. It seems the older I become, the more I'm drawn to them. I've learned to co-exist alongside them, but my recurring nightmare as a child paralyzed me, and I dreaded falling asleep.

Whenever I closed my eyes, they'd explode from within their sockets, and warm brain matter rolled down my cheeks. I'd fall to my knees and pound at the floor until a second me lucidly appeared, and my first body melted into a pile of keys. The undamaged me would walk to the pile of keys, select one at random, and face a padlocked, spiraling doorway. She'd place the key in the hole and turn it until it clicked, but I'd wake up before I could ever enter through the doorway.

Mason once confided in me that his recurring nightmare consisted of being sewn together, barely held together by a thread thinner than hair. He'd struggle helplessly against an unknown attacker, but his body would separate into bloody pieces. The assailant picked up his limbs, torso, and head and set them into jars of water. Before he drowned, he'd wake up.

One shift, we woke up screaming in unison, found each other through the darkness of our room, and huddled together.

"Sam, it happened again—my whole body fell apart."

My fingers combed through his inky-black hair. "It was only a drift, and you're safe. It's not real. It's never real."

His innocent nine-year-old frame was weightless as it pressed against my own shaking body, burning an inescapable sense of existential dread into my core while we waited for Ruth and Jerald to comfort us like they always did.

"Did you have those awful drifts again?" Ruth had asked, wiping away our tears.

Jerald leaned into the doorway, his silver eyes finding mine. "Can I read you a Grand Story?"

No matter how afraid I felt after a nightmare, my answer was to hear a story, as was Mason's at first. After a while, the stories began to bore him, and he and Ruth played card games or opted for baking odds and ends to rid him of the fear he felt after his nightmare.

"Once upon the surface when the sun went to sleep, stars shared the sky with the moon, and there used to be night," Jerald had read from a handwritten journal.

With his rhythmic voice and emphasis on the strange words, so much mystery came behind whatever suns, stars, skies, and moons were. I dreamt of what true daylight and nighttime felt like instead of being reminded that the only source of light Foxtrot provides is manufactured. Programmed to power on for sixteen hours for a wakeful shift, then power off for a sleep shift for the rest.

Of course, it's difficult to imagine a world with natural light created by the sun and natural darkness created from its absence, not fluorescent lights buzzing from the ceiling. Still, Jerald promised me such a thing existed.

No matter how many times I had already heard any of his Grand Stories, he'd patiently repeat them, filling me with wonder each time. But on one sleep shift, he had a book I had never seen before—a book with images and texts dedicated to the surface, with pages of daylight and nighttime. We weren't allowed to talk about the book outside the four of us, but as Mason and I traced pictures into our own journals, we laughed about how otherworldly the animals had been.

I've tried to find that book in the library these last few weeks, but it's been in vain. I can't ask a librarian for help without sinking for it, and Ruth has been so lost lately that I haven't found the courage to bring up another memory.

Jerald had explained everything he learned about the surface from that book, into the galaxies and beyond, and I dreamt of insects, planets, and everything in between.

"Can I go live up there, Jerry?" I asked.

"Of course you can, my little bug. But not yet. You need to be able to fly first."

"What does flying have to do with anything? I don't even know how to swim."

"You can learn to do both. When you're older and

stronger, I'll show you the sun, the moon, the stars, and true night. We'll all go together," he promised.

3

As if I'm the moon and Mason is the tide, he's waiting for me outside the school. "Do you have another letter to show me, or are we stuck talking about normal things?" I ask him. If he was a miserable person to be around, I'd find a way to ditch him every chance I got. But he's my favorite person. Who needs friends when you have a twin.

"No letters this time." He matches my stride, progressing through Sec-Five. "We could talk about what foods we need to pick up at the commissary or which rerun to watch."

I sigh, my thoughts too busy to entertain the normalcy. "My new student is grieving her mother. I don't know how to help her, and I wish that I did. I'd trade everything I own if it meant I could take that pain from her." I kick an empty fizzy-can to the side.

"That's pretty heavy, Sam. Are you doing okay?"

"I'd be lying if I said her pain doesn't hit close. Losing a parent, no matter the age, is a type of grief that makes you question yourself. It makes you question what you're capable of overcoming. I hope she has the support she needs."

The commotion ahead of us stops his response from leaving his lips. We pay heed to two Watchmen escorting a man in zip ties to a Watchman shuttle outside of our apartment complex.

"Looks like they caught Deranged Desmond," Mason says coldly. The daggers in my eyes pierce him.

Strands of Desmond's snowy hair fall free from his bun, hiding some of his heat-flushed face. His usual jeans are newly ripped at the knees, and his shirt is dusty across his chest. Did Desmond resist arrest—or did the two Watchmen force him to the ground.

Being homeless is illegal, but Desmond has been a well-kept secret in the neighborhood for some time now, which is surprising since extra ration cards are dangled for anyone tempted to report a crime. But Desmond hasn't been a nuisance, he mostly keeps to himself. Rambling about some odd thing or another. He may be a little deranged, but he's polite and, unfortunately, of Indicating age.

When I finally learned the truth of how Foxtrot maintains population control, vexation burrowed deep in my bones and never left. A one-way ticket to being a victim of the ocean is narrowed down to two options: be a criminal or have an Indicator. It's a choice to be a criminal but not to have an Indicator.

In simple terms and according to the Warden, an Indicator means someone isn't worth the trouble of keeping alive. If someone needs consistent medication for any disease, requires a complex surgery, has a difficult, terminal, or chronic illness, or suffers from any kind of mental health disorder, like Desmond, they're considered irreparable and placed in the Vat. Fortunately, anxiety is "allowed"—seems most of the population can't avoid it—but Atlantic-forbid a child is born with a chromosomal condition. The Warden has the infants placed into tiny, clear caskets to serve a life sentence before theirs can start.

There's an awful place in Sector One where anyone considered a criminal or has a verified Indicator is held awaiting the deep. Once placed in the Vat, all anyone can do is wait to die. No one knows how to swim or how to stop their lungs from collapsing from the immense pressure of the ocean. The people in the Vat remind the rest of us who dare witness a sinking that there are rules and a system for a reason, but I struggle to find that purpose.

When the opportunity arises, the Warden pulls an emergency release lever conveniently located in his office, never facing the cruel reality he's condemned with his vulgar display of power. Within minutes of pulling the lever, anyone in the Vat is sucked into the ocean, on display through the half-moon Observatory, struggling in vain to stay alive. Mason believes I'm morbid because I purposely watch sinkings, but I can only hope if I were to die horribly and alone, someone with kind eyes would be there to help share that brief burden, even if there's nothing they could do to stop it.

The requirements to survive may be strict, but all you

have to do is what you're told because even with population control, the Warden can't allow Foxtrot to become extinct. Where would his power come from if there was no one left alive? All you have to do is what they say. No fault in that system.

The practice of remanding Indicators is nefarious, but the most widely accepted Indicator is once someone reaches the too-soon age of seventy. There are no resources to care for senior citizens, and the Vat patiently awaits their enforced surrender. Judging by the appearance and erratic behavior in front of me, Desmond stands accused of the crime of homelessness and has two Indicators: senior age and mental health. But that doesn't mean he has no right to live.

"There is life," Desmond wildly shouts at no one. "Up, up, and up. You must go up!"

Mason and I simultaneously halt our movement, allowing the Watchmen more space to work. Desmond loses his footing, tripping at my feet. From his back and through a gray, wiry beard, he whispers, "Go up."

Uneasiness tenses through my shoulders. The Watchmen lift him and place him into the shuttle, leaving me unable to shake the wildness in his eyes.

A Watchman wearing black gloves slams the shuttle door shut with unnecessary force. Through the small window, Desmond shoulder thrusts the back door, but the attempt at escaping leads to a cascade of emotions. One moment, he's laughing and mouthing something to me once more. The next, he's crying and screaming, all sound staying with him in his death-sentenced shuttle. The vehicle pulls away, and he finds my sympathetic eyes for the last time and points up.

"What did he say to you?" Mason asks, picking up our pace.

I pull open the double doors of our building, the tension tight on my skin passing through the lobby. The confusion in my voice is impossible to hide. "I think he said, *go up*."

Mason rests his hand on top of my head, patting it lightly. It's something silly he used to do and hasn't done since we were kids, but it's comforting, nonetheless. Once he hit his growth spurt and skyrocketed in height, he would tease that when he touched the top of my head, he could see my brain and read my thoughts. He must have felt my nerves.

He presses twenty-one for our floor and humors me. "Well, we are going up."

"What do you think he meant by that? Go up?"

"I don't know if any of what he said ever made sense. I think he was Deranged Desmond for a reason, and it's as easy as that." He's not interested in this conversation. He has a bad habit of prematurely ending our discussions and knows I don't like it when he does it.

Still, I'm left with my thoughts until the elevator stops on the fifteenth floor. An older woman with opalescent hair shuffles into the elevator, pressing the button for the first floor.

"We're still going up, but we're only a few floors away.

It looks like you're stuck with us," I joke, admiring the glow surrounding her.

"Oh, don't fuss over me. I enjoy the company." She waves her hand, a calm silence encasing us as we ascend. "I heard my friend Desmond yelling from outside my window. Did you see him while you were out front?" The innocence in her voice fills the elevator. She looks directly at me as if knowing I have the answer.

Wedged between a dividing line of admitting what happened or being dishonest, I lose eye contact to think. I should lie to her. Warping the truth is better than explaining it. I could tell her someone else had been shouting outside her window because that's not hard to believe. But what if she saw it was Desmond? Then she'll know I'm lying, and I'm not sure it's worth the trouble. My silver tongue isn't in the mood for games.

I'm still shaken from Desmond's hickory eyes locked onto mine. As if he were thinking of countless things to say, but was on borrowed time and didn't know what to say first. Or if he should at all. Or maybe he was simply deranged, I'll never know. What I don't want to give is an avoidable lie to this woman. If someone I knew had been detained, I'd want to know.

Deciding against the easier choice of lying to her to move past it, I clear my throat, keeping my voice quiet. "We passed Desmond on the way in. Watchmen put him in zip ties."

Her voice shakes, from anger or sorrow, there's no

way to tell. "That's a shame. I've known Desmond for decades. He's never bothered anyone. I suppose madness will overcome a person surrounded by such unnecessary death." A trembling finger rests on her lips. She holds a vacant stare, as if she too is thinking of countless things to say. "He used to be a writer, you know. Before his mind became ... occupied," she continues, as if remembering where she was. "He wrote beautiful stories that filled journals, and he gave them to me to keep safe after he lost his home. He knew I'd never lose them. They were particularly important. It breaks my heart he'll be sunk." She sweeps away a tear from her cheek.

The space in the elevator is cramped and delicate, as if any movement will send us hurtling into a universe full of white noise. Anxiety is a wonderful friend of mine, and I don't know how to respond.

She's grieving the loss of her friend by way of this conversation, the least I can do is give her company. Besides, I love stories. I'm interested in what *Deranged Desmond* would have written about, though if the stories are anything like his usual bouts of paranoia or of cameras being hidden inside mashed potatoes, I'll have to swallow the laugh.

I keep my voice sensitive. "What kind of stories?" My knuckles cover my mouth to hide an impending smirk, my ribcage meeting a loaded swat from Mason. He's shaking his head, warning me to back off, reminding me to leave it alone. I give him a scowl and a middle finger.

"All sorts of stories," the woman continues, unfazed by

my grunt of pain. "Stories about the surface that will be lost once I'm gone, sadly. I only have a year left before I reach Indicating age." She gives an unprompted downward nod, a hint of despair lingering on her lips.

My jaw turns slack. What did she say?

"Of the surface?" I blurt out. "Are you saying Desmond wrote about the surface?"

We are taught that the surface is the past and Foxtrot is the now. This is all there is, this is all we need, and there is nothing more, it just is. But what this is right now? This conversation? It only makes sense in a way it shouldn't.

"What unit do you live in?" I ask before she can respond. "I can stop by, and we could—"

The elevator comes to a halt. Mason shoves me through the open doors to the hallway of our level. I wrangle myself from his grasp and make eye contact with the strange woman, who gives another downward nod as the doors close.

"Why can't you leave well enough alone? You made her cry, Samara. Why do you always have to keep pushing people?" His normally cautious eyes turn to stone.

"She needed someone to talk to, can't you see that?" *Deflect, deflect, deflect.* "She said Desmond was her friend, and she was clearly upset. There are other people here besides you and me, you know. You should be more neighborly. I'd think twice before putting your hands on me again, Mason. I bite."

The nerve he has to physically remove me from the

elevator. He knows, he *knows* I don't like being touched by force. He knows the trauma I've buried and the memories I couldn't burn.

"You're telling me that had nothing to do with her mentioning a journal that sounds like the stories Jerald used to tell us? Because I thought you wanted to keep making her cry since you're still obsessed with those stories, and maybe Deranged Desmond wrote the same shit. Am I getting any warmer?" His slice of attitude is impenetrable.

The whole walk through the empty hallway full of peeling wallpaper, cracked concrete flooring, and dusty fake plants on crumbling wooden shelves, I try collecting my thoughts to form a calm response for him, but all I can think about is his audacity.

He unlocks our front door and, in an effort to redeem himself, turns to me with regret-filled eyes. "I'm sorry. I didn't mean for it to come out like that. I loved Jerald, but I knew they were stories. Sometimes I wonder if you knew that too."

With a stone-cold stare, I open my palm to the ceiling, motioning for the keys. "I'm going to check the mail." Without a fight, he places the keys in my hand and enters the apartment.

My legs have a mind of their own, carrying me back to the elevator. I repeatedly press the button to open it. The soft chime rings, and I stagger through the doors, pressing the level one button, hoping no one else is summoning the elevator.

If I can swindle the woman into telling me her unit number, I'll circle back and wait for her outside her front door. Discussing anything about the surface in a public setting is a depth-wish. But what if she doesn't want to tell me more? What if that was all she had to say.

It doesn't matter—I need to see those journals. I'll get her unit number, and if she doesn't want to talk to me more, I'll try again on another shift. Or come back during a sleep shift and sneak into—*what am I thinking? What am I doing? What the hell am I doing?*

Watching the numbers slowly count down to one, I calm myself and exhale deeply once the doors open. She's standing at the communal post box where all our housing numbers are on display, her mailbox open. She stands nearby, sorting through it.

I casually approach her and stop, pretending to find the right key for my mailbox, reminding myself not to hover as I steal a glance at her unit number. Quick inventory, and I'll make a plan later.

"Floor 15, unit 7," she says under her breath without straying from sorting.

"What's that now?"

"Aren't you looking for my unit number so you can break in to find Desmond's journals?"

I'm unprepared for a conversation. I can't let her hear the deceit stuck in my teeth. "Ma'am, that is a bold statement and quite the accusation. Breaking and entering is a serious crime, one that would send me to the Vat within hours. In

case you aren't able to see properly, I'm checking my mail."
My hands are steady, holding up the post key as evidence.

"Oh. In that case, I think we both know the post boxes
for floors twenty through thirty are over on that shelf."
She tilts her head to the side. "Weren't you going to the
twenty-first floor with your brother?"

She must've seen the illuminated button in the elevator
showing what floor we live on, but how does she know
Mason is my brother? I suppose our neighbors could've
heard our countless squabbles in the lobby or elevator over
the years we've lived here.

"I was going to the twenty-first floor with him, but
remembered my other neighbor Mr. Sawyer had asked me
to …" I clear my throat, searching for the lie. "He asked me
to—"

"—You're Jerald's girl, aren't you?" She discards her
mail to the nearby shelf, her hazel-green eyes full of love and
pain. I nod in confusion. "Floor 15, Unit 7," she repeats.
"I'm going out for a bit to see an old friend. Since you're no
longer breaking in, I can tell you that Desmond's journals are
in a tin on top of the fridge." She gently hands me the key to
her apartment. "Deadbolt it when you're finished, and tell
your mother Ruth that Sonia says hello."

4

"Floor 15, Unit 7," I repeat aloud, willing myself not to forget. In hindsight, taking the stairs to the fifteenth floor was a poor decision, but after Sonia left, my mind took off at a gallop, and I couldn't stand still any longer waiting for the elevator.

On the fifth-floor landing, I pause to catch my breath. Another perk of living underwater means the fluorescent lights and circulated oxygen breed generations of weaker bodies, I'm sure of it. Long forgotten are the ancestors with natural strength and hearty growth.

I read somewhere that the Husk was modeled after a 'football field' blueprint, roughly a hundred yards. If I were to jog the length of it, I'd be winded. Who am I to take fifteen flights of stairs?

The chipping steel on the handrail floods the cement-enclosed area with a stale stench of rust. I stare at the concrete staircase above, questioning if the hesitation is because I'm not up for the challenge or if it's worth trying. I wipe my sweating palms on my pants, taking a few steps back to the level below.

My *heads* side of the coin spins and spins with logic: Circle back to the elevator and take it to the fifteenth floor. Or go back to the twenty-first floor and blow all of this off as a lapse of judgment. That woman is a stranger. Who am I to enter her home and go through her things? Why does it matter what Desmond wrote in his journals.

But she gave me her key and mentioned Jerald and Ruth. If I turn back now, I'll always wonder *what if*.

My reliably impulsive *tails* lands. I close my eyes and take a deep breath, mentally preparing for the daunting legwork ahead.

Two hundred and thirteen steps later, the landing of the fifteenth floor is beneath my feet, along with burning legs on the verge of turning gelatin and a heartbeat of hummingbird wings. I've never had a reason to step foot on the fifteenth floor, and the worn-down, uniquely smelling beige carpeting is the first thing I notice. The second is the wallpaper.

It's different from mine on the twenty-first floor because instead of being a tacky yellow littered with geometric shapes, it's a charming lavender decorated with hand-painted petals of a flower. How the musty carpet and wonderful wallpaper coexist in the same hallway is beyond my understanding. With the key to her apartment in hand, I stop at her front door, mentally questioning why it's painted a different shade of white.

It's slight, discrete, and unnoticeable to the untrained eye, but I know this shade discrepancy. I was raised in a home with the same color door. "It looks the same," my twelve-year-old self had complained to Jerald as we quietly painted our front door together during lights-out.

"It only looks the same if you're not looking," he whispered back. "This color resembles the feathers of a dove, my little bug. Like the birds on the surface."

The memory of his voice lovingly carries through my head and simultaneously fills my heart with a biting fury.

Last month, Jerald was found dead in the main corridor outside the Arboretum, and a cosmic piece of me died with him. I love Ruth with everything I am, but Jerald earned a piece of my heart capable of love I didn't understand until it was lost.

After Jerald's passing, a ravenous flame ignited inside of me, blazing with suicidal rage. I fantasized about setting fire to all of Foxtrot to rid everyone inside because nothing made sense without him anymore. I needed to smash the windows to bits and flood the facility with salt water and tears to drown every single person.

And although grief is an apex predator lying in wait, sharing the shadows with the burden of the new reality it thrives in, I refused to give in to the temptation to end it all. Grief was mine and mine alone to overcome. I surrendered to the sadness and adapted to life without him.

To keep his memory alive, I wrote down all the Grand Stories I'd memorized, but with that insignificant memento came unyielding questions: How did he find a book of the surface? Where did the book come from? Why did we trace images and copy paragraphs into separate journals? Why couldn't we talk about it with anyone else? What did he do with it when we were done? Why didn't Ruth know where it came from?

I should have asked him when he was still alive, I'm sure he would have told me. That's the funny thing about death, it reminds us of everything we never said. But now, after meeting a stranger who also shares stories of the surface, I'm flooded with conflicting emotions unlocking Sonia's door.

Judging by her decor, she lives a modest life. It's refreshing since so many people live in homes that are borderline hoarder pits, fearful they will eventually be without. She's not Senseless Sonia being chummy with Deranged Desmond. The simplicity of how she lives validates my case of nerves that I'm not chasing a pipedream. She has everything she needs and nothing more. A corner lamp illuminates the living room, highlighting one recliner positioned in front of a television and a small coffee table with one red teacup placed on a single coaster.

My curiosity for exploring the rest of her home is outweighed by the fact that she's trusting me to find Desmond's journals and nothing more. I shove aside my intrusive thoughts to snoop, disappointed the temptation was there to do anything other than what I was allowed to come in for. What I thought about breaking in for.

To the right of the living room and past an empty coat rack, the corner of the stove is visible. Gently closing the front door, I ease into the quaint kitchen. Everything inside her apartment assures me Sonia lives alone, but I'm cautious about making noise.

I don't know how watchful her neighbors are. For all I know, someone has seen me enter this apartment, and a Watchman is on their way to place me in zip ties. *Stop being paranoid.*

Surprisingly enough, the tin box is on top of the fridge, exactly where Sonia said it would be. The distrustful lump in my skull created a scenario where this task would lead to a scavenger hunt down a rabbit hole because this seemed too good to be true. But I stand corrected.

Adrenaline and anticipation shake my hands from their cocktail. Reaching for the top of the refrigerator, I grab the tin box and set it on the counter, but the first thing inside isn't what I expected.

Inside a sealed glass placard is a pristine dollar bill. I've never seen one in person, only in pictures from the book of the surface. Once civilization evacuated to Alpha through Zulu, all traditional currencies went extinct. Money doesn't mean much down here. Whoever preserved this dollar bill must have thought this piece of history would prove invaluable. It could still be worth something. Stopping myself from pocketing the dollar bill, I set it aside and pick up a journal from the top of the stack.

Some type of insect is sketched on the front cover, an insect with two pairs of membranous wings, a robust body, and two antennae.

Brushing my fingers through the thin pages, a

turned-down corner of a page organically opens. Thunder clashes in my chest. I read a snippet from its page:

They don't want us asking questions because they're keeping secrets from all of us. There has to be more to life than all of this. If we ...

Setting the journal aside, I rummage through at least ten more, all sharing sketched variations of the same insect on the front cover.

Some show the wings extended beyond the abdomen, others have the insect upside down, six slender legs jutting out of the almond-shaped body. Most journals have many of the same insects drawn on them, depicting them in different stages of flight.

Picking up another at random and fluttering through its pages, I land on a page in the middle of the journal, but this entry has different handwriting:

I went to the drop to swap journals, but it was empty. I didn't know what else to do. I took this one back. I'll check again in a few hours, but I worry ...

Feverishly reading the rest of the page, I flip to the next, absorbing nothing and everything all at once until stopping on another excerpt with the same handwriting. The date is what catches my eye:

16 February
The drop is still empty. I have to assume that location has been compromised. I'm afraid watchful eyes have gotten him because now that I have time to think, I haven't seen him for two entire shifts. I know it's risky, but I'll keep looking for him. I have to because he would do the same for any of us. I know that he ...

My heart booms skimming the rest of the paragraph, searching for a name I'm sure is in here. A name that is going to unlock a hidden door deep in my core. I turn to the next page with hyperfocus, devouring every single word until his full name stares back at me.

5

Unlatching the front door of my apartment, I find Mason asleep on the couch. He must've thought I'd be back a lot sooner. And I would've been, had it not been for my insatiable thirst to keep reading journals in Sonia's kitchen.

Knowing him as well as I know myself, he would've corralled me into a conversation to convince me I should forgive him the moment I stepped inside. Luckily, he didn't stir when I entered. I'm not brave enough to prove he was wrong, and I'm not in the mood for dancing around the truth.

Despite these conflicting feelings, if he'd been awake when I came in, I would've word-vomited everything to him until there was nothing left inside my brain because these questions are pounding against my skull. I long for sympathetic eyes to watch me drown within this Pandora's Box I've opened.

Gently setting my satchel on the cabinet near the door, I quietly remove my shoes, place the keys on the key ring, and walk to my room, glancing at the clock at the end of the hall—2140. Plenty of time to shower before lights-out.

Though seemingly never-ending, the rule on electricity is the most reasonable. It's strictly enforced to be shut off by 2200 at the end of each wakeful shift to allow the current-powered turbines to recharge Foxtrot's generators.

Standing in the shower, the hot water dilutes my thoughts. For a moment, surrounded by smothering steam, a sob silently escapes. Why was *Jerald Quinn* written in that journal? My heart is screaming that this hollowness spilling from me is contagious and will swallow me whole.

Absorbing the uneasiness, I procrastinate getting dressed. Partly because the air against my wet body reminds me I'm not as numb as I feel on the inside, but mostly because I'm almost out of clean laundry. Digging through the last remnants from my dresser, I put on an old pair of sweatpants, a sports bra, and an oversized t-shirt, making a mental note to do laundry the next wakeful shift.

Lying on my bed, staring at the ceiling fan haphazardly wobbling above, I come to terms that my thoughts will not settle any time soon. There's no use fighting a wave destined to crash, and my thoughts spin with the fan blade. Around and around and around on an endless rotation.

This uncertainty is making me sick. My mouth is sandpaper, my loose clothing suddenly constricting, and the strands of my wet hair are snakes coiling down to tighten around my throat. I need something to drink.

Mason is awake, reading on the couch. "Hey, pal," I say awkwardly, pouring a glass of desalinated water.

The best way to move past our disputes is to rip off

the bandage to let the wound breathe, but he doesn't reply. I guzzle the first glass and fill a second, savoring this one because the bandage will come off once I'm finished. The silence is too loud.

Turning around to face him, my confidence morphs into glass like the cup in my hand a second ago, both shattering to pieces at my feet.

My satchel is open at his feet, his voice a dangerous calm on the verge of exploding. "What is this?" He throws one of Desmond's journals to the ground.

Shit, shit, shit. "I was going to tell—"

"—Damn it, Samara. How did you get these journals, and why do you have this placard? What the hell is wrong with you?"

The lights-out siren chirps in its usual two-part intervals, partially drowning out the last bit of his question. He likely said *what the fuck is wrong with you.* But to ease my anxiety, I'll pretend he said *hell.*

Without losing eye contact, we both reach for the closest switch and turn off the remaining lights in the apartment. The tension in the pitch blackness is claustrophobic, vibrating with razor blades. It feels as if I'm choking on my tongue, which now seems too large for my mouth.

"After realizing you lied about checking the mail, I went back to the Husk. Something was off with you. You were cagey while we were there, like you were hiding something. I spoke to Maeve," he says through the darkness. "I couldn't stop thinking about how defensive and secretive you were. She told me you asked for a name."

My hand reaches for the coolness of the kitchen counter to center my mounting anxiety. I must have been gone for hours. Longer than I thought. Longer than I meant to be. I take little comfort knowing he can't see me trembling—from nerves, adrenaline, or panic—or a mixture of them all. Both syllables of his name seem unreachable. "Mason."

"Please don't interrupt me. I'm not mad. I promise I'm not mad. I'm trying to work this out, the least you can do is hear me out and let me finish." He takes a deep, shaking breath. "I know who you're looking for. I went to the Sector Hub, entered his name, and it generated his address. It's him, isn't it?"

I don't know the *him* he's talking about. Thinking back to everything leading up to this, Maeve is a pawn in the scheme of things. She knows people who know people. At most, she's a go-between. He can't know, can he? I remain silent.

"You're looking for our biological father, aren't you? Is that who Nathan Marlow is?" His insecurity with the unknown behind our birth becomes vibrantly clear.

Ruth and Jerald had explained to us that our biological mother was in love. As fate would have it, her husband was as sterile as our mother was fertile, and the dream of creating a family turned into a castle in the sky as his vigor was replaced with limitation. And although impossibly opposite in what they'd hoped for in life, they were simply atoms lining up.

Her husband settled on our mother's persistence of artificial insemination from a donor, and his deep-seated insecurity was placed in the back of his hidden, Indicating mind. Within weeks of the procedure, we were two embryos surrounded by love and bliss. Unbeknownst to her, it was one-sided.

It wasn't until she was encompassed with the glow of pregnancy that her husband's Indicator revealed itself. His inner conflicts devoured him, and our mother's reassurances lay wasted on her lips as he swung from metal pipes in their kitchen from a synthetic rope.

I've never felt inclined to reach out to our biological father to see any resemblance or to have a relationship. To me, he's the name on an application. A name of many, one of thousands. I'm fulfilled with what Ruth and Jerald have given us.

We've had them in our lives since we were nine, and they've been alongside us longer than our time without them. For the last seventeen years, we've known their love and support, but Mason has passively questioned his lineage, especially after losing our mother to complications during childbirth.

Sometimes there are no answers to festering questions, and Mason hasn't accepted that yet, even decades later. If I could see him right now, I know with my entire twin heart he's fidgeting with his fingers and teeter with the idea of agreeing with him for the sake of ending this conversation—he can't see the bald-faced lie through the darkness.

But my secret is already out, no sense in trying to keep it hidden. "No, Mason. That's not the name of our biological father."

"Then who is Nathan Marlow, and why are you looking for him?"

I'm back at my crossroads of honesty and deceit. If Mason knows the real reason I wanted the name, he'll weaponize his love for me as a deterrent from following through with any of it. He'll remind me that being impulsive isn't the logical way to live, that there are no bragging rights with being the *tails*.

He'll tell me to listen to reason, even though reason and logic and rationality are what anchors me to this existence. He'll remind me to follow the rules and to do as *they* say because *they* say it.

But I crave control. It's my only constant. After everything I've read at Sonia's, it's time he knows that I won't be swayed. "Mason, do you love me?" I know the answer, but I need to hear it.

Anxiety dances in his tone. "Of course I love you."

I shift the two-ton weights between my feet. "Do you want me to be happy, even if that means I need to be free?"

"Samara, please. Tell me what's going on. You can trust me. Whatever it is, we can figure this out."

"I need to go to the surface." The words spill out of me, the air suffocatingly thin awaiting his response.

"What?"

"I can't live here anymore."

"What does that mean you can't live here? Where is *here*? With me? If you don't want to live with me that's fine. But the surface? Are you trying to kill yourself? Atlantic be damned Samara, you sound absurd."

I can sense his heart hammering through the acidic words he's spewing, but confidently say, "I'm not trying to die. I need to live like Jerald promised me was possible."

"You're going to go against the fact that the surface was destroyed and trust the fairy tales enough to risk your life? Do you hear yourself?"

"I need to fly, not drown. This can't be all there is, there has to be more out there."

"What are you saying? Why are you being so cryptic? More importantly, what if you're wrong?"

"Because he ..." I gently touch my throat to help swallow the lump of fear that won't let the words get past. "Because Jerald was mentioned by name in one of those journals, and it has to mean something."

"Let me repeat that back to you. Deranged Desmond wrote about Jerald in a journal that you found in a stranger's home, and that's enough for you to leave me for a suicide mission?" He's questioning his sanity while I convince him of mine.

"I don't know if Desmond was the one who wrote in them. Each journal and about every entry had different handwriting. They all had an insect with wings drawn on them. Why would they all share that drawing? That doesn't matter right now." I break that chain of thought, negating his chance to interrupt. "The bottom line is Desmond and Jerald both had journals and wrote about the surface. Think about it, Mason. Why are there journals hidden in drops? Who is collecting these journals? There's so much we don't know."

"All of that sounds pretty fucking deranged to me, Sam. Who cares about journals in drops and whatever that insect is. I'm wondering how all of that convinced you to go to the surface."

He's growing impatient with me. I need to remind him how this all started, everything leading up to it, and what I learned at Sonia's. I must be as brave as the bulls I used to draw to prove I'm not on a suicide mission.

"I've always felt like I didn't belong in Foxtrot. And they weren't stories, Mason. We saw the book of the surface when we were kids. We've seen what we're being stripped from, you have to remember?" I demand, hoping to lessen the fog surrounding his repressed memories.

"I remember Jerald's Grand Stories and the imagination and make-believe we shared when we drew together, yes."

I lean against the refrigerator, processing what he's saying. Maybe my other half is more distant from me than I thought. "You don't remember the book of the surface full of pictures and text that we copied and traced into journals? And not the regular Foxtrot Studies, where it's vague interpretations of the surface and natural disasters that almost wiped us out. I'm talking about *the book* of *the surface*. The one with animal kingdoms, insects, and marine life. Mountain ranges, airplanes, and countries. Continents, cultural diversity, and religions. Into the galaxies!"

"I barely remember anything from that book. Jerald said we couldn't talk about it, so I didn't talk about it. I didn't think about it after we were done with it. That was what, fifteen years ago? I hardly remember anything from that book. I don't *want* to remember that book because I don't think we were supposed to have it. There's a reason Foxtrot Studies are 'regular'. Science, math, history, and language arts are the most reasonable curriculums, the very ones you teach. Not this book of the surface shit. I remember drawing with you, but I either fell back asleep when Jerald read or did something else with Ruth. I never felt like any of it was real," he confesses, and I take a step back.

I was obsessed with that book and Grand Stories when I was younger, but I didn't realize how disconnected he was from them. We've been living separate lives, each in our own bubble, never realizing how close but distant we were from each other. Jerald did tell us we weren't allowed to speak of that book, and Mason is proving to be true to his *too afraid to break a rule* mantra. I don't know why I expected anything less.

"You may not remember, but I know what I saw. I know what I read. Ever since Jerald died, I needed answers as to why he stopped sharing stories the older I got. About why he became more secretive and dismissive whenever I mentioned anything about the surface. When I opened Desmond's journals, something clicked into place." I take a deep breath. "Desmond, or whoever, dated one of those entries. One said a drop was empty on the sixteenth of February and that Jerald hadn't been seen for two shifts. Do you remember what happened on the sixteenth of February?" I need to drive this point home. I know he remembers that date.

The pain in his voice matches the dread we shared in that building. "That's when we identified Jerald's body with Ruth at the morgue."

"You're goddamn right it is. This has to mean something."

"But who is Nathan Marlow, and what does he have to do with any of this? Why have you been hiding that? Why keep it to yourself?" he asks cautiously, circling back to the origin of our dispute.

"Nathan Marlow is Jerald's Watchman partner. I didn't know he had a partner, did you?" I don't wait for his response. "I was saying goodbye to Ruth the last time we stopped by, and after I hugged her, she said, *his partner betrayed him*. But then she changed the subject. I didn't want to press it, but I had to know who she was talking about. I didn't want to tell you without looking into it first because what if it was nothing? That's why I went to Maeve. I was going to find Nathan Marlow and ask if he knows anything, but then you showed up, and Sonia—"

"—Sonia?"

"The woman in the elevator. And for the record, I

didn't break in. She gave me her key and told me where to find Desmond's journals, and now I have more questions than answers. What if Jerald was caught trying to get a damn journal from a drop? What if he found out something he wasn't supposed to? Something they would kill—"

The shuffling sound of Mason moving closer to me through the darkness shuts me up. His hand is on top of my head, sinking my floating thoughts back down to the floor. I angrily wipe an unwanted tear from my cheek, loosening the tension in my shoulders with small rotations.

The sharpness in his voice dulls to an approachable point. "Sam, this is a lot to take in. Let's talk about it next shift."

He's doing it again. Ending the conversation because he doesn't have the patience to finish it. The lack of mental energy drains from my body. I disappear into my room.

6

"I barely slept," Mason says through a yawn, shoving a slice of melon into his mouth once it passes. "I couldn't stop thinking about everything you said. I know you'll keep looking into this because you're too stubborn for your own good." He takes a moment to let that jab sink in, and to finish chewing. "But I won't tell anyone. You have to know I can't help you with any of this, Sam. I start my first patrol in Sector One in an hour." An unnecessary reminder. He's told me seventeen times already. "I can't be involved without risking everything I've worked for. Did you ever stop to think how this could affect me? Do you have a plan?"

Can't or *won't* help me? His loyalties could lie with either me or his new duty, but I've been anticipating this conversation, still unsure how to approach it. A part of me is relieved not to keep secrets from him, but a larger part is ashamed he's aware of the mess I am. How he's managing to accept my warpath for answers is harder to swallow than this lab-fresh mystery meat slathered in ketchup.

"I wasn't expecting you to help me, but as far as having a plan, I haven't figured that part out yet," I admit, switching my clothes to the dryer. "I'm stopping by Ruth's after class to see if I can borrow Jerald's journal to find a connection. I'm sure you'll still be on patrol, but I wanted to remind you not to wait for me after school." I give him a cheeky smile and a thumbs up, but he doesn't laugh. Either he's regretting knowing my secrets, or he's convinced I'm losing my mind, and I'd bet my nail polish on the latter. I pat his shoulder lightly. "I better go. Don't want to be late for my field trip."

"Sam?" he says through a bite. "Be sure to tame that scowl of yours at the museum. You don't want to ruin the fun for the kids." He throws his head back and laughs.

———— ◆◇◆ ————

My second-grade class is booming with excitement. I never imagined that little whispers of landslides and giggles about tsunamis could be so adorable. How strange those words are to them.

"Soo-name-is," they argue.

"*Tsunami*," I correct, pointing to the spelling on the board.

Nineteen students are present, except I should have twenty. The class settles, and I peek into the hallway to check if she's running late, but a barren hallway of gray lockers stares back at me. "Did anyone see Wren on the walk to school?" I ask the group, most of them shaking their heads.

"No, but I heard my mom say she's glad Wren left that one place. It's that place where all the kids live because no one wants them. Does that help?" a student asks.

"It does! Thank you so much for letting me know. Are we all ready for the field trip?" I smile, trying to quell the suspicion in my gut.

Scenarios pulse through my mind. Wren has only been in my class for three shifts, four if she were here now. That's hardly enough time for her to be processed, let alone placed in foster care and transferred to another sector. It's not impossible, but if she's been adopted the principal would've let me know by now. Paperwork must be provided on a student's behavior and progress to the next teacher.

I didn't sleep well after the confrontation with Mason. Normally, I wouldn't complain since it's rare for me to experience a decent sleep shift, but I've been wading in conspiracies. A busy mind makes for a creative nightmare. I dreamt my arms were amputated to the elbows, my mouth sewn shut, and teeth dislodging from my gums. I woke up massaging my throat to help swallow them down. I went to the roof and sat in the quiet for hours.

But there's nothing abnormal about a child not being in attendance. There will be an email from the principal explaining her absence, or at the very least confirming a transfer or adoption.

Logging into the intranet, double-clicking the email icon, and madly browsing through my inbox, there's nothing from Principal Martin Jeup with the subject line of *insert name here has been transferred*, as I've seen countless times before. My heart sinks into my stomach. I can't explain this feeling, but something is wrong. Someone would've told me … something. It's a rule. If anyone has to follow all the damn rules around here, it's the school.

Dialing the teacher's number in the adjacent room, I clear my throat while it rings, making my voice convincingly weak. "Hi, Miss Zoe, it's Miss Samara. I don't know what's happening, but something is off. I woke up with my stomach in knots. I know we're both scheduled for the museum, but I don't think I can make it. I don't want to let the kids down. They're so looking forward to going. Do you mind taking my class on the field trip to Sector One? I'd hate to get anyone else sick. I can push through if this is inconvenient for you, no problem at all." If there's one thing I've learned about Miss Zoe, it's that she's a germaphobe.

"Oh. Oh no, no don't bother to, eh, oh that's terrible." She clears her throat. "Yes, I have a teacher's aide with me. We have plenty of eyes to watch over two classrooms. Do you have a fever? Or do you think it was something you ate?"

If you count a bloodthirsty hunger for answers, then yes, it's something I ate. I keep my voice casually professional. "I'm feeling terrible, but I don't think it's contagious." I cough. "Forget I called, Miss Zoe. I'll push through it. I haven't been to the museum in years, I would hate to miss this."

"No, no, no!" she shrieks. "Please, Miss Samara. I will take your class, and we can schedule another trip for when you're feeling better. Please go home."

I unscrew the lid on my water bottle and take a small

sip, letting it slowly pass down my throat, and make a strange gurgling sound. It's supposed to resemble phlegm, but she won't know the difference. "You are too kind, Miss Zoe. You're right. It's best if I go home and lie down. I'll bring the children over first."

"No, that's quite all right. Don't come over here. Have them wait in the hallway. Go home and rest!" Her voice is muffled as if she's covering her mouth.

I cup mine, holding in a laugh. Sometimes it's too easy to be deceitful. Clapping my hands, I help gather everyone's things. "Class, Miss Zoe will be taking you on the field trip. I'd like all of us to collect our packs and form a line."

Escorting my class to the hallway, Miss Zoe promptly shoos me away with a handkerchief, another covering her nose. She takes one glimpse at the sweat ring around my neck and nearly faints. Her aide, standing halfway in their classroom, is yanked into the hallway, Miss Zoe swapping places with her. Pouring water on my shirt might've been overkill.

Keeping the illusion of being out of sorts with one hand on my stomach and the other on my hip, I saunter from the school zone with the speed of a tortoise. Once the school is out of sight, I run as fast as my legs can carry me in these inconvenient sandals I put on to match this unlike-me romper I wore for the field trip I'm no longer going on.

A field trip that would've placed me in Sec-One where I was planning to conveniently, but briefly, slip away to confirm Nathan Marlow's address. Why I didn't wear my usual pants and t-shirt with sneakers is beyond me. I regret not dressing like myself.

After nearly a mile of power-walking, the sign for the Sector Five Foxtrot Foster Agency comes into view. I enter the building with a convincing pleasantry, replacing the confusion across my face.

A lone, beautiful woman sitting behind a large wooden desk greets me. "Welcome! We at Sec-Five F.F.A thank you for coming by to explore your adoption options. What can I help you with?"

A conscious, forceful smile nearly reaches my neck. "I'm looking for a young girl, her name is Wren Bracken." I spell her full name to avoid confusion. "She's from Sector Two, but temporarily in Sec-Five."

The receptionist's attention shifts from me to the computer in front of her, humming under her breath as she types. As I wait for her to confirm Wren's adoption, I admire the golden braids wrapped across the top of her head. I doubt I could replicate it—my braiding skills are passable, but barely.

Her humming stops. Sympathy flashes through her amber eyes, painted as if she has to remind herself to keep her composure. "I must apologize, but she's no longer in this sector. It appears she's been adopted. Isn't that wonderful?"

The avoidance of eye contact isn't overlooked. She smiles through me, spinning the bracelet on her wrist. Is she suppressing nerves? No, she's been helpful. Professional. She's doing her job, I'm overthinking this. Wren has been adopted, that's the answer.

The receptionist interlocks her fingers, squeezing the tops of each knuckle. Her nervous tell is minimal, but it's there. She's hiding something.

Suspicion tingles the back of my head. "That's so lovely to hear! I made her a doll and was hoping to give it to her. Can you tell me who adopted her? I'd love to see her." My fake excitement is enough to make me nauseous.

"We have a non-disclosure policy, I must apologize. If you leave the doll here, I'll get in touch with the family to get it to her."

Another deterrence. I reach into my pockets, searching for a doll I don't have. "You are too helpful. You know, Wren is such a wonderful young lady, she—do I smell coffee?" I perk up with a playful grin, lazily crossing my arms.

"Why, yes. I'm down to my last pot, but I'm happy to share. Would you like a cup?" She gestures to the shelf behind her.

Her helpfulness is enough to prolong this prickly conversation. I feed into the awkwardness, crinkling my nose with a wave of my hand. "I hate to impose. Are you sure?"

"Oh yes, yes. It's nothing." She scribbles on a notepad to order more coffee. "Stay right here, I'll get you a cup." She walks to the machine to make me a beverage.

Patiently standing in front of her desk, I look around the lobby, pretending to admire the staged photographs of happy families, and set my eyes back on the receptionist.

"Syrup?" she calls over her shoulder.

"A dash!"

There are two security cameras in the lobby—one at the entrance and one above me. The receptionist's desk is free of paperwork, except for an almost finished crossword puzzle and a notepad with reminders and doodles of faces. The pens are neatly arranged, the stapler is tucked next to a hole-punch, and there's a box of tissues with the one on top ornately folded. She's been awfully busy.

"Lots of visitors this shift?" I ask, tapping my fingers.

"You're the first one," she clucks.

Interesting. If I'm the first visitor, how could Wren have been adopted? I keep my tone breezy. "Besides the family that came for the adoption, of course."

She half-turns to me, holding that vacant smile. I relax my body language, leaning on her desk. She clears her throat. "The family was here earlier, first thing this shift!" Returning to the desk holding two ceramic mugs, she extends one to me. "Here you are, my dear."

A red herring swims by. I reach for the cup, a smile burning my cheeks. Feigning ignorance, I lean over her desk, squinting. "Thank you so much. Audrey, is it?" Before she can acknowledge her nametag I can clearly read, the mug slips from my hands. Hot liquid splashes, ceramic breaks, and the handle soars across the desk, knocking over the pen cup. I was aiming for the chair, but this will do.

I skirt behind her desk to clean it up. "Oh my Foxtrot, Audrey, I am so sorry for the mess."

"Miss, you can't be back here."

"Please, Audrey, let me help." Taking tissue from its box, I lap the puddle. "You've been so kind, and now I've ruined everything. I need to make this right." I awkwardly push the liquid off the desk into my hand as she stands still, frozen like a long-ago iceberg. Sensing she's frazzled, I take hold of this opportunity. "I'm so irresponsible. How could I do such a senseless thing? I hate myself," I cry out, impressed at how quickly I can create and diffuse a situation.

Her hand rests on my shoulder, patting me reassuringly. "It's a little spill, don't be too hard on yourself. Let me help." She collects bits of ceramic, discarding the broken pieces in the bin.

I steal a glance at her screen. A photograph of Wren with, IRREPARABLE. CURRENT LOCATION: VAT flashes in red letters above her image.

I step out from behind her desk, swallowing my confusion. "I can't apologize enough, Audrey."

"Don't mind it too much, it was an easy fix. Did you want to leave the doll with me?"

I pat my empty pockets, summoning an innocent face. "I must have left it at my apartment. I'll be right back." She picks up the receiver and dials a number, offering a shrouded, forced smile. "Please don't," I whisper, but I don't think she heard me.

I never imagined this is how I would die. I thought I'd go out doing something meaningful and worthwhile, not another notch in the Vat's tally. How can I convince her not to call a Watchman when all I've done is manipulate her the moment I stepped inside this building? Maybe I should do everyone the favor and finally sink.

"Hello, Mr. Rocha, this is Audrey calling from the Sec-Five F.F.A."

My lungs prepare for their collapse as I patiently wait to be sentenced to the deep.

There's no use in hiding; I'm in the security footage. If I'm lucky enough to make it home, all I'd do is wait to die. I can't escape a Watchman with a bounty on my head. For most of my life, I've fantasized about escaping to a cabin in the mountains or a beaten-down shack hidden in a meadow. As much as I wish for it, there's none of that here. If a broadcast gets put out, I wouldn't be able to hide in another sector. The public would sniff out I'm from Sec-Five and turn me in for a reward. It's cutthroat down here.

Through the bubbling panic in my ears, Audrey gives me a wave goodbye from her phone call as if I'm interrupting. "I'm well, thank you," she says into the receiver. "I have a small issue over here." I give her a half-wave in return, my face scrunched in confusion. "And miss," her voice booms at me from across the empty lobby, "if you can't return before lights-out, we open at 0700."

Pushing the door open and stepping out onto the sidewalk, a remnant of her conversation follows me as the doors close: "I need to place another order of your dark roast coffee to be delivered to ..."

7

Situated in the main corridor between all five sectors, the Arboretum is breathtaking. I pause to appreciate the serenity behind the glass on my way to Sec-One.

Within the colossal snow globe, an ecosystem is perfectly preserved, with leaves carelessly floating to the ground. In the early era of Foxtrot, when the human population was high and morale not as low, livestock was kept in the Arboretum. The thought of fresh meat from cattle and poultry is something I can't wrap my head around.

The consumption rate of meat and lack of breeding in captivity was unmatched, and eventually, all the animals died off. In their wake, maple trees, spruces, willows, beeches, and firs have been maintained in the massive terrarium, and they're marvelous, aiding the oxygen spreading through the ducts. Of course, in the informational pamphlets, they're simply named *trees*. No discerning factors so no one is curious about the types of species. Still, I admire each one and recognize their individuality.

Nestled between a pond, hundreds of fruit trees and berry bushes thrive, the willows taking up a hillside overlooking the cornfields and nut groves. Nearest to the maples and surrounded by one of many vegetable gardens, a freshwater creek moves effortlessly. Jerald once told me that even though it's manufactured, the stream's sound is organic, moving exactly nowhere and everywhere in a casual yet hurried flow.

After Jerald's passing, I often found Ruth standing here, mourning from her own widow's peak, gazing into the lush enclosure. I'd gently take her back home. Ruth reminds me of willows in a way, because they're both peaceful, the long foliage akin to her sandy-blonde hair. But also because her soul used to weep here. I've lost count of how many times I've collected her from this spot.

Standing here, peering into the vastness, can make a person feel incredibly small. How can we exist alongside these wooden giants and think Foxtrot is all there is? Ruth must have felt closer to Jerald here because it reminded her of his spirit because that's what I'm feeling now. Jerald *is* the trees. He's the creek, the pond, the berries. He's all of this in front of me because he believed there was more.

He was growth, he was hope, and he was killed. His body found in the main corridor.

Authorities said it was a random act of violence during his patrol because surely, that's how any Watchman could die. Case closed, no formal complaint, no investigation to find the killer. As if what happened to him was as common as a sinking. It was the first alleged incident of a Watchman suffering a coup de grâce at the hands of a citizen in decades.

Breaking my gaze from the Arboretum, I move with determination to the entrance of Sector One until the sound of laughing children halts me. The laughter is familiar and innocent. I've heard those tiny voices hundreds of times.

Vigilant on Miss Zoe, her aide, and my oblivious class, I watch them take the stairs to the catwalk above the Arboretum. Backing into a women's public restroom, my back collides into something padded.

I spin around to face a Watchman. "I didn't—"

"—I'm sorry, I didn't mean to startle you, ma'am. I was following up on a complaint of vandalism, but it's clear. I must be in the wrong restroom. It's my first patrol shift, and I'm already making mistakes. Don't tell my sergeant." She cups her mouth to hide a smirk. "You can use these facilities." Her cedar-tinted lips and long black braids nearly jumpstart my pulse.

Her beauty outshines the hideous Watchman uniform she's wearing. She apologized to *me* for bumping into *her*, *and* she has a sense of humor? Unusual for a Watchman. I'd imagine if it were any other guard, I'd be in the detention facility because I shared the same air as them, and they sure as hell wouldn't admit they made a mistake. Color me intrigued.

"There's no vandalism in there?" I ask. She crosses her arms, tapping her ribs. "There are no absurd drawings in the stalls or napkins clogging the sink?" She shakes her head, smiling with almond eyes. "You're telling me the trash bin isn't flipped over, and someone didn't smear anything on the mirrors? Is a stall door at least dented or off its hinge?"

"Hate to tell you, but the whole thing is clean."

"Well, this is absurd."

She removes a hand, extending it to me. "Aubert. Olivia Aubert."

I meet her for the handshake. "Samara."

"Nice to meet you, Samara. Do you usually walk backward into restrooms?"

"Not usually, no. But sometimes I do it for fun. Do Watchmen usually treat civilians with so much respect?"

Why did I say that? If there was ever a time and place to prevent my thoughts from leaving my mouth, it would be now. First patrol shift or not, she's still one of Warden Gryme's watchdogs.

"I think we both know the answer to that." Her fingertips tap against her thighs. "I know Watchmen are pegged to be aggressive and uncaring, but I don't want to be grouped in with that. We're all people, you know. Watchmen and the public don't have to be at odds. I want to help change it all."

"I hope you're right," I say tightly. That's all I can offer. *Good luck with that* seems more fitting, but I've already overstayed this conversation.

"I better get back to my assignment. My partner must be wondering where I'm at." With that, she gives me a downward nod and disappears from sight.

The restroom is disappointingly clean and surprisingly empty. I glance at the watch on my wrist. Most everyone is working the monotonous nine-to-five. In the next hour or so, this restroom will be busy during lunch break. Everyone is working except me because I faked an illness to get out of class, and now I'm hiding in a restroom to avoid said class because they're in the area I was supposed to be in to sneak off to find someone's address—I'm a mess.

I splash icy water on my cheeks, lightly pressing where it's the puffiest. The water beads over the prominent scar across my right cheek, a once grisly wound gifted to me from a long-ago adult who got too handsy. Selfish men don't like it when a child fights back, especially when that child rakes their fingernails down his face. Sometimes I can still feel the blade, still hear him shouting at me to *lay still* or else he'd cut me. I'd take that knife again on any shift. I'd rake my nails down his face thrice over if I could, then claw both his eyes out for the fun of it.

Scanning the surrounding area for my class, hoping to make a quick getaway, my collarbone meets the forearm of a male Watchman, abruptly stopping my movement. Active Watchmen where I live in Sec-Five are far and few in between unless someone is being restrained, but Sector One being the training sector for all Watchmen means this vile section is teeming with them, and they're eager to stir up trouble.

I've been told it wasn't always like this. In the early years of humans living in this doomsday bunker, there were no Watchmen or Wardens or endless laws dictating how to live. Sec-One used to be like the other four, another place to live in while waiting out the destruction of the sun. When relief never came, refugees realized the odds of rescue were slim, and panic ensued. People stole from each other and killed one another. The first Warden Gryme was voted in by the public, and Foxtrot became militarized under his regime.

"State your purpose," the Watchman demands, his features sharp and orderly. He's older than me, somewhere in his late thirties. An unusual hostility surrounds him, one that warns me that he will not show me his tell. I'll have to downplay myself.

I paint on my best pout. "Can you help me?"

"State your purpose," he repeats through small lips surrounded by a prickly, honey-brown beard, contrasting against his cerulean uniform.

Absorbing his tone, I slant my weight into my left hip, making myself shorter. "I've been trying to find my class," I lie. "We went to the museum, but I must have gotten turned around." I point to nothing in particular.

"Badge," he commands, a black-gloved hand reaching out.

This is the second time a Watchman has worn black gloves as part of the uniform. The odds of this man being the same Watchman who detained Desmond are far too high for my liking. If he had been that aggressive in detaining a senior citizen, what's to stop him from doing the same to me—or worse. Digging into my pockets, I pull out my Sec-Five teacher's lanyard and place it in his palm.

He inspects it, gives me a once-over, and hands it back. "You're from Sec-Five?"

Well done, you can read. I nod, holding in the sarcasm.

"I can't place it, but you look familiar. Have we met? Do you have a sister? Do you visit Sec-One often?" he asks in rapid-fire.

Who does he think he is interrogating me? The embroidered F patched on his right shoulder stands for Foxtrot, but *fuckhead* would be more fitting. The embellishment of FTO below is what's concerning. This man is a Field Training Officer. He trains Watchmen how to carry out the rules and regulations bestowed by the Warden and gets away with manslaughter for both criminals and Indicators alike.

My facial expression is unmoving. Bored. Unbothered. "The answer to all of your questions is *no.*"

Watchmen are trained for security and public execution, but their god-complex makes them believe everyone should worship them. This man's facial expression tells me he's unsatisfied with my quick explanation. Though being indirect is in my bailiwick, something inside of me is cautioning that this Watchman is dangerous. It's only a whisper of a warning, but I hear it, nonetheless. I need him to back off or I'll get myself cornered.

"I do not believe we've met before. I do not have a sister because I'm an only child, and I don't visit Sec-One." I add.

It's straightforward enough to end this unsolicited examination of my personal life, but he's persistent. "I'm in Sec-Five a lot. We could've passed by each other at some point. I know teachers live close to the school for an easy commute, maybe that's where I've seen you. How can you be sure we've never met? Who are your parents?"

"How is that any of your goddamn business? Is it a crime to take children to the museum? If it is, you should arrest me now." I display my wrists facing up, taunting him to zip tie me. My wickedness earns a look of disapproval.

"Non-residential lanyards are required to be visibly worn on your person at all times when outside your sector," he says sharply. "If you're seen without it again, I'll personally escort you to the detention facility, no questions asked." His unsettling, deep blue eyes send centipedes crawling on top of my skin.

I want to shout a zillion things at him and simultaneously pull out his powerful eyes, but I don't. Instead, I simply say *thank you*, and place the lanyard around my neck, though now it's more of a noose.

Sector One is alien with its tall, immaculate buildings and banners of the current Warden Gryme's face tacked to some, his grinning mug portraying immorality. There's no litter or cracks on the pavement, and it doesn't smell of arduous work.

It's maintained and well-lit, not aged and refurbished with unreliable shift lighting. Only the best for the residents in Sector One where the Warden lives and his Watchmen train. How wonderful for them all.

A large sign outside the building housing the Vat reads: WELCOME. OBSERVATORY. VAT. GIFTSHOP.

Barbaric.

I inhale deeply, exhale slowly. I don't have a plan, but I need to be here. I need answers, need to know what's happening with Wren if she's in there. I hope to the Atlantic she's not. I've been inside this building too many times to count, but it's never an easy task. I've seen lives being lost to this ocean, and I've seen the families of the sunken succumb to mental blight, lifeless in sorrow and drowning themselves in spirits.

A sinking is open to the public, but gaining access to the Vat itself is impossible unless personally ushered inside. Years ago, the family of a sunken retaliated and attacked the Watchmen who stood outside the Vat. The family was restrained, and to prove a point, Warden Calum Gryme decreed that they, too, shall be sunk. Within an hour, an entire family line was erased from Foxtrot.

A daring act of defiance such as that had never been tried before and hasn't since. Not a single soul thought the consequences would be a death sentence. At most, an extended stay at the detention facility long enough to remind them to stay in line but never meeting the deep. Security tightened outside the Vat whenever there was a sinking, but after some years without incident, the workforce was assigned elsewhere. Only trainees or semi-retired Watchmen maintain this beat since all they do is stand and stare at the entrance. Lucky me.

This building is stuffy, oozing with the scent of death. My breath shudders at the sight of the two Watchmen guarding the Vat. They're both standing with immaculate posture, each holding a baton across their chest, both staring at me.

"Excuse me, which way is the Observatory?" I ask the male Watchman, though I know exactly where it is.

"Down the hall and to the left, ma'am," Mason says, his voice vacantly monotone. I swallow a giggle, continuing down the familiar hall.

Entering the darkened lobby, a sense of dread pools in my stomach. The Observatory offers an up-close view of a sinking for the public. It's a half-moon window in the shape of a dome, extending toward the boundless ocean. From the right angle, part of the Vat can be seen.

Stepping into the Observatory is like stepping into a portal to another dimension. A shiver runs down my spine. The outer spotlights provide an illuminating effect, and the heavy contrast against the dark ocean is dizzying. When the lever is pulled and a soul vacuumed from the Vat, the bright lights outside the Observatory create a section perfectly lit for an audience.

I despise all of this, but will myself to look toward the Vat.

Wren's fragile frame is wrapped in on itself, cross-legged in a catatonic state on the floor, her wine-red hair a tangled mess across her shoulders. I step further into the Observatory's window to see what she's holding in her hands and if my eyes are deceiving me, but they're not. She's covered in blood from her elbows down to her fingertips.

8

My limbs are heavy and tingling. I glide down the hall back to the entrance of the building where the two rookies on watch guard the Vat. "Excuse me, I was wondering when the next sinking is?" I ask them, blinking between the two for an answer from either.

Olivia's posture seems more Watchman than it did outside the restroom, and Mason's is stiff and unmoving. First patrol shift or not, one of them is bound to know the answer. I'd imagine that's part of the job.

Mason stares past me at the entrance door. "There's a sign in the Observatory lobby that displays the next time of a sinking, ma'am."

"I was in there and didn't see a sign. Can you show me where it's at?"

"We cannot leave our station to assist the public unless there's an emergency, ma'am."

I remind myself not to stomp retreating to the lobby. Pausing in the hallway near the gift shop to slow my beating heart, I lean against the wall, picking through my satchel to think. *We cannot leave our station to assist the public unless there's an emergency.*

If Mason won't meet me here, I'll force him to come to me. Crouching down, a blood-curdling scream erupts from my throat. With my back to the boots thundering down the hall, I close my eyes and scream again, my voice cracking and fluctuating in pitch. Collapsing to my knees, two arms scoop my weight off the floor, gently positioning me upright.

"Samara, what's wrong?" Olivia asks, moving aside the displaced hair from my face. The back of her hand searches for a fever I don't have. A thin film of regret forms on my tongue. I meet her worried gaze.

Forced weariness leaks from my lips, my silver tongue regaining traction. "It felt like my head shattered. I've never had this happen. I should rest here for a minute. Is the other Watchman coming to help?"

She shouldn't know that Mason is my brother, and I don't know how to gauge her. I expected Mason to come to my aid, but maybe he sent Olivia instead. If Mason were here, I could have talked him into answering my questions. But her?

"I've never heard anyone scream like that. I was worried," she admits. "Watchman Quinn will not be assisting. Is there anything I can do to help?"

What do I say to this stranger? I can barely focus on a response because she's tapping her nails on her baton. Is this her nervous tell, or is she simply impatient? Trusting my gut, I ask, "Why is that little girl inside the Vat? What could she have done to deserve this?" Not that anyone *deserves* the Vat, but this woman is a Watchman. I'll use her lingo against her if it means getting an answer.

Olivia stops tapping. She places a hand under my arm and lifts me to my feet. Standing in front of me, studying me as I study her, she says, "I shouldn't be telling you this, but I know I can trust you."

My teeth clamp, suppressing the cackle. Trust me? Why does she need to trust me? Better yet, how does she know she can trust me? I could be an infamous, yet-to-be-discovered serial maniac for all she knows.

Olivia scans our surroundings. "She's been sentenced to the deep because she killed a Watchman."

My raised brow nearly touches the ceiling. "She did what now?"

"We can't stand here talking. Here, wrap your arm around me and keep holding your head. Maybe limp a little. Let's go to the Observatory lobby."

I oblige.

Sitting me on a cement bench in the darkened room, she maintains a military posture. "Last wakeful shift at 1330, the little girl was found at her old home in Sector Two. A neighbor called in, stating the front door to the residence was open, fearing a burglary. When Watchman Sampson arrived on the scene, she radioed in that she had eyes on a female juvenile sitting in a child's room and didn't require backup. At 1400 with no radio response, two additional Watchmen were dispatched to the location." She takes a deep breath as if reliving a terrible image she can't escape from. "When backup arrived, they found Watchman Sampson lying on her back in a child's room, her tactical knife lodged through her temple. The letter M was carved into her right cheek, so deep her teeth were visible. Another M was sliced through her left cheek, and her mouth was gaping open."

Staring at Olivia with my mouth wide open, my hand absentmindedly traces the letters on my cheeks. Wren spelled Mom.

"That can't be right. Wren is what, eight years old?"

"The girl was sitting on the bed covered in blood, holding a small kitchen knife and a knapsack. She kept apologizing for doing the 'bad thing'. The Watchmen coaxed her into giving them the knife, but she begged for them to let her keep the knapsack. They received an order to transport her to the Vat. Even after they restrained her, she kept screaming at them to see her mom."

Her knapsack. A knapsack that I reminded her she didn't have, and a field trip she felt jaded from because she didn't have parents to sign the permission slip. I stood by as she left my classroom in tears as if I had no control of the situation, but I did. I should have done more, and now I have to live with that.

"Can I get her out? Please, Olivia. Is there any way? I'll do anything."

Damn it, why didn't I sign that permission slip for her? Why didn't I comfort her more?

"There's nothing we can do to save her without joining her in the Vat. I've put eyes and ears into all the resources I could think of." Her voice is unusually somber for someone with orders to kill a child. For someone who is a Watchman.

I stand up, matching her height. "Why would you risk doing any of that? Why would a Watchman care about doing anything besides what they're ordered to do? How can you hope to be the change when you're no better than any of the other Watchmen? Who the hell are you?"

"I am everyone, and you are?" she says, leaving me dumbfounded.

"What kind of answer is that?" I demand, taking a step back. She dips her chin. *Twice* now, she's given me that nod. The first time it happened, it made sense. Our conversation outside the restroom had ended and she was leaving. A professional goodbye. But this? "And why do you keep doing that?"

Approaching boots interrupt our odd twist of conversation. We aren't alone anymore. "Status report, Aubert," a somewhat familiar, authoritative voice says from behind her.

Olivia faces the man, her frame blocking my view. "I was assisting a member of the public, sir, who had a possible medical condition arise."

"If she's clear, report back to your station outside the Vat immediately. That's an order."

With another downward nod directed at me, Olivia retreats to her post.

My focus is drawn to the male Watchman standing a few feet away. It's the same Watchman who demanded my teacher's lanyard. The same one who said I looked familiar. The one with black gloves. If I didn't know any better, I'd say this man is orbiting me.

His tone is callous and lazy. "Do you need medical assistance?"

"I'm fine, thank you," I say cordially, but *I don't need help from a fuzzy, kiwi-faced murder-machine* is what I wanted to say.

"As you were," he orders me. As if I'm his to order.

The defiant lump in my skull took it as a challenge. "What's your name? I don't believe I caught it the last time we met."

He lifts his chin high, looking down at me as if considering whether I'm worth his time. "Locke," he finally says. "Parker Locke." He's viciously hellish; I can feel it. Full of dark matter and a demonic spirit—and not in a fun way.

I intended to hustle information from him, but every single cell inside my body is begging me to leave this man alone. The warning whispers grow ever louder, threatening to consume me whole. This man is the embodiment of death. He could have me sunk because he was bored.

I change my tone, switching to one I despise using. Submissive. "Thank you for your time, Watchman Locke. Before I leave, can you tell me when the next sinking is?"

"1200 this shift. As you were," he dismisses me, leaving me alone in the room bounded by uncertainty and doubt.

9

A child will be sentenced to death in less than an hour.

I need to talk to her. I need to apologize for seeing her hurt and not stepping up to help. For not comforting her in class out of fear someone would see, that someone would report it. *Teachers teach*, the Warden says. *Teachers don't reconcile.*

I'm a coward. I should have done more. If I did, maybe it'd be me in the Vat instead of her.

Storming back to the entrance of the building in a manner in which I can only assume is my *I'm on a mission* walk, I'm pleased at the lack of Watchman Locke and only Mason and Olivia stand outside the Vat. My two familiars.

"Open the door. I need to talk to my student in there," I impatiently tell Mason, motioning for him to move.

Pointing an index finger at me, his newly found Watchman tone slips through. "Ma'am, you need to—"

"—Mason, I swear to whatever higher being you believe in, that if you keep giving me these bullshit Watchman responses, I'll snap that finger of yours off and shove it—"

"—There's an intercom on the wall," Olivia says. My

fists loosen. Breaking my stare from Mason, I incline my head toward her, dictating my facial expressions to stand down. "There's an intercom and a monitor with a live feed to the Vat. The other person can't reply, but they can hear you."

"Watchman Aubert, what do you think you're doing?" Mason spits out. "Don't assist her. Do I need to remind you that the public is unauthorized to use Watchman resources? It's our first patrol shift, and you're breaking code for someone who strolled in here like we owe her an explanation on how we run this beat. Can't you see she's comically a try-hard? Clearly, she's someone who needs to be reminded she's important, otherwise she'll show up unannounced where she's not wanted. She's one of those people who don't respect authority, and if she's not creating problems for herself, she's surrounding herself with drama. She's a nobody. She's a civilian who needs to learn her place and *go home*." He doesn't break his immaculate posture, staring at the entrance door in front of him as if waiting for a massive sea creature to break it down with razor-sharp tentacles and gash out Olivia's tongue for giving me an answer.

I've known Mason to be cautious and reserved, afraid of breaking rules, but I never thought he'd openly reject me. At the very least, he could have stood by and said nothing as I assessed this unmanageable situation. He didn't have to degrade my character as if he'd wanted to say it for years. I've sacrificed so much of my sanity to make sure he feels safe, but when it's my turn to be vulnerable, he can't help but still be afraid of the unknown and push back against me.

Yet here is Olivia, a stranger I've barely met, risking so much and for what reason? I've never needed Mason in the ways he's needed me. I accepted that relationship long ago. I am older, after all. The obligation to shelter him is woven into my DNA.

It's not uncommon for me to skip meals because it means his rations are secure. More times than not, promising him I had already eaten and wasn't hungry, even as my stomach protested. I've learned to bandage his physical and mental wounds while ignoring my own. Made sure each of his insecurities were tightly wrapped with a bow and a kiss. I've spent most of my life defending him against himself and others, speaking up and for him when he couldn't find the right words, but it took him being a Watchman for me to understand how selfish he can be.

The rose-colored lenses I've been wearing crack. Seems like he doesn't need me anymore now that he's discovered his courage.

"How do I use the intercom?" I ask Olivia.

"There's a panel in the hallway around that corner, right past Watchman Quinn. It's used by Watchmen when inmates are unruly with one another." The scorn in her voice at the use of the word *inmate* doesn't go unheard. "Promise me you'll be quick. The cameras rotate between these rooms, but there's a tight window to avoid being seen. Do you understand what I'm telling you?"

"I understand what you're saying." *As if it's hard to*

follow. "How will you know when the camera rotates off that hallway and I can go back?" I ask, curious how she will have the answer to that with all the great answers she seems to have.

Tilting her head to one of the two radios attached to her right shoulder, she inaudibly whispers into the smaller of them. "Go, now. I'll alert you when it's time to exit."

It's as if I'm floating toward the hallway, my mind too busy to form a thought, my legs on autopilot, one foot in front of the other.

Passing by Mason, he tests his luck at coercing me, gripping my upper arm. "Sam, please," he whispers. "*Go home.* Go home, and we'll talk later. Can you do that? Can you do that for me?"

"Do not touch me." Venom drips from my mouth. "This is the last time I warn you, Watchman Quinn." I jerk free from his unwelcome grasp, leaving him stunned at the entrance.

The hallway isn't a hallway, it's more of an alcove. A chair, a keyboard, and a monitor. With a shaking finger hovering over the intercom, I swallow most of my anxiety and hold down the button. "Wren? It's Miss Samara."

Lifting her head from her lap, she searches the empty chamber for the source of my voice. Standing, she sways her head rhythmically, her fingertips swirling above as if she's a marionette, then points to the vast, dark ocean. It's as if it's singing to her like a Siren, luring her to an infinite sleep.

"You're so very brave, Wren," I say, trying not to sound

81

upset.

Atlantic be damned, what do I say? It feels like entire shifts are sweeping past me as I think of what to say. Of what I need to say and what I should be saying. I need to stop overthinking and let my heart take control. She's going to be with her mom in the ocean.

"That's a wonderful knapsack your mom made for you. I'm so happy you were able to get it back."

This has nothing to do with me, I can't let her hear the agony in my voice. She knows what's happening and she's ready to meet the deep to reunite with her mom in the next realm.

Regardless of how someone dies, the Vat disposes of the bodies. The underwater current is strong enough to pull them along, so they aren't left hovering in plain sight as they're swept away into the unknown. I need to believe that she'll be reunited with her mom. Somehow, somewhere out in the Atlantic, their bodies will collide, and they'll be at rest together. They have to be.

"Don't try to hold your breath when you're out in the ocean," I coach her.

Too many adults struggle when there's no point. Instead of accepting their absolute death, they waste precious time in a panic to stop the inevitable, shaving anxious seconds off their limited life span.

"You're going to hear a loud buzzer. It'll play three times, then red lights will spin above you. When the buzzer stops, the chamber you're standing in will fill with water, but

remember you're brave. Remember your mom is waiting for you somewhere on the other side of the window, and you'll be together again. Hold tight to your pack when the water comes in. Everything will happen fast, but keep your eyes closed and look for your mom in your mind. She'll find you."
I've never felt so helplessly gut-wrenched in my entire life.

Knowing she'll be released from this submerged plane of existence, a subtle tinge of jealousy shudders through me. What does that feel like, the emptiness of an endless sleep? To no longer be confined in Foxtrot but instead guided by a magnetic pull to a gentle rest, free of anger and hurt. Free from the biting fear that I'll never be good enough. I hope it's a soothing, vibrating darkness. A kind of darkness that swallows—

A strange, static sound echoes from the entrance, followed by my name in a whisper, reeling me back to reality. Although unfamiliar with the sound, I understand it to be Olivia's signal. I'm out of time.

———◄○►———

I stood in the Observatory until the red lights from the Vat no longer reflected off the darkness of the water. Until the water-tight chamber was filled enough to prompt the remote lever pull. Until the side doors opened, and she was vacuumed into the ocean, drifting past me.

Her fiery-red hair floated around her as she was pulled into the openness, the Watchman's blood a crimson cloud washing off her skin. She kept her eyes tightly closed, clenching the knapsack against her chest. Whether she consciously gripped it or if her body was caving in on itself, I'm not sure. But she looked peaceful.

I stood there as her body moved through the near-black nothingness, going exactly nowhere and everywhere in a casual yet hurried flow in the underwater current until she was out of sight. Until the spotlights in front of me shut off, and all that was left was my reflection against the Observatory window.

10

My adopted home is filled with the ghosts of laughter and memories, but Ruth tries her best to keep it alive. She refused to move once it became a skeleton, keeping all of Jerald's belongings, as well as mine and Mason's, and still meanders through the rooms as if searching for a purpose.

Ruth opens the front door, peeking around me for my vacant half. "My girl, did I get my shifts mixed up again? I wasn't expecting you or your brother for dinner until the next shift." Excitement bubbles out of her. She brings me in for a hug, making me feel like a child again, safe in her embrace.

"I wanted to talk to you about something. Is this a bad time? I can come back if you're busy. I'm sorry, I should have called first," I ramble, feeling like an unexpected visitor.

"There's never a bad time for you. Come on." She lovingly takes my hand, leading me inside. I cherish the split-second spark in my chest cavity that's been engulfed with desolation since leaving the Vat.

As Wren disappeared into the deep, the last shred of hope I might've been holding onto was left in the

Observatory. Though usually a welcome sight, I brushed past Mason and left the building without saying a word to him or Olivia. I didn't have time to stop and diffuse my rapid thoughts.

Ruth hands me a plate of potato crisps, factory-made Foxtrot meat, and a fizzy drink on the couch. "What's on your mind, my girl?"

I'm confident she's never lied to me. At least, not an actual lie. Parents sneak harmless lies to their children to lessen the truth, but I'll watch for her tell, if she has one. I pride myself on reading people and noticing when they're nervous, but I hope I don't pick up on one.

A potato crisp crumbles between my fingers. "The Warden sunk one of my students." I meant to take a bite, but saying that confession aloud made it all too real.

Her expressive eyes succumb to misery. "I know."

Without questioning her directly, I ask, "You know? But it ... it happened less than an hour ago. How could you know?"

"There's a lot I know that you don't, and I think it's time you did. I'll be right back." She gently grips my shoulder, walking past.

The sudden loss of Wren and this unexpected riddle from Ruth are making me parched. It's hard to swallow these potato crisps and unnaturally developed meat. My feet tap against the floor, my mouth feeling too heavy, the trivial food an added weight. It's as if my skin is dripping from me, my soul turning to liquid. I stare blankly across the room at nothing.

Ruth returns to the living room, holding a cardboard box in her arms. She places it on the table in front of us, her hands resting on the box, guarding its secrets. "I think you should explore this on your own. I'll make up your bed. Stay here while you dig through all that, doesn't matter how long it takes. I'll be around if you need me to help answer any questions." She kisses me on the forehead, leaving me alone in the living room.

It's nice being back home. I can't fathom seeing Mason back at our apartment. I'd rather be surrounded by Ruth's loving energy than Mason's neurotic negativity.

She's a nobody, he said. *Someone who needs to be reminded she's important.*

I don't need to feel important, I need to feel ... purpose. I crave control, crave the weightlessness of impulsivity. *He* needs to feel important, that's why he trained to be a Watchman. He's a fucking shithead.

Overwhelming hesitation keeps me still. I glare at the box, contemplating whether or not I want to open it. Ruth hands me an oversized, roasted-sienna crew-neck sweatshirt. "You can keep that, my love."

Tears spill down my cheeks. I put on Jerald's sweatshirt, pressing my face into the sleeves and wiping away my gloom, nodding my head in thanks. I needed this strength.

Removing my face from the fabric, I stare at the box again. It's not too large, not too small, but plenty big to hold secrets. Secrets I'm hesitant to discover. I open the folds, diving into the unknown.

There are at least fifteen journals. Some the size of my hand, others more traditional in length, more than half sharing the height between the two, and all of them have that winged insect sketched on the front. Selecting a journal on top, I read the first page:

12, February

My dear Ruth, it's time you knew the truth. I should have told you sooner, but I needed to keep you and the twins safe. I know I became distant, and for that I am truly sorry, my love. There's so much I need to tell you before it's too late. These secrets can't sink with me if there's a chance you may see the surface. If you're reading this, it's because I've passed on, and I imagine you've stumbled across this hidden box. In here, you'll find journals with everything you need to piece all this together, but before you read any further, please remember I love you. I have always loved you. I will love you forever.

I set the journal on the coffee table and close my eyes, wondering if I should be reading this. It's too personal. But Ruth gave me this box knowing this journal was here. She's sharing this with me. I continue reading:

In this box, you'll find my personal journals detailing findings, as well as shared journals between like-minded individuals. Let me start by saying this: the surface is alive, my Ruth. All we have to do is swim. I know that sounds impossible, but please hear me out.

Honestly, I don't know where to start, but the beginning is best. It was before we adopted the twins. I was a rookie when I overheard a conversation about the surface and thought the same thing you're probably thinking: Didn't the surface die? The two individuals were convinced it reset itself, all we had to do was reach it. They explained they were recruits of a movement and shared their theories with me—I couldn't help but join.

Have you noticed there's an insect drawn on the cover of each of these journals? Those were insects that also used to live under the surface for most of their lives. They are us. We are Cicadas. There are too many curious minds for Foxtrot to contain. I knew what I was signing up for, but if it meant there was a chance I could stand next to you beneath a tree with the wind caressing our faces, I had to try. Please my love, know I had to try.

Tears flood my vision. My forehead finds comfort in my palms, billions of questions exploding in my head like fireworks. I straighten my stiff posture on the couch, an icy prickle shooting up my spine. I massage my lower back, twisting my torso, tilting my head side to side.

Nightmares last sleep shift, check. Hauling my out-of-shape ass down to the foster agency, check. Walking miles to Sec-One to get to the Vat, check. Standing in the Observatory too long while digesting and accepting a child was sunk, check. Hunching over a farewell letter written by someone I loved so deeply the pain is cycling through me again, check and check.

Trudging to the kitchen, I find Ruth sitting at the dining table, staring at a photograph of all four of us in her hands. "How far did you get?" she asks.

I absentmindedly dig through the pantry for food. "He was explaining the insects drawn on the journals. How he joined some kind of movement."

The word feels strange in my mouth. *Movement* makes it seem like a collaborative understanding. Are there a lot of people who think about the surface? Who are these people? *Where* are these people?

"There should be grits in there somewhere. If you like, I can make them for you."

I set the paper bag on the counter, opening a cupboard for a bowl. "I don't mind. Thank you though. It'll help me process what I've read."

"Please, Sammy. Let me make it for you. I would love to."

Sensing she needs the distraction more than I do, I close the cupboard, giving her a smile. I rub the lower part of my back. "If it's all right, I'll be in my room with the journals. I'd rather lie down to read than hunch over the couch."

She smiles, wiping away a tear. "I'll bring it to your room when it's ready."

After we adopted the twins, I knew I had to save them from this place, save all four of us. I began with the Grand Stories, hoping they would become passionate about the surface. Do you remember when I found the book of the surface? Of course you do. You nearly took off my head when I brought it home! I should've told you then instead of lying, but I've shared the information we copied amongst the movement. The Cicadas were able to read about the true surface, not the type of surface the Warden tells us.

Cicadas share journals, detailing investigations. We hide them in drops to rotate them, but we can only assume a lot were confiscated because too many drops were empty when they shouldn't have been. We all agreed to hide as many journals as possible among the members.

It's a sad truth, but some people were careless and used our true names in the entries instead of our aliases. It's a mistake that's claimed many. The Cicadas whose identities were revealed were sunk without explanation, and the Watchmen not in alliance with us followed the orders from Gryme. Others' deaths were staged for reasons I can't explain. Why produce an end when a sinking is more common? Everyone is on edge, and over the years some have become too afraid to remain in the movement. They're blending in and hiding within Foxtrot, severing themselves from the cause and taking our secrets with them.

I'm afraid to admit I recently found my full name in a journal. I blacked it out, but there's no telling who has already seen it. I couldn't rip the page out, it had too much information on both sides to ruin because my name was there. My friend Ocelot told me she saw my name in a different journal, and that someone else told her they saw it in yet another. We tried to remove those journals from rotation, but there's no telling where those journals ended up. I'm afraid some are still out there. This could be my undoing. If Warden Gryme finds out ...

I'm telling you all of this in case something happens to me. So you can find peace or answers or at the very least know the truth. I've asked my most trusted friend to check in on you should something happen to me. If someone introduces themselves to you as Root, they're safe. Root will explain to you how to find a Cicada in public if you ever need help.

The movement is large, but I have a few close friends who you can trust above all. They are a force. They are loyal to the cause, loyal to me as I am to them. It's an inner circle of friendship within the movement, their kin included. It's not a large circle, a handful of people, but their front doors are painted a different shade of white, like ours.

These journals have further proof of the new surface, escape plans, and theories. Read them with caution, I beg of you. To become a Cicada means there's a bounty, and the price may be a soul. After losing so many people, I stopped telling the twins my Grand Stories. I couldn't risk putting them in danger without having a plan. Sometimes I fear Sammy has resented me because of it.

I know this is asking a lot, but if she ever comes to you looking for answers, please let her read these journals. She's *always been attracted to the surface, though I can only blame myself for that. Please let her find the answers she's searching for and support whatever path she takes. She's not meant to live here. None of us are.*

I love you,

-J

Soft knocking on the bedroom door reels me back. Ruth enters the room with a bed tray full of goodies. In a ceramic bowl, walnuts and syrup top the grits with a smiley face, the way she used to do when I was younger. Dried apricots and pickled cucumbers lay in tasty rows, banana and apple slices next to the potato crisps, and a small ramekin of chocolate-covered almonds.

She makes sure to fill our totes with goodies after each visit, but I didn't realize she was this well off from the commissary allotment she receives from Jerald's service with the Watchmen. Maybe she feels as if this is a special occasion. Or maybe the mundane preparation of this platter was a moment she could spend taking care of someone again instead of being stuck in her head. Either way, I'm grateful.

"Thank you." I set the journal on the bed and pick up the bowl, swallowing down the perfectly made grits. "I finished Jerald's entry."

She sighs, joining me on the bed. "I can't say I was too surprised when I read it. Even if I didn't know for sure, my intuition felt like he was hiding something. Not in a way that points to infidelity, but more so he was shielding me, shielding us from the horrors he might have seen on the job. I had suspicions it was in our best interest not to know. I didn't pressure him. I trusted him. I never imagined it was to this extent."

"A secret movement is a lot to take in, I wasn't expecting this either. Have you contacted any of the Cicadas?"

"I have." Another spark ignites in my chest. "Samara, will you be pursuing this outside of the journals? Because if you are, I'll tell you everything I know. But if you're not, and no one will blame you if you don't, I'll leave well enough alone."

A chocolate-covered almond spins between my fingers. Knowing the cost of joining could be my soul is a heavy burden I wasn't prepared to face. If I impulsively pull the trigger and explore this movement, I could very well end up on the same side as Jerald. He was stronger than me. He was capable and discrete. Atlantic, he was a *Watchman*. And now he's dead.

My withered *heads* side of the coin spins with logic: Who am I to try my hand at this movement if Jerald wasn't able to? I can't take on this task. This is too big for me, there's no shame in admitting that. I can't join a movement and sneak under the Warden and his Watchmen. Who's to say I won't be caught? That I won't sink because of this?

My *tails* side of the coin spins and spins with impulse: Joining this movement can fulfill the desire for purpose, for meaning. Whether the surface is or was, something has to be up there. Jerald can't die for nothing. All the Cicadas who were caught can't die for nothing. Death is not something to fear, it's something to respect. Everyone dies. But it has to matter ... *I* matter.

My *tails* finally lands. Jerald was right, I'm not meant to live here. None of us are. Confidence replaces my anxiety. "I want to join the movement."

"Then it won't be for nothing." She places a hand on her chest. "It won't be for nothing."

11

"Desmond was a Cicada recruit?" I blurt out through a mouthful of apple slices. "Deranged Desmond, or do you mean another Desmond?"

"He wasn't always unbalanced, you know," Ruth says. "He wasn't always deranged. Keeping so many secrets and being helpless against the demise of friends can leave a trail of paranoia and survivor's guilt. Death always collects its due, and it eventually occupies the mind. It can rot and fester, bleeding through one's reality and spilling madness in its wake. It would help if you were more patient with those who have lost their way." She gives me a tight smile that reminds me not to cast aspersions.

"I met a woman in my complex who said something similar—about Desmond's mind being occupied. She told me to tell you she said hello," I mumble, feeling twice ashamed I haven't been more empathetic to Desmond's struggles.

Ruth smirks, stealing a pickled cucumber from the bed tray. "You must have met Sonia, then."

My encounter with Sonia repaints itself in my mind's

eye. Her willingness to let me explore her apartment and the unprompted information about Desmond's stories are so clear in my memory. Had she not said anything, had we ridden the elevator in silence, I would've never gone to her apartment in search of Desmond's stories. But they weren't stories. They were shared, secret, life-changing discoveries she hid for him because he couldn't escape the emptiness devouring him.

Curiosity strikes. "Who else is a Cicada?"

She clears crumbs from the bed in a sweeping motion. "I don't know for sure, but I know there are many. I've only met with Jerald's inner circle so far, and they've been waiting for you to come around. To start asking questions and become a Cicada."

That doesn't make sense. Not in the slightest. I breathe past my throbbing heart. "I don't even know who his close friends are. They don't know *me*. Why have they been waiting for me to join?"

"After reading through these journals and talking with his friends, I learned how much you inspired Jerald. He loved you and your brother completely. Our family was whole, the four of us, and he refused to accept this was the life we were meant to live. He saw that same flame ignite in you. He was confident you'd become a Cicada, that you'd be drawn to the pull. His inner circle knows all about Apricus." The golden hue behind her green eyes shines.

"Apricus?" The word is unusual in my mouth.

Linguistics is a dormant field. It belongs only to those

whom the Warden has approved to study it. As much as I wanted to learn the ways of a polyglot, my application was denied four times. Exploring the science of languages eludes me, but I know the word isn't *approved*—it's not English. I repeat it aloud, keeping the *A* and *i* soft. It's another strange word I get to keep.

"In Latin, it means *having lots of sunshine.* When you were little, you once asked how sunshine felt, how it smelled, and if it tasted like warm lemon cookies. That innocence inspired Jerald to nickname you Apricus to his friends. I'm sure you read the part about aliases and what happens when a name is slipped." She rubs her arms, warding off a nonexistent draft. "With sunshine comes an incredible heat. A fiery existence that can't be put out, not even with all the water from all the oceans combined. Jerald noticed that fire and believed you could apply it to the movement. Many parents are involved in the movement, hoping for a better life for their children. Most of them are adults now who grew up sharing the same beliefs. I've been waiting for sunshine to give light to this dreadful gloom. The Cicadas are lucky you've joined, Sammy. You can help save us all."

"But I don't know how to save anyone. I couldn't save Wren." Her name is a sledgehammer, nearly knocking me to the ground. "I'm made of fire because I welcome any anger and all the hurt because it's what I've taught myself is normal. If anything, I'm destined to live a rage-filled life, unable to fully trust anyone. How am I supposed to help *save* anyone when I'm barely a functioning adult? I'm twenty-six and live with my brother because I'm terrified of living alone. I can't sleep without waking up from screaming. I need to be in control all the time that I guiltlessly manipulate anyone to gain an edge. I'm not a good person!" Mouthfuls of doubt ooze from me, unsure if my vision of seeing myself on the surface is enough to bring anyone with me.

"Everything you've been through has led you to where you need to be. You're a survivor, my girl. You've lived with the beast of self-doubt for so long, it has convinced you that you're worthless, but you're not. You're indispensable as a daughter, a sister, and a friend. Even if you can't see the fire or feel it, others can. You've learned to dance in the flames instead of being consumed. Trust yourself." She brushes the bangs from her viridian eyes.

I stare at the floor, processing what she's saying, not entirely believing her. *Fire,* she says. "You're supposed to say things like that." I toss an apple slice her way. She catches it and takes a bite. If being full of *fire* means burning everything in my path because I'm afraid to rebuild, then sure. But I'd say I'm full of spite. I change the subject. "Who isn't a Cicada?"

I already know the name of at least one person.

She crosses a leg and leans against the bedframe, respecting the shift in conversation. "I'm sure you can guess that your brother doesn't know of the movement. Until necessary, I ask you to keep it to yourself. We both know how sensitive to change he is. I worry he'll push back or create waves where they're not needed." She reaches forward and steals a cucumber. I don't interrupt her thought process to gloat. Instead, I swallow my words and bite my tongue, waiting for her to continue.

"The Watchmen in our alliance assure us that Cicadas aren't common knowledge, but there are specific Watchmen assigned to infiltrate the movement. Those Watchmen have free reign in all sectors in search of a weak spot, so keep your wits about. Warden Gryme's Prime Watchmen must be avoided entirely."

Gryme's Primes—fucking narcissist. "Are there a lot of these *Primes*? How do I know who to avoid?"

"There are only four, but that's four too many. They're like bloodhounds. You remember those canines from the book of the surface?"

Uneasiness tenses in my shoulders. Bloodhounds were scent hounds bred to track and hunt, known to be relentless. I give her a worrisome nod.

"The Cicadas have learned three of their full names but only three of their identities. Prime Watchman Gideon is a sneaky one, no one has been able to figure out his full name or what he looks like. He's not as familiar as the other three. Someone known only by last name is a dangerous person. We imagine his activity is more behind the scenes."

A mystery Prime. How am I supposed to avoid a wraith? "And the three others?"

"Prime Watchman Lilly Sampson is the only woman. Or *was*, I should say. She's no longer a threat. Rumor has it a little girl put a tactical knife through her temple." A cunning smile slips past her lips. My eyes widen in disbelief at the sight of it. "Don't gawk at me, Sammy. It's terrible what happened, even more so that it was an innocent child who snapped and fell into that darkness. One less Prime means more Cicadas will live. Your student saved the lives of many by sacrificing her own, even if she didn't know she was doing it. Warden Gryme is a coward for ordering the fate of a child out of spite because she eliminated one of his *special* Watchmen." Ruth takes a deep breath, shaking off a shiver.

"Another Prime is Watchman Parker Locke. He's the youngest of them all and the most active. I don't know how to properly explain him to you, but there is something ... dark ... about him. As if he was selected to be a Prime simply for his lust for people to sink. He seems to be obsessed with death. He's known to accuse people of being Cicadas, even when they're not. He plants evidence on them to 'prove' it to the Warden. The Warden doesn't question it, of course. He trusts Prime Watchman Locke to do his bidding." Her fist meets the mattress, the dishes on the bed tray clattering. I stack them neatly off to the side.

I felt his darkness outside the restroom. My instincts spiked. He had an aura, one that whispered the imminence of death. He had the strangest questions for me when we first met. *I can't place it, but you look familiar. Who are your parents?* Maybe he recognized me since I'm connected to Jerald. I keep that information to myself, nodding for Ruth to continue.

"The last Prime is Watchman Nathan Marlow. He's the

leader of the Primes and was Jerald's partner. There's no proof, but I know he had a hand in Jerald's death. I can feel it." Her nostrils flare, jaw clenching. She stares at the wall behind me. "Watchman Marlow is a trapdoor spider. If he ever visits me, it'll be the last thing he ever does." She abruptly stands, jolting me from her fierce trance. "I've gotten myself worked up, Sammy. I'm sorry. I know this is a lot to take in. I'll grab us the tea."

"Are you—"

"—Lemon? Syrup?"

"Wait, are you sure that you're—"

"—I'll keep it plain and bring the toppings on the side. How does that sound?" She blinks away the tears trying to break free.

Clearing my throat, I stand and hug her. "That sounds perfect." She closes the door behind her.

Staring at the journals on the bed, I pace around the room. There's nothing ominous about joining a movement while being hunted down by bloodhounds. Nothing unsettling about The Trapdoor Spider, The Death Whisperer, or The Wraith.

Who needs normal—what *is* normal? My normal is to wake up, go to work, and go home. Wake up, teach what I'm told, and go home. Wake up when I'm told, teach what I'm told, go home when I'm told. Because *they* said.

What about what I have to say? This movement makes more sense the more I think about it. Don't do something because *they* said to do it; *try* something else. To the Atlantic with the risks, I need to *do* something meaningful.

Ruth standing beside me doesn't register until she puts a hand on my shoulder. "It's almost lights-out. I'd love it if you spent the sleep shift here. It'll be like old times." She hands me the cup and plate of sliced lemons, a spoonful of syrup on the side. We sip the tea and reminisce until the lights-out siren chirps.

Lying in my childhood bed, listening to the rhythm of the fan blades with heavy eyelids, I pray to whatever god is still listening to not give me nightmares.

12

Principal Jeup,

I hope the start of your wakeful shift is treating you well. I was anticipating being back in class to teach, but I regret to inform you that I'm not feeling well enough to return. After my unexpected departure, I'm embarrassed to tell you that a stomach ailment has me confined to the restroom. I will not be able to make it to work this shift, or the next. I fear I'll be too distracted to teach. Most importantly, I don't wish to pass this sickness off to the children. I'll let you know as soon as my symptoms improve and when I can return, but if I'm honest, there's no end in sight. Thank you for understanding,

Miss Samara

A little bit too formal, but I giggle at the theatrics and shut Ruth's laptop. Closing the door of my childhood bedroom, nostalgia runs my fingers across the dusty dresser and aligns the mismatched and too-small shoes at the base of the door. The little girl who used to dream of the surface still flows through my veins. I can't silence her any longer. *I matter.*

Humming over a skillet of sizzling onions and tomatoes, Ruth pours rehydrated powdered eggs into a frying pan from a bowl held too high above her head. I lean into the doorframe. "I have to admit, that's impressive."

"They taste better the higher they fall. Don't tell anyone, but gravity is the secret ingredient. Takes the powder right out of them. They'll be farm-fresh, and that's a fact," she snickers.

"Gravity, huh? I read somewhere that if you pour them from that height, it's the velocity that gets them so velvety. Also, hot sauce. The hot sauce helps." My serious face fails me.

Laughing with Ruth is a much-needed cleanse. The last time I genuinely laughed is a moment in time I can't recall. Eating the bouncy and still powdery eggs feeds that contagious laughter, along with my sanity and stomach.

Piercing a peppery tomato with my fork, I indulge in its sweet acidity. "Can I borrow some clothes? I think I'll head home in a bit to gather some things, but I'm hoping to avoid Mason for as long as I can."

"Of course you can. May I ask why you're avoiding your brother?" She has a curious yet motherly tone, staring at me from across the table.

I examine my near-empty plate in search of a distraction. She's saying, *May I ask* as a courtesy. She's not asking for permission. She's carefully telling me to fill her in on my built-up animosity she must have noticed.

Without overthinking the response, instead, letting it

run like fluid from my lips, I ask, "Have you ever felt like your heart and brain are in a death match to win?" I pause so my voice doesn't crack. "I don't know how to explain it, but my heart is pounding through my chest that I need Mason to do any of this because he's the best version of myself. But my brain is screaming that he's someone to keep at arm's length. And they both make sense, but they don't make sense together. I don't know which one to listen to."

She moves aside her plate, lacing her hands on the table. "Well, let's break that down a bit. Why does your heart tell you that you need him? Surely you're capable on your own."

"Because he's my person. My best friend, my—"

"—Crutch, safety net, safe place?" The interjection is without judgment.

"Yes," I admit, gulping down orange juice.

"That's a rare connection to share with someone. If you separate yourself from him, what does your heart say?"

The easy answer is that we rely on each other too much, but I'm not convinced that's the root of these clashing feelings. I take a moment to think. "He's not the better extension of me. He's more of a skeleton key, there when I need him and tucked away when I don't. He can be logical and reasonable, but so can I. And I can be impulsive and arbitrary, but so can he. We're identically opposite but a complete jigsaw piece when put together."

I have to admit, this reminds me of an impromptu therapy session. With each unpredictable toss of the coin, *heads* or *tails* can land and take turns.

"Sounds right to me," she says, interrupting my thoughts. "Now let's figure out your brain. Why is it screaming at you to keep him at bay?"

The abiding annoyance is crisp on my tongue. "Because he's content with following the rules."

"Samara, let's try that again," she says, softly reminding me to separate myself from him and my passive thoughts.

"Because I need to protect him," I finally say, once the question finishes squirming through all the gyri and sulci surrounding my brain. "I don't know what's ahead, and I can't bring him along. That's not fair for him."

"Have you considered speaking with him? I'm sure you have a lot to say, as does he. In the end, we both know you won't leave him behind."

Speak to him? No.

Yell at him? Yes.

Maybe my half-truths at the Husk, sneaking around at Sonia's, and my surprise visit to the Vat threw him off-kilter. His comments at the Vat were hurtful, but I should've been more understanding of the situation I forced us into.

My knee-jerk reaction to feeling betrayed by his pushback may have been unjust. I risked being caught on surveillance by entering the Watchman hallway because of my lack of impulse control. I'd have been annoyed, too, if the roles were reversed. I might have said nastier comments than the ones he gave me.

He must have been trying to deter me with his comments because he was afraid for me. More selfishly, afraid of what would happen to him if he no longer had me because I've felt that way before. I've been afraid of what would become of me if I reached the pits of my despair, fearful of how my rage would taste if faced with another loss. I don't think I'd be able to withstand it. I wouldn't survive it.

If I had been caught, I would've been nothing more than a waterlogged corpse doomed to hover wherever the current took me. I should've given him the benefit of the doubt, he might've surprised me.

Maybe my heart and brain haven't been fighting. Maybe they've been trying to create a symphony of emotions that complement each other if I listen.

13

Passing through the lobby, my ears are on high alert, listening for Mason's familiar gait and the keys jangling on his belt loop. I doubt he's here at all. His acceptance letter said to report at 0800 to his trainer each shift, and it's well past that. He shouldn't be here, but I'm cautious of a coincidence. I have secrets in my satchel. Secrets I don't want to share with him. Secrets I can't share with anyone ... yet.

Weaving through my neighbors, I channel an air of nonchalance, mumbling greetings and compliments to them. *Oh yes, lovely wakeful shift. Green is* your *color. How are the kids?*

Small talk can sink.

The older gentleman at the post boxes spots my ridiculous behavior, glaring down at me through caterpillar eyebrows. I point two fingers at him with a shake of the wrists and a wink. "Looking as charming as ever, Mr. Sawyer."

Pressing the elevator button, the indicator above displays a red X. Out of service again. Who knows how long until it's fixed—if at all. Stepping away from the elevator, I open the familiar door to the left, revealing my old nemesis. The seemingly never-ending stairs to the fifteenth floor are less daunting than before. I'm less anxious about taking on the cardio, but I prepared this time.

Stopping in the stairwell outside of the sixth floor, I sit cross-legged on the cement landing. Digging into my satchel, I retrieve a Cicada journal. Ruth said to wait until I got home to read more, but there's no one in here with me, no cameras in the corners. Besides, I'll hear someone coming. Briefly pausing to catch my breath, I finish the last page I fell asleep to at Ruth's:

Mars and I were finally able to get into the wing where the emergency escape capsules are stored. It took some creativity and a lot of patience, but we documented it. I'll sketch the layout and give it to Root.

The good news is there were a lot. More than you can imagine. We split up into sections, and between the two of us, counted seventy-three interfaces that responded to touch commands, but that's not even half of what's there. At least three people can fit in each, four if someone doesn't mind a tight squeeze. Maybe five with a child.

The bad news is a lot of them had cracked screens and exposed wiring. I think we can assume they were sabotaged. I'm sure someone could fix them, but it'd be risky. We only had a thirty-minute window to get in and out. We need to lay low for a while, but we'll recheck this wing to see if we can fix them.

~~Saturn~~

I almost forgot. Ocelot got us a type of sticker. But I guess it isn't a sticker, it's like a wad? If it's rolled a few times it'll stick to anything. We stuck them to the underside of the vessels that responded to touch commands.

If you're facing the front of the capsule, reach beneath it and feel under its belly, under the seat nearest the controls. You'll feel the sticker. It's recycled and textured. It'll feel like you're touching a raisin. Kind of. Those are the capsules that lit up.

Saturn

All the effort, correspondence, and involvement put into this movement is bigger than I expected. They seem coordinated and determined. They're risking their lives for a *sketch* to pass along to someone else. How would someone gain access to an escape wing?

This is the first I've heard of such a wing, and I've read Foxtrot's schematics—Atlantic, I have to *teach* the schematics. How else would the Warden remind everyone that he keeps us safe in this starfish-shaped facility without imbuing our youth.

Pushing past the temptation to read more, I shut the journal, tucking it away in my satchel, and continue my cardio to Sonia's. My fingers absentmindedly tap against the pockets of it across my torso, resting on my hip. Tap-tap. I crack my neck and knuckles to release the gnawing pull. Tap-tap-tap. One foot in front of the other, I slide the satchel from the front of my body, letting it rest on my backside.

Out of sight, out of mind. If I can't see it, it's no longer there. Tap-tap-tap-tap.

My possessed fingers find my satchel on my back with ease and death grip its straps, swinging it frontside again. There's no harm in reading a bit more. I'll stop on the seventh-floor landing to rest, it's only a few steps away. Besides, these entries are easy to finish, most are a few quick paragraphs.

Giving in to the urge on the seventh-floor landing, I blindly rummage in my sack and get cozy on the cement. With my legs outstretched, the right over the left, my eager eyes consume a few more paragraphs:

There's a rumor of a detonation switch being controlled from the command center to prevent a successful escape. No one can prove it or disprove it. It could be a scare tactic. We won't know until ...

"Ahem."

... we try. We need to prepare ourselves that we may not reach the surface with the escape capsules alone. There are compact respirators hidden somewhere in Foxtrot. Some say it looks like a squid is hugging your face. Once I find the wing for the breathing equipment, all we have to do is ...

"Excuse me," an unfamiliar voice echoes through the stairwell.

I instinctively slam the journal shut, placing it underneath my body. If being inconspicuous was awarded with a smiley face on top of an exam paper for a job well done, I would have precisely zero smiley faces.

A woman is halfway in the landing with me, struggling to enter through the crack of the door from the seventh-floor hallway. I give her an innocent smile. "Hi there."

"Your feet are in the way," she chides. "I can't open the door. You're a thin little thing, but your feet are made of lead. Didn't you hear me clear my throat?" A hint of annoyance lingers on the question.

"No, I didn't hear you. I've been busy finishing my lesson plan and must've been stuck in my head. Here, let me move." Pulling my legs in faster than I can finish the sentence, I simultaneously stand upright and step on the Cicada journal, covering it with my feet.

"This is a strange place to be finishing a lesson plan. Don't you think it would make more sense for you to be somewhere else?" Her judgmental tone follows her into the landing with a limp, favoring her left leg. A tote of oranges swings on her wrist, a stern face warning *I can smell lies*.

To add to my last-minute charade, I reach down and pick up my satchel, careful not to move my feet too much, and pull out my school planner I'm never without. "The next lesson is about Warden Calum Gryme and how he was empowered to be our leader. You see, it's important to teach our youth that he comes from a lineage of leaders, each of his predecessors within his bloodline. His family was destined for greatness." A volcano builds inside of me, ready to erupt. I swallow down the lava. "It's hard to pick a favorite because it's undeniable they've all done so much to keep us all safe, but since Warden Calum Gryme is the leader I've grown up with, he's my favorite. When he hosts the Tri-Annual Sector Appreciation, I get pinpricks! The kids love it when I explain the—"

"—Fascinating," she breathes. Brushing past me, her tote of oranges knocks against my elbow as she hobbles down the flight of stairs.

Standing still with a shit-eating grin and lesson plan in hand, I wait until the top of her hair is no longer visible before carefully stepping off the journal. Tucking it into my satchel, I can't escape the overwhelming shame of being so careless. Tightly closing my eyes, I try to burn the last words I said from my memory.

Though it's true Calum Gryme became Warden after his father's death simply by being born, as I'm sure one of his sons will become our next Warden once he expires, it's repulsive to imagine admiring him in any way. But that's what I'm told to teach—what I'm forced to teach.

Praise Warden Calum Gryme, the man who murders anyone who finds his talons.

14

The off-white door is a welcoming sight. It feels *right* to trust everything I've read, to trust all of what Ruth has told me, and to trust the movement because it doesn't make sense not to. How can so many people sharing the same thought be wrong? How can anything about the surface be *wrong*?

My knuckles barely touch the door. It swings open, and delicate arms pull me inside. "Samara," Sonia whispers into my chest through an embrace, her hair tickling my chin.

Unsure of what to do, I reciprocate the hug, nimbly hopping to close the door with my foot. "Seems like you were expecting me." The palms of my hands pat her shoulder blades. It's not that I don't like being hugged. Well, I *usually* don't, but I don't know why we're hugging. I'm cautious and skeptical about this sudden embrace. She's a stranger I've only met one other time.

Her right hand sweeps the living room, gesturing to the two steaming mugs on the coffee table and the single recliner with a newly added floor cushion. "I'm so happy you're here. Come, sit."

I take a seat on the floor cushion and Sonia takes hers

in the recliner. We both pick up the cups, sipping the tea. It reminds me of the one Ruth makes, warm and rich with a hint of lemon. Contemplating what to ask first, patiently waiting for the right moment as we drink the tea, I charge my silver tongue. I could play with the conversation—see how far I could get before she realizes she shouldn't be telling me something. A well-planted question can unlock many doors.

"Did you know I would be stopping by?" I ask, deciding against deception. I need to practice being more direct, even if I have to force self-confidence. The path to manipulating my way into answers is well beaten, but I have to teach myself how to be more capable instead of dancing between guessing games and waiting for someone to falter. I don't want to come across as untrustworthy because even though Jerald spoke so highly of me to his closest friends, I still need to prove myself. I need to control the flames and learn to feed them.

"Ruth sent me an encrypted email, but don't worry. It's safe. Over the years, Cicadas have set up a network of untraceable codes. I've taught your mother so we can communicate with each other. You must understand that a woman my age can't be walking for miles between all five sectors, digging through drops. It's a miracle I can still use my fingers to type, but I manage," she whispers with ease, leaning back in the recliner and rocking.

"What did the email say? I want to be in the know so I don't accidentally slip up." My hands jut around as I speak. "Sonia, why are we whispering?"

She giggles, her fingertips touching her lips to hide a smirk. Her tone increases in volume. "Old habits, I suppose. This floor is safe. My closest neighbors on either side are six doors down the hall. We don't have to be whispering."

There's a glow around her, encompassing her with serenity and comfort. She's what I imagine an autumn wind would feel like, refreshing and inviting. In the brief moments I've spent with her before and the time I've shared with her now, I know she's a generous soul who'd sacrifice her life for someone she loves.

Sometimes, when I reflect on my trauma, I wish I could wipe it all away and start anew, free of hindrance and anger. But other times, such as this, I'm grateful I was forced to learn the ability to read people for my gain because it hasn't led me astray yet.

"Hand me the computer, will you? It's under there." She points to the table in front of us, pulling my focus back to the living room.

Blindly reaching underneath, I feel for the laptop and in one fluid motion, pick up the computer, stand to place it in Sonia's lap, and resume my seat on the floor cushion.

"You're quick on your feet, I see. That'll come in handy. Believe it or not, I used to be spritely myself. But that's neither here nor there. Let's see where that email went." She opens her laptop, muttering under her breath about passwords and buttons. After what felt entirely too long for my tapping, impatient feet, she says, "Dear me, I can't see anything." Reaching for her reading glasses on the end table next to her, she gingerly unfolds the plastic arms, breathes warm air onto them, and wipes them clean on her shirt. Putting them on, she squints at the screen, time slowly melting away into an unreachable corner. I find myself leaning closer to her, nearly bursting with anticipation. "I've got it now. Would you like me to read it to you, or do you prefer to read it to yourself?" She removes the glasses from her face, unaware I'm moments away from exploding into a million impatient pieces.

"I'll read it to myself." I gently take the computer from her and resume my seat on the floor cushion with the laptop in my lap, and finally read the email from Ruth:

Sonia, the first of the month will be here sooner than you know. You should welcome it with open arms, it's here! I think I'll put fresh lemons on my list for next month's allotment order.

All my best, Ruth

Reading it a few more times, I can't piece together how Sonia knew I'd be here. It makes sense to speak in riddles through email because I'm sure it could be hacked, but it's unclear to me, even as someone vaguely familiar with the movement. "I don't understand," I say curtly, reading it a fourth time.

Sonia chuckles, motioning to the laptop with wiggling fingers. She finishes her ritual of unfolding the glasses, cleaning them, and putting them back on. "I'd say that's a good thing. Let me explain." She places a finger on the screen and reads it to herself, that finger of hers an inchworm against the brightness following the text. "*The first of the month will be here sooner than you know,*" she reads aloud. "She means you, Samara. As the firstborn twin, you're the first of the month. She's saying you'll be stopping by." She takes a moment to run her fingers across the screen, slowly nodding. "When she wrote, *you should welcome it with open arms, it's here. S*he's telling me you'd like to become a Cicada. Of course, I welcome you. She paid tribute to Jerald when she wrote she'd order fresh lemons. You are Apricus, after all. I'm sure the sun tastes of warm, lemon cookies." She shuts the laptop and resumes her rocking.

All the effort to let Sonia know I'd be here is so simple yet detailed. I can't discredit Ruth's motherly instinct, considering the time stamp on the email from her was minutes after I left her home. I'm a little impressed and, honestly, a bit inspired. "Now that I'm here, what's the first thing I need to know?"

"The most important thing to know is how to find a Cicada in public. We have a watchword, and it's a simple one. If you see a downward nod, it's a signal to approach. Ask them, *Who are you?* If they're in the movement, their response will be, *I am everyone, and you are?* If they're not a Cicada, well I suppose they'll introduce themselves like normal. Speaking of introductions, I almost forgot. Wait here." She gently removes herself from the recliner, declining my silent offer to help.

I remain in the living room, my peripherals following her into the kitchen. A cabinet creaks open and softly closes shut. She returns to the living room with yet another journal.

"Before you think terribly of me, understand I run a tight ship. I'm sure you think these journals are lying around, but that's only because I knew you were coming. Any other shift, these are so well hidden that even if Warden Gryme and all his Watchmen or Primes marched in here, they wouldn't find a single one. Can I tell you a secret?" A delightful smile slips from me. "When I looked out my window and saw Desmond being detained, I was overjoyed to see you there, too. I put the tin box on top of the fridge because I knew you'd be in the elevator. I didn't know how I'd get you in here at first, but after we talked a bit, I gambled on you coming to find me. That's why I waited at the post boxes. I would've been knocking on your door if you hadn't come."

There's a bubbling in my stomach, either from flattery or uneasiness. It's strange to know she was waiting for me—waiting to intercept—but her intent lacks malice. She seems close to Ruth, and knowing her front door is painted a different shade of white, she's one of Jerald's closest friends. I remind myself not to be suspicious. If they both trust her, I do too.

15

My fingers flutter through seemingly endless pages from a journal labeled *recipes*. "Let me see if I have these right: I am *Apricus*. Ruth is *Vivere*, Jerald was *Spes*. Desmond is *Link*, Maeve is *Ocelot*, and you're *Root*?"

Countless names fill almost every page, front to back, top to bottom, the ink blurring together in a hypnotizing way. Every name in here is a person risking their life to reach for something bigger than themselves. To reach for the surface.

"Those are the ones you've told me you've met so far," she answers from behind, joining me in the kitchen with a vegetable tray.

"I'm not too creative when it comes to nicknames, but where did these all come from? Are people naming themselves, or are people naming them? How did you get Root?" Her alias reassures me not to be suspicious of her. *Root* was the name Jerald mentioned in his journal, his most trusted friend.

"The simple answer is, it's a little bit of both. Some of the nicknames were given, like mine. It's been so long, but Desmond gave me this name and ..." Her head turns slightly as if an icy prickle pinched her neck. I remain silent, pretending to be oblivious to her tell. Passion pushes through her hurt. "He once told me I am too grounded to be stuck underwater."

"That's a wonderful way to put it," I tread, relieving the tension and creating an opening. "Can I ask why Desmond's name was Link?" It's a sensitive subject, but I have to tell her what happened at the Vat.

"He was a Cicada recruit, a connection. He was a wonderful man before he lost his way. Before he ..." She fixes her hair, staring at the table as if trying to catch a memory shifting across her vision.

I weigh the options of telling her. If I'm wrong, false hope will crush her faster than being sunk. But if I'm right, then maybe there's a chance he can still be saved.

"I have something to tell you." She pops a grape tomato in her mouth, chewing slowly, and focusing her attention back on me. "When I was at the Vat, Desmond wasn't in the chamber. It was only a student of mine. I didn't realize it until now, but why wasn't he in there with her? Collective sinkings are more common than a one-off. Maybe we can find where they're keeping him and help him hide in another sector. We could—" My mouth moves faster than my thoughts can process. Atlantic, *what* can anyone do? Once marked for the Vat, the ferryman always collects the toll.

"Thank you for feeling like you had to tell me that,

sweet girl. Desmond's sinking has been scheduled for another shift. He's seventy-one, which means he's a year overdue of Indicating age. I don't expect you to know this, you have some forty-odd years left, but senior citizens are given a free shift before they're sunk. Enough time to gather their affairs, say their goodbyes, and a hot meal from an exclusive menu. There's nothing to be done for my friend. Cicadas can fly faster than your nimble legs can carry you." I'm confident she's not condescending, but I'm slightly defeated. "I'll let you know when we find out more, but until then, let's focus on what we do have control over. Where were we?" she asks herself.

No matter how impatient I feel, I remind myself this must happen more often than I've given it thought. "Oh, nicknames," she says, interrupting my wandering. I snack to quiet my thoughts. "Some nicknames are given, others chosen. Your mother Ruth, for instance, learned your name was a loose translation from Latin, as was Jerald's. She followed suit. Yours means sunshine, Jerald's was hope, and hers is to live. Many family units share commonalities between names. Take for example Maeve, and her daughter Olivia."

I nearly choke on the fibrous broccoli at the unexpected mention of Olivia. I politely spit it into a napkin in the palm of my hand. "Are you talking about Watchman Aubert? Olivia is Maeve's daughter?" The familial resemblance interlocks across my vision.

"The same one." Sonia takes a bite of a crunchy

snap pea. "Maeve is *Ocelot*. Observant, careful, hiding in plain sight and blending in. *Oncilla* is her daughter. She's stubborn but can hold the world's weight with her inner strength. Are you surprised to hear of a mother-daughter duo?"

"It doesn't surprise me, but I've met Olivia. I didn't realize she was Maeve's daughter." Now that I give it some thought, Maeve has never mentioned having a family. But why would she if she's hiding in plain sight?

I am everyone, and you are? Olivia responded in the Observatory. For someone proud to be so preceptive, I'm sorely lacking in the piecing things together department.

"You've met Oncilla? She's joined the Cicadas recently, but I've known her since she was a girl. I can tell you for certain that she is wonderful. She's always sort of known of the movement because of Maeve, of course. But she wanted to become a Watchman before joining to prove something to herself. She had a phrase, a mantra if you will: *Stoop and become a Watchman to rise and become a Cicada*." She clears napkins from the table, adjusting the glasses on her face. "Never mind about all that, I'm rambling. Samara, now that you've joined, it's time to prepare you for the tasks ahead." Her fragile hands find mine from across the table, her coolness zapping my warmth.

"This is …" I stumble through my thoughts. "All of this is happening so fast. Why am I being told of the Cicadas now? Why didn't anyone mention it sooner?"

She steals a pepper from the tray. "Jerald's inner circle

promised him we wouldn't influence you to join, but Maeve was concerned. She told Ruth and me that you were looking for a name at the Husk, but Watchman Nathan Marlow is not a name to know blindly. Count your blessings it was Maeve you asked. I'm sure you had good intentions, but we couldn't allow you to explore that on your own. Your mother, Maeve, and I agreed it was time to break that promise, just a bit."

If Mason were here, he'd blame me for not leaving well enough alone, once again. But this time it opened something else, it opened the movement. Ruth's comment about Jerald's partner betraying him only came about because I kept pestering her to complain about the lack of investigation.

If Mason hadn't followed me to the Husk, muddying my sleuthing for Watchman Marlow, I would've gathered the Prime's address and explored answers on my own. What would have happened if I'd found Watchman Marlow and asked him about Jerald's passing without knowing he was a Prime? Without knowing he's a bloodhound, a trapdoor spider, hunting Cicadas? Would he have thought me innocent, or accused me of being in a movement I knew nothing about? Would I have been sunk, or given death by design? I risked my life to chase an impulse. Atlantic, what is wrong with me. How can I be a reliable player in this movement when I am so selfishly careless.

My whole life, I've been seething with rage on the verge of erupting, insatiable for hurt to arrive and end the tension that wakes me from nightmares, pulling me back to this reality. How can Sonia, Ruth, Maeve, or any of the Cicadas trust I am capable based on the word of Jerald when I'm simply an angry person who demands more in life.

Escaping the beast living deep in my brain that craves self-pity, I look up from my lap to find a pure smile from Sonia. I tuck my hair behind my ear, adjusting my posture. "I'm not full of charisma or leadership, but I can take direction if someone tells me what needs to be done and how to help. Tell me what I need to do."

I cannot feed my self-loathing beast morsels of doubt unless I wish to join it in the shadows. I will not allow my past to define me. My body may be a roadmap of healed scars from my abusers—of chipped teeth and mended bones—but I have no control over that. The long-ago healed bruises, the invisible palm prints—the wounds left in my heart and mind—I have control of those marks. I have control over how to apply them to my life.

My skin is not tattooed with the fingerprints of those who took advantage of my innocence. I am not forged from bits of broken glass and severed promises. To the depths with this unwanted weight. I'll cut the rope I've woven from around my neck and let the anchor sink without me. I'm tired of being surrounded by water. It's suffocating, compact, and all there is beyond the windows of Foxtrot. My curiosity needs to be fed. It needs to breathe and dance.

16

Sonia's instructions were clear: Plan to be away from home for a few shifts, pack light but strategic, and meet Maeve at the Husk for further direction. I didn't ask what she meant by *pack strategic* because I didn't want to seem like I *didn't know* what she meant—even though I don't. Instead, I nodded with an understanding. The whole walk up the six flights of stairs to my unit, I cursed myself under my breath. Note to self: ask clarifying questions even if they're embarrassing. Be humble.

Having already rehearsed the conversation a hundred times in my head, I unlock my apartment. "Mason?"

My only greeting is silence.

Light spills from the bathroom, providing a faint line of sight. Moving through the darkened hallway with careful, silent steps, I stop in the middle and turn to my left, resting my fingertips on his door. I consciously form them into a knuckle to knock, but as I prepare to disrupt the quiet apartment, my fingers release, resting on the back of my neck.

I must pack first to prove to him I'm as determined as

I'm trying to prove to myself. I must set the plan in motion before inviting any of his questions. What am I going to do, barge in there and say, *I know you said some shitty things to me, and I know I've been shitty to you, but I've joined a movement and I'm heading up to the surface now.*

Unintentionally rolling my eyes, whether at Mason behind the door or at myself, I walk to my bedroom. My foot hits the base of my closed door, which is usually open. "Mason, you can close your door to ignore me, but if you were in my room, I'll kick you in your shin." I turn the knob on my door to open it but it barely opens enough to fit my arm through. I close the door and try to open it again, but it stops itself.

Taking in a deep, frustrated breath, I march to the front of the hallway and flip the light switch on. With my shoulder to the frame of my bedroom door, I push and push against the unknown resistance until I stumble inside.

Anger floods me.

The drawers of my dresser are scattered across the floor, surrounded by clothes and shattered pieces of the ceiling light and fan blades. My mattress is overturned and tilted sideways, its frame misplaced and barely inches from the door. My comforter is shredded, sprawling across the floor covered in broken glass from my vanity, and the closet doors are detached, leaning against the opposite wall.

In the corner of the room, illuminated by the crack of light from the hallway, my small handheld chest of keepsakes is split in two. Rushing into the darkened room, stepping over the obstacles strewn about, my knees absorb my weight. I pick up the broken, now empty, handcrafted chest Jerald had made for me. The recipe for my homemade nail polish, a pull tab from the first sugary drink Mason and I had shared when we were younger, our adoption papers, and the earrings Ruth passed down to me had lived in that chest.

I long to search my room for my missing items, but a whispering voice is telling me they won't be found here. Mason would've hidden them. It would force me to play nice to get my things back. He can throw his predictable tantrums, but I won't feed into his childishness. He says foul things to my face about my character, and he pulls this shit? I could strangle him. If anyone deserves their room to be flipped, it's his. By me.

Taking a flashlight from a drawer, I imagine the look on Mason's face after I kick him in the shin with a to-go bag hanging off my shoulder. Stepping over all the broken glass, maneuvering around corners of misplaced furniture, I find my backpack on the floor of my closet and think of items to shove into it.

Aside from clothing and nonperishables, I'm failing to find an answer as to what constitutes as strategic, and the fact that I don't know what I'm doing sets in. I'm a homebody. I've never had to pack for anything that wasn't already pre-planned, organized, and set into motion. There's never anywhere to go. Work, home, commissary, Ruth's.

But I *have* to go to those places. I have to work to earn ration cards to buy the food from the commissary. I don't *have* to go to Ruth's, I rather enjoy being there. She's my lighthouse—and she makes better food than I do.

But sometimes I mix it up. Sometimes I go to the library, sometimes to the roof. But those are all planned excursions. I don't ... go ... somewhere else. And it sounds like Cicadas are always *going* somewhere. Exploring escape wings and searching for respirators, coordinating drop locations in all five sectors—who am I to do any of that.

Stealing a moment from the brief panic, I listen for my inner voice throbbing in my ears: lightweight, durable clothing. Comfortable sneakers. Food, reusable water bottle. Bandages, painkillers, antibacterial ointment. Hair ties, lip balm. ID card, lucky nail polish. A flashlight, the Cicada journals from my satchel—ditch the satchel. There's no need to carry an extra bag. The dollar bill in case I need to trade. Jerald's pocketknife from Mason's room.

Simple enough, and effectively strategic.

Dressing and doubling up on socks, I put on my comfortable shoes and gather the remaining supplies off my mental checklist, avoiding Mason's room altogether as I pass by for the first-aid items in the bathroom. I'll confront him once I finish packing, but only after I secure Jerald's knife from his room.

Mason is too logical. If he knows I'm leaving, he won't let me borrow his heirloom. He'll have so many questions that I don't feel like answering, and Maeve will mummify awaiting my arrival.

With bandages, ointment, lip balm, painkillers, and hair

ties secured in the front pocket of my backpack, I head for the kitchen for the rest. Opening the pantry, the options are scarce. The *meat* on the top shelf doesn't look too tasty, but it will have to suffice. The freeze-dried fruit, assortment of nuts, jam-filled pastries, and ready-to-eat rice should mellow out the tang. Canned soup should do in a pinch. It's added weight, but I'd rather be safe. I snag the can-opener. This rag-tag group of calories is almost questionable, but I'll steal from the Husk if it comes down to it.

Rummaging through the junk drawer for the last items on my list and with Foxtrot jerky between my teeth, I march to Mason's room to face my fraternal opponent.

Losing the motherly tone I've accidentally inherited over the years, I knock vigorously. "Mason, I need to talk to you. Now." No response. I knock again, a little harder and with less patience. "Mason Jackson Quinn, you must not understand. Whether you open this door or not, I will be coming in there. I'm warning you, as a courtesy, because I respect other people's personal space and don't barge in."

The surrounding silence is enough to make my ears ring violently. With a heavy sigh, I turn the doorknob, entering his room with resolve. "You're forcing me to treat you like a child. You realize that, right?" I ask the clean, vacant room.

17

Eeriness and déjà vu settle in my stomach. Although here for a purpose I never thought possible, it's less of a chore this time. Usually, I come here with Mason to trade for odds and ends to sustain some need in my life, but now I'm here as a stepping stone to reach for something more than the basics. To reach for the surface.

I've only ever been to the Husk alone once before, but it was enough to make me aware of my surroundings. Though I pay no attention to the desperate catcalling as I make my way through the crowd, the chilling reminder of unpredictability weighs heavily on my skin. Clamoring and shoulder bumping are expected, but I will not be a victim of a mugging with nothing more to show than a cut lip and a bruised ego. Not again. I keep my focus on high alert.

Sharing the front pocket of my sweatshirt, my fingers open and close Jerald's knife, my head swiveling around, taking mental pictures of every face I pass. Blending into the crowd, my eyes are drawn to a jewelry stand. No one else would have a set of handmade earrings made of polished ball bearings, soldered into copper washers with a *Q* for Quinn engraved on the front unless they're mine. And they are. Mason will have both his shins kicked. Twice.

"Where did you get these?" I ask the merchant behind the booth, pointing to the earrings. He's too busy sitting down and picking his fingernails to be bothered. I move past a woman and rest my palms on the table. "I said, where did you get these earrings?" It smells of body odor in his space, rancid and sour. I keep my composure unfaltering.

"It doesn't matter where I got them. What matters is what you're willing to trade for them," the merchant huffs, setting aside the nail clippers and swigging a mouthful of spirits straight from the bottle.

"Did a guy trade you for these? Tall, prickly head, and a shit-eating grin?" A smirk slips past my lips envisioning Mason.

The merchant slams the bottle on the table, green liquid spilling from the top and reaching my fingertips. "Lady, if you're not going to trade me for anything, I suggest you take your own shit-eating grin on over to the section of mind-your-own-goddamn-business. It's right around that corner." He points to the public restroom.

A wicked laugh escapes my chest. The sweeping fog of anger from Mason trashing my room and pawning my jewelry to this disgusting man thins. "Fair enough." I wipe my hands on my pants. "You see, these are mine. And I was wondering if whoever you got these from fits that description."

"Seems to me like these are not *yours*, and that's because

they're mine. Like I said, don't matter who I got them from. What have you got that's worth them?"

"I assure you, these are *mine*, passed down from my mother, and I can prove it to you. Turn them over. There will be four painted dots on the back. One brown, two greens, and a silver. The colors of my family's eyes." A brown and green for Mason and me, another green for Ruth, silver for Jerald. I painted them myself when I was younger, sealing them with clear nail polish.

"That's a nice story and all, but I could give two fucks about your whining. What do you have to trade? I'm not going to ask again, lady. You're taking my time away from the other customers."

I look around his empty booth, at all his *customers* wanting to trade for his moldy wooden beads, rusty anklets, and dazzling pasta necklaces. I sigh. "Can't I have them back?"

"Have them?" He scoffs. "Not a chance. Find me a case of tobacco and give me a kiss and they're yours. Haven't had either for over a decade."

"Why don't I find you a bar of soap instead, you give me my earrings, and we call it even?"

"You got a mouth on you, don't you, Samara?"

I stifle a gasp. "What did you say?"

"I said you got a mouth on you, *Samara Quinn*. You should learn how to use it properly."

He hasn't given a downward nod, but he shouldn't know my name. Is he a Cicada? I tempt fate. "Who are you?"

"Name's Kline Grant. It says so right here on my badge." He points a freshly clean yet still questionably dirty index finger to his merchant's ID clipped to his chest. Reaching across the table, his grubby fingers graze my hip, lingering a bit too long. "And yours says Samara Quinn. You're even smiling in this picture. Must've been thinking about me." He releases his grip, and my Sec-Five ID card retracts back to my hip.

A smile of ill will replaces my fleeting moment of embarrassment. Not only is he *not* a Cicada, but his repulsive hands touched me. As if I'm his to touch. Why can't people keep their hands to themselves? I twirl my hair and pout. "I can be so empty-headed sometimes. I don't know how to find any tobacco, but I do have painkillers and lips that crave yours."

He licks his lips as if he's a predator with a fresh kill. "I'd like some tobacco, but I'll take the painkillers. I want six, and make sure to use your tongue."

I nibble on my bottom lip. "Is there any other way?"

Bubbling red takes over my vision. I blink it away, giving him a sultry gaze. Swinging my pack frontside, I find my strategically packed first-aid items. I'm aware I must practice being less manipulative, but I don't have to practice that impulse now. Not when this man has something that belongs to me, and especially not when he thinks I'm desperate enough to kiss him.

Opening the container and finding seven painkillers, I screw the lid back on and place it in my sweater pocket.

Maneuvering my pack to my back, I sashay behind his booth and join him, keeping his eye contact. He pats his thigh, motioning for me to come over. Invitation accepted.

Undressing me with his carnivorous eyes, I shyly straddle his lap, my fingers swirling through his greasy hair. "I have to tell you a secret first," I whisper in his ear.

"I like secrets," he coos.

My fingertips touch his lips to silence him. "My secret is, I already know how to use my mouth. It's my favorite thing to play with." I press my cheek against his and arch my back. His palms trail up my spine, but I fight against the reflex to stand up. A deceitful moan slips out of me, soft and delicate. I reach behind my back and press my chest against his, feeling for his hands; his oily, unwashed hands. I take hold of them and pin them beneath my thighs, rocking forward, then slide mine back into my front pocket. The rings on his fingers roll beneath my pressure. He winces, sucking in air through his teeth. "Kline, is something the matter? Do you want me to get off?"

"Mmm," he grumbles, eyes closed and a despicable smile curling up. "No, girl. Stay where you are. I can take a little bit of pain."

Gripping a handful of his hair, I gently crane his neck back. "I have something for you that's better than my mouth." With my face in front of his, our lips nearly touching, I breathe balmy air onto his exposed neck. "How empowering do you think it is to slit a man's throat?" My pocketknife is open, firmly pressing against his skin.

He squirms beneath me, trying to lift me off. With a powerful grip on his hair, I keep my weight centered, pressing the knife harder against his flesh. "Don't move too much, we don't want any accidents. It'll be a small cut, a flash of pain. A bright, white fire. I'm in control of this, not you. But we don't want any accidents. I'm only going to ask you one more time. Who gave you those earrings?"

His body relaxes, as if coming to terms with the situation. "It was a guy," he stammers. "Some guy. I've never seen him before."

I angle the knife to its tip. "Not good enough, Kline."

"I don't know! I don't know, some guy. Late twenties, early to mid-thirties. Lady, I don't fucking know!"

"Did he look like me?"

"What?"

"Did he *look* like *me*?"

"I didn't pay much attention. He was here, then he wasn't, I swear to god I don't remember what he looked like."

Swearing to gods is tasteless. Doesn't he know they all left us to die in Foxtrot? "What did he trade you for?"

"Nothing. He didn't trade me for anything. Didn't want anything in exchange. He came up, tossed them on my table, and left. Lady, I *swear*."

That's ... odd. Why wouldn't Mason trade for anything? To prove a point? To be the shithead that he is? Here I sit, straddling this man's lap with a knife to his throat to get an answer he doesn't have. This was a horrible idea. But this man has something of mine, something he shouldn't. Something he wasn't willing to give back from kindness alone. He didn't *look* at the back of the earrings to confirm they were mine.

The offer he gave me was as useless as the makeshift government—he knows it's impossible to find tobacco. I'd have better odds of finding prehistoric bones in my closet.

My counteroffer for him may have been one-sided, as I would never give him any painkillers, let alone six. Painkillers are as common as non-asshole Watchmen—sure, they're there, but not usually.

There's an anger vibrating through my body from everything that's happened these last few shifts. I'm craving control, and if that means standing my ground, then goddamn it, I am going to be impulsive.

A quick, lateral cut the length of my finger tears across his flesh. Shallow enough to only need a bandage, but enough to prove a point. I slide off his lap, pocketing my earrings.

Inspiration finds me. "And Kline?" The tone in my voice increases in pitch, caressing the vowel in his name. He's still as a statue, the sleeve of his shirt pressing into his neck, eyes as wide as an owl's. "If you mention any of this to anyone or if you try to find me, I'll make sure to give you that kiss. But only after I sew your lips shut."

18

"Took you a little while, but I'm glad you found the real me." Maeve teases with a grin, signaling me to enter behind her booth with a head tilt. I've never stepped behind a merchant's booth before, only ever as a passerby, aside from my encounter with the ever-so-charming kiss seeker.

Her booth is an optical illusion. From the outside, it looks like there's hardly enough space for an adult, let alone two, but from within, it's much larger. Shelves and racks in the center and to the sides break up the horseshoe pattern, making it a small maze with a woman's touch. Judging by all the items for trade, all the items that can be seen from this side of the table, being a merchant for women's needs is a front.

She has rations and ration cards. Flashlights, strange mechanical items, clothing, batteries, and so much more. Nothing is overcrowding or overflowing, and it's not claustrophobic. It's wonderful and organized and chaotic. Everything is where it needs to be, with room to spare. She's a one-stop shop. Here I was thinking she only traded sanitary products and secrets for nail polish. Maeve the

Ocelot, hiding in plain sight.

Following her past a makeshift privacy screen made of blankets hanging from plastic pipes, out of sight from the thundering Husk beyond its thin fabric, the three of us stand in a triangle formation. Despite my best efforts, a smile slips from me. I should've anticipated this. I would've put on better clothes. Information between Cicadas *does* fly faster than my legs can carry me.

"Do you prefer *Samara* or your alias, *Apricus?*" Olivia asks.

"That depends. Should I call you *Watchman Aubert, Olivia*, or *Oncilla?*"

She smirks. "Everyone calls me Liv. I know, another name to remember."

"I'd rather not be grouped in with everyone," I say coyly.

Maeve playfully swats the air at us and takes a seat on an end table. "I'm happy you're here, Samara. I hope you're not too upset with me."

"Upset with you? Why would you think that?"

She tucks a braid behind her ear. "It was difficult for me to see you go about your business in the Husk without telling you I knew Jerald. To see my closest friend's daughter be in so much pain from losing him and be impartial toward you. To treat you like any other customer. Many of us shared that loss, that heartache. I could've been there for you." Her hand extends to me, blue-painted nails shimmering in the light.

Taking her hand, I kneel beside her. "I'm not upset

with you for anything, Maeve. You made him a promise not to influence me to join the movement, and you kept it. You honored him, even when it was hard to do so. I'd be a madwoman if I felt wronged because of that."

The freckles on her nose wrinkle, a tight, pained smile slipping past. She clears her throat, nodding her head. "Now you've gone and brought up another skeleton in my closet. It felt like a breach of trust to tell your mother and Sonia you were asking for Nathan Marlow's name. Are you feeling like a madwoman about that?"

A quick laugh escapes my chest. "Are you asking if I'm upset that you stopped me from finding a Prime's address?"

"They're nastier than demons," Olivia breathes. "Watchman Locke was an overseer at the academy. It made my skin itchy whenever I interacted with him." She shakes off a shiver. "And good riddance to Watchman Sampson. Do you know she used to arrest people so she could confiscate their ration cards and shred them? Most of the rookies thought she was *so fucking cool* for doing it." She releases her fists, tapping the tips of her fingers on her thumb.

We may be concealed behind this booth, but speaking about Primes aloud in a public setting seems too risky. I redirect the tense conversation. "Watchman Olivia Aubert, Cicada in disguise," I whisper, flashing my palms to her and making a half circle in the air.

"Believe it or not, I did it for the fashion. You've seen me in uniform so tell me, did the cerulean cargo pants and hand-me-down, too big of a button-up do the trick? Did I seem *authoritative?* Don't answer that." Her laugh is light and carefree. She lowers her voice. "Having another Cicada on the inside was too tempting to pass up. It was short-lived, but I learned a lot."

Confusion scrunches my face. "Short-lived?"

"Samara," Maeve says. "Sonia asked you to meet me because I have something important to tell you. I need you to understand that Cicadas have active eyes on the situation, but I am asking you not to meddle, under any circumstance. We must all stay undetected." The tone in her voice mimics that of a warning bell.

My ears buzz. It feels as if I'm about to be told bad news. Is Ruth okay? Has more information on Jerald come to light? Meddle with what? Did I do something wrong? Maeve's eyebrow curves up, studying me as I think, waiting for my response. "I promise not to meddle."

She glances at Olivia, impatience jittering off my skin. "Your brother has been discharged from the Watchmen and black-listed," she finally says.

"That's ..." *Not something I considered.* "... What?"

"Shortly after you left the Vat, Olivia was ordered to report to the Sec-Op facility. She was permanently discharged from her position. They told her it was due to poor performance and misconduct at the Vat to allow a member of the public to go down a Watchman hallway and use the intercom." I swallow hard, the reality of my impulsiveness setting in. "They said she wasn't an ideal candidate for keeping sectors safe because she failed her first patrol shift. No disciplinary actions, immediate termination."

"That doesn't mean—"

"—Mason received the order, same as I did," Olivia says. "We walked to Sec-Op together. I was told to go into the office first, alone. They stripped me of my gear and escorted me through a separate exit. I haven't seen him since."

That was a few shifts ago, wasn't it? I haven't seen him either. "Has anyone talked to him?"

"I don't believe so, but Cicada scouts followed him for some time as a precaution," Maeve says. "Mason didn't take well to being discharged. He reacted poorly. Lashed out and vandalized the front of homes at random as he exited Sec-One. The scouts abandoned his trail once he was back in his sector."

It's my fault Mason was discharged. He worked tirelessly to earn his position, and even if I don't understand why being a Watchman *meant* something to him, by rules of proxy, it should have meant something to me, too.

Atlantic, that's why he trashed my room. Sort of immature and a little wild to think, but I can forgive his outburst. I should find him and talk to him. See if he—no. Sonia gave me instructions. How reliable will I be if I break away to do something else? To do something *I* would rather do. *Priorities*. Mason is an adult; I'm an adult. I'll find him another shift.

"I'm sorry you were caught in the middle of all that," I say to Olivia. "I didn't think about what would happen to you or Mason when I was going down that hallway."

"You wanted to see your student. I can't blame you for that. I told you outside the restroom I wanted to be the change, that Watchmen and the public don't have to be at odds. I wouldn't have been able to sleep if I didn't at least try. I'll find another way to be useful in the movement," she says with ease.

I give her a nod in thanks. "Sonia said you had some direction for me," I say to Maeve. "What is it?"

"I have directions for both of you." Confusion flashes in Olivia's eyes. "I wanted to surprise you, Liv. Besides, I didn't want to have to say it twice. Two giggles from one tickle."

"Two giggles from one tickle?" Olivia cups her mouth. "And I thought you saying, *mash two potatoes with one fork* the other shift was bad enough." She mouths *sorry* to me.

"I like it." I wink at Maeve. "What are the two giggles?"

"Liv has been familiar with the movement most of her life but has joined only a few shifts ago. Same as you, Samara. You're nymphs—you're baby Cicadas, and you're not the only ones. There's been an influx of recruits recently, within the last year or so. All grown children of those who joined long ago. It's inspiring to have the movement come alive again. It's been silent for decades." She places a hand on her chest, staring vacantly behind us.

Olivia steps forward, gently squeezing Maeve's hands. "We don't have to talk about that."

Maeve blinks, swallowing hard. "I'm sorry, I was remembering ... that's a tale for another time." I bury my questions, accepting that whatever Maeve can't bring herself to say is not something to pry at. I'm practicing being stoic, after all. "We welcome all members, no matter their age, but not everyone is fit to be in the forefront of the movement. Humans are quirky. We can be clumsy, even when we try our best. There's a Test that helps place members, one that allows them to contribute in areas where their natural attributes shine. Some people do best in the background, others spearheading as recruits. It's a balance we try to find so that everyone can help."

"You've never mentioned anything about a Test," Olivia says.

"Like I said, two giggles." Maeve winks back at me. "The Test is something new we've been doing, but it seems to be working. It's more organized this way. Don't furrow your brows like that, Liv. You'll do fine. The Test is impossible to fail."

"What is this Test?" I ask.

Scenarios flit through my mind. Is math involved? I'm fairly decent at math. Is it a physical test? If I'm lucky, it's a test of penmanship. My handwriting is fantastic. I could fill out Cicada journals with ease. Some of those entries are questionable. At Ruth's, I couldn't figure out if someone wrote, *there's a shift change at zero-hundred*, or if it said, *there's a shit charge at zeno-mundro.* Thank the Atlantic for context clues.

Maybe the Test focuses on who can recite all the Warden Gryme's in chronological order. That, I can do:

incompetent asshole, incompetent asshole, incompetent asshole. Don't forget about the incompetent asshole. Hopefully, the Test is about who can be more sarcastic.

"The Test is in two parts, but I don't want to ruin the surprise. Your directions are to meet with Cicadas who go by Sandstone and Flint in Sector Two within the hour. They're veterans and have the first Test scheduled with six nymphs, you two included. You better get moving."

19

A Test. If I can hand them out once a week, I can at least *take* one. Especially one that's impossible to fail. What's the worst that happens, I'm a background player in the movement? Doesn't seem like a horrible thought, not sure if I could hold the responsibility of being a recruit. My permanent scowl doesn't scream: I'm approachable! Let's talk in secret about the surface!

"What do you think?" Olivia asks, our strides in sync.

"About the Test? I'd rather grade papers."

"Don't like tests?"

I like to be prepared. I like control. I like to be wistful and a tad impulsive. "I don't *not* like tests, but I don't like surprises."

"I think it's adventurous." She twirls and cups her heart. "Before I trained to be a Watchman, I used to work at the library. It was easy work, but it didn't scratch that itch, you know? I wanted something challenging." I nod my head as we cross the threshold of Sec-Two. "Do you like teaching?"

"I do." I shove my hands into my pockets, debating

whether I should hold back on being honest.

Do I like being forced to teach propaganda? Forced to tell the young minds in this bunker that Warden Gryme keeps us *safe*, his rules and the Watchmen keep us *safe*. Foxtrot is all we need, there is nothing more, and there will never be anything more. And don't question anything too much, because that makes you curious, and curiosity is a crime. Do what you're *told*, listen to what we *say*. Don't bother—

"Samara?" She's in front of me, a hand propped under her elbow, the other on her neck.

"Sorry," I say with a tight smile, heat flushing in my cheeks. "Sometimes my mind wanders. Yes, I enjoy teaching. Children are innocent to all this." My hand waves in the air. "They don't see what adults see. They don't feel ... inconvenienced. They get to worry about how much glue to use for their papier-mâché projects, not worrying about how to earn enough ration cards to get a meal. It might sound selfish, but it gives me a purpose to be the one who gets to distract them from it all." My shoulders relax, my smile more genuine. A bit of honesty mixed with cynical thoughts makes a healthy concoction.

"It doesn't sound selfish at all. If you think about it, the movement is like a distraction. It gives us hope and purpose. Where would we be without either?"

We take the alley behind residentials, nearing the rendezvous at the commissary. I crane my head back, taking in all three stories. "Without a purpose, I'd jump from the roof of that building and hope for a quick death." I cackle, but Olivia falls behind a few steps. Twisting my body to face her, my knee bangs on a crate. "I'm joking."

Am I?

Her brows knit together, studying me. Seconds later, her gaze glides past me, a light returning to her eyes. Her chin dips down. "We're here."

Four adults stand in a casual semi-circle, their lips moving. Two others lean against the outside wall of the commissary, an arm's length away but adding to the conversation. To anyone else, they're six people in the sea of people inside Foxtrot. To anyone else, those six people giving a downward nod in intervals politely greet Olivia and me—to anyone else, those six people are not Cicadas.

A burly man with a patchy beard and too-big glasses waves us over, his tan and black flannel rising above his waist. The woman beside him steps forward, wearing a smile sweet as syrup. "Glad you can make it. I'm Sandstone, this is Flint," she half-whispers, tilting her head to the man and pointing to the commissary as if that's what we're discussing. She spins on her heels, a golden strand breaking from behind her ear. "Over there, we have Anglerfish, Squid, Magnolia, and Poppy." She's careful to point to the large letters spelling out *commissary* at the top of the building, coinciding with where the remainder of the group is positioned below it.

Standing below the *C,* Anglerfish, a male somewhere in his thirties with olive skin and a cutting jawline, nods to us.

Under an *M,* the only other male and youngest of everyone, Squid flashes us a smile. Dimples in both cheeks and a mole on his right temple. He looks to be hardly twenty.

Leaning against the building below an *S,* Magnolia seems to be sucking on an invisible lemon, her sapphire eyes assessing us with crossed arms.

Finally, leaning beneath the *Y,* Poppy finishes braiding her fiery-orange hair, then puts her hands in her overall pockets and shifts her weight to her toes and heels.

Pointing to the metal sign outside the building displaying the hours of operation, Sandstone throws her voice like a ventriloquist. "In a few minutes, we'll all be taking our leave. Choose amongst yourselves which of the two of you will go last, then wait five minutes after Poppy walks away and start for the back of the building. There's less foot traffic. We can speak more openly and prepare you for the first part of the Test." She takes hold of Flint's arm, and the both of them stroll away.

"I'll go last," Olivia says before I can volunteer. "Should we introduce ourselves?" She side-eyes the other Cicadas.

Mimicking Sandstone's deceptive movements, I point to the building and step around the pedestrians in my path as Olivia breaks away to pick up litter off the street. Scanning for my target between the four other nymphs, I set my eyes on the one pretending not to see me coming. Kneeling beside Magnolia, I tighten my shoelaces. "I'm—"

"—No."

Noted. I stand, taking a flyer from the periodical box. Pretending to study the current inventory of the commissary, I lean on the same wall as Poppy. "The pomegranate trees have fruited." I show her the flyer.

"I'm allergic to pomegranates." She leaves me to stand near Magnolia, both of them whispering about something.

Can people be allergic to pomegranates?

Understanding the dismissal, I keep my composure and continue to read the flyer, appearing unbothered. I should've gone to Anglerfish or Squid first, but Magnolia seemed like a challenge, Poppy at least an in. I glaze over the flyer, flipping through it to buy myself time to charge my silver tongue.

Olivia laughs behind me. Glancing up from the flyer, Squid walks backward behind the commissary, shaking his head with a grin. Olivia pushes against Anglerfish's upper shoulder, her head tilted back, black braids swaying with the movement. She crosses her arms, scanning the area, then locks eyes with me. Gripping Anglerfish's forearm, she leans in to tell him something.

I study the flyer again, nodding my head with quizzical eyebrows. Potatoes, apples, zucchini. Oh look, peaches are back in rotation. *What the hell am I doing being sidelined by other recruits?* Putting the flyer back in the box, I will myself not to hiss at Magnolia and Poppy as I join Olivia and Anglerfish.

"You got them to talk to you?" he asks, nodding to the

two women.

"I got them to ignore me." I channel my Foxtrot-famous shit-eating grin.

"I've known them for all of thirty minutes and can attest they aren't the friendliest duo. Flint says they're lifelong friends. I don't think they talk to anyone but each other." Magnolia strolls past us, rounding the corner behind the commissary. "I'm up next," Anglerfish says. "Five whole minutes to avoid talking about what we want to talk about. At least until we get behind the building." He flashes a smile.

"Anything interesting in the flyer, or were you pretending?" Olivia nudges me. She's observant, I'll give her that.

"All of it was interesting. It was full of ... the usual." I shrug.

"Anglerfish was saying he's the oldest out of six."

"Five," he corrects. "What about you? Any siblings?"

"It's only me," Olivia says. "My mom said I was enough trouble growing up, and she couldn't imagine having more. I tell her she's missing out." She squints her eyes with a cheeky smile, angling the tops of her hands beneath her chin.

"Let me guess, you're an only child too?" Anglerfish asks me. "Are my parents the only ones brave enough to raise a pack of wildlings?"

Not feeling up for the banter, I display two fingers and angle my body away, glancing at my watch. Camaraderie isn't necessary to accomplish tasks—people don't need to get to know me. I don't need to *know* any of them. I rely on myself—I barely trust myself—but I've managed this far in life. Most shifts, I like myself enough to get by. Adding extra people into the mix is a recipe I don't have the ingredients for.

Joining a movement doesn't mean my reclusive habits are suddenly killed off. I can take direction, and my direction right now is to meet the veterans behind the commissary five minutes after Poppy leaves, not make idle chitchat. It's not essential to be friends with any Cicadas, we just have to synergize. Any type of relationship means there's a risk for loss, and I can't afford that mental block. Burning bridges before they're built means there's no need for reinforcement. Healthy? Probably not.

Anglerfish clicks his tongue and whistles. "I'll see you both back there."

Olivia waves him down with her free hand, the other tucked under an elbow. She clears her throat, and I incline my head to her. "You don't have to do that, you know," she says.

"Do what?"

"Search for reasons to push people away."

"It's easier than letting anyone in." Damnit, why did I say that. What is it about her that makes my thoughts fall from my mouth. "Let's not talk about it. We're here to take a Test, let's get through it."

I don't need friendships. Once we're placed in the movement, who's to say Olivia and I are even in the same assignments? Why bother putting in the effort.

Poppy walks past us. Five more minutes.

20

The back of the commissary is an area I've never explored. Usually, I'm in and out of the building, huffing through the aisles as I count my ration cards, shoving produce into homemade totes while Mason gets bags of dried goods from the top shelves.

Fresh produce costs less than a can of beans, but that's because it only lasts a few shifts and has to be bought more frequently. I tried convincing Mason once that fresh produce was *more* expensive and that we should stick to the jars, bags, and cans of food because I've done the math. But he held firm that the benefits of fresh produce outweighed the repeated cost.

A single ration card is equal to a pound of common fruits or vegetables, whereas two ration cards can buy a pound of dried beans, nuts, dehydrated fruits, or rice. *Three* ration cards mean the good stuff: a few ounces of sweets, Foxtrot jerky, or a couple jars of pickled goods.

Why spend single ration cards multiple times on items that have to be eaten quickly, when we could save up the singles and turn them into doubles or triples and eat something more filling and less often? Mason says there's a balance. He says that we should enjoy the vitamins and nutrients from fruits and vegetables, even if we have to buy them more often.

I can see the logic, but if we didn't live together, I'd save up my ration cards. My pantry would be full of shelf-stable items and my kitchen counter free of fruit.

Save for the six other Cicadas, a passerby here and there, and a dumpster with three padlocks, the alley is empty. Of course the dumpster is locked. Why hand out foods nearing expiration to those in need when monopolizing it is much more ethical.

Olivia turns the corner and joins my side, a nonchalant glaze in her eyes. With all eight of us now present, Sandstone hands out brochures for the museum in Sec-One at random from a stack of at least twenty.

Flint steps forward, peeling a banana, his voice hushed. "As you all know, we communicate through journals. But, collecting them from a drop can be dangerous. Not everyone is cut out to be the relay. There are a handful of runners in the whole movement."

Among the six of us, it seems I'm the only one curious enough to open the brochure while he speaks, the rest staring at him with fixed concentration. The page for the volcano exhibition has a turned-down corner and handwriting on its fold: *Sec-Four, nineteenth.*

"The first Test is designed to challenge your resolve. If you open your brochures, you'll find instructions—ah—seems Apricus is one step ahead. Can you read the code aloud?" I do as instructed. "Location and area," he continues. "Most all drops are within the designated alley in vents or eye-level ducts. Your Test is to collect a journal from the drop and bring it back here. It goes without saying to avoid being caught."

That's the first Test? Sneak around Sec-Four in search of contraband. I might as well march into Gryme's office to make an appointment for my sinking.

Glancing between the five others, I'm not the only one feeling hesitant. Squid paces around, smacking his brochure in his palm. Anglerfish reads his directive to himself and closes his eyes, then opens the brochure to read it again as if he's afraid he's gotten it wrong. Magnolia and Poppy speak amongst themselves in whispers, pointing to their dog-eared pages, sharing nods and shakes of the head. Olivia's fingers tap against the spine of hers, wrinkles in her forehead and a sway on her heels.

"What if we can't do it?" Squid asks, his voice shaky. "What if we *don't* do the Test?"

Sandstone steps in front of him, gently halting his frantic movement with a palm on his shoulder. "You don't have to do anything you're not comfortable with. Taking the Test or not taking the Test is still part of the same Test. You will find your place in the movement, I promise you that." She opens her palm for his brochure, allowing him a patient choice. Chewing on the inside of his lip, his eyes dart between us. He reaches to place the brochure in her palm, then pulls it back. Opening it once more, he reads it to himself and hands it to her. "This is not a failure on your part, Squid. It's brave to share your feelings. We don't want anyone feeling like they don't have a voice."

"Where was it?" Magnolia hisses, startling me. "Where was your drop location?"

Squid chews on his cheeks as if debating whether he has to explain himself. "Sector One," he finally says. "Sec-One, Sec-Op." I stifle a gasp, Magnolia's eyes dropping to the ground. "I'll go to any other drop. Any sector, any alley, but please. I can't go into Sec-Op. That's too many ... too many Watchmen. Can I pick from another location?" His pleading wrenches my heart.

Flint shakes his head, hands sliding into his pockets. "The hardest part about accepting our roles is that we don't always get to choose an easier option. There's a risk in all of this. If a runner can't be trusted to collect from a drop, no matter the location, then it's not a good fit. Trust your gut, Squid. You know yourself better than anyone. If you feel as if being a relay is too big a task, we'll assign you somewhere as important."

"I can't—no." Squid takes a deep breath. "I *won't* do it. I want to help somewhere else."

His change of vocabulary is admirable. He must believe he *can* do it, but his mind is made up that he *won't*. There's a difference between accepting personal defeat and adapting to it. I respect his decision, and from the way Olivia nods her head with a friendly smile aimed at him, I assume she feels the same.

Sandstone hands the rest of us small totes, shoving bags of rice and herbs into each from hers. "When you find the drop, check your surroundings before gathering the journal. Place it at the bottom of the tote and meet us back here in a few hours. Good luck." With that, she takes her leave, Flint and Squid behind.

In the time it takes to shift my attention back to the remaining nymphs, Magnolia and Poppy are rounding the corner. They didn't tell any of us where they were heading, and maybe that's best, but I hope they do well. "Where's your drop?" I ask Anglerfish.

"A few alleys from here." His smirk is shrouded. "Sec-Two, twelfth."

"Why did you seem nervous if your location is where you're already at?" The words are out of my mouth before I can tame them. I could have phrased them to be less ... sharp. But he doesn't have to walk miles to and from another sector with illegal material in his tote—what does he have to be worried about?

He sighs, adjusting the strap on his shoulder. "It's almost the end of a work shift and people need groceries. The commissary will be buzzing louder than the Husk. That's a lot of eyes if you ask me."

My thoughts reach to grab hold of the apology balloon floating away.

"You'll do fine," Olivia says. "They'll be so busy milling about, they won't pay attention to you. To keep busy while you wait for the rest of us, you could wander the commissary and pick out some snacks when you're done." She reaches into her pocket, digging out four ration cards. "Pick out something sweet." She winks at him. He takes the cards and gives her an exaggerated bow, then leaves to find his drop. My tongue may be made of silver, but hers is syrup.

I slice into the awkward silence once we're alone. "Where's your drop?"

Her side-long glance is sharp. "You have to stop doing that."

"And what is it that I'm doing?"

"Sounding so miserable all the time."

"That's not fair, I'm only miserable half the time." My shit-eating grin releases hers. "Are you going to tell me where your drop is?"

"Sec-Four, first. Yours?"

"Sec-Four, nineteenth."

"Sounds like we're partners."

"I wouldn't say we're *partners*." I sweep my arm forward, encouraging her to lead the way. "We are two people leaving at the same time and heading for the same general location, trying to accomplish the same task."

She accepts the offer with a dainty curtsy, stepping past me and around the dumpster. "Sounds like we're partners."

21

It's simple.

All I have to do is meet Olivia back at the threshold of Sec-Four once I'm finished *not* being caught searching for a journal that's shared between Cicadas. Oh, what's a Cicada? It's a movement of people who believe the surface is livable, and for some unknown reason, the Warden doesn't want anyone to know. And by the way, he has Prime Watchmen assigned to murder anyone if they *suspect* you're involved.

My heart thrums in my chest, so violently it pulses in my toes. Am I sweating? The sleeve of my sweatshirt glides over my forehead, collecting the beads. I pull the fabric over my head, securing it around my waist with a tug. Tilting my head side to side, I release the tension in my shoulders with small rotations. I'm a person walking through Sector Four with all the other people walking through Sector Four, passing by fifth avenue, and no one is staring at me.

On the sidewalk ahead, a trash collector takes bags out of bins and tosses them into a shuttle. A woman with a screaming baby on her hip calls for the toddler behind her eating strawberries to keep up. Volunteers hang up yet another redundant banner, reminding everyone of the *200 Bicentennial Bash!*

Why does it need to say two hundred and bicentennial? Might as well have it say *Two-Hundred, Two-Hundred Bash!*

To their credit, this banner isn't as hideous. The two is a two, and the zeroes are straight. There aren't any stains, and the fabric isn't as wrinkled—I can forgive their misspelling of *bicetenial* from that alone. Can't expect everyone to know that there are twelve letters, not ten.

Across the street, a man throws a fizzy can down at his feet, the woman in front of him yelling about something. Children laugh with each other, hopping in and out of chalk boxes drawn on the ground. A woman jogs past, pursed lips and two fingers pressed to her neck. Cleaners outside apartment buildings and storefronts wipe down the windows and sweep away litter.

The fluorescent lights above hum and buzz.

The circulated oxygen is heavy and stale.

Close by, the ocean presses in, dark and cold.

Normal. Everything is normal.

Walking backward, I double-check to make sure I read the street sign right. If I passed eighteenth avenue, then I'm almost to nineteenth. Normally, I'd complain about anxiety, but for once, I'm grateful for it. I've walked over a mile in less than ten minutes without realizing it because I'm gliding through Sector Four with a messy mind to keep the company.

Milling about. We're all milling about. I'm blending

in. I am not taking a left to cut down nineteenth avenue to collect a journal from a drop. No—I'm turning down nineteenth because this is the shortcut to get to one of the textile shops.

The alley is near empty, save for a few stragglers here and there. Jerald once told me a frightful Grand Story—during a wakeful shift, of course—about the living dead. How there used to be movies about corpses reanimating. When they came back from the dead and weren't eating human flesh, they'd turn dormant and stand around waiting for stimulus. *Zombies*, he said. Another word I kept to myself.

The strangers in the alley are much like that, boredom carved so deeply in their faces it's impossible to tell if they're conscious. Maybe they've had too much to drink. Even better. I slip past them, eyes ahead scouting for vents but cognizant of their gaze. I steal a glance over my shoulder to assess the stragglers shuffling away. I might as well have been a dust mite.

Leaning against the opposite wall, I debate which vent to try first. Three to choose from. I can't risk checking all three, not without being seen, at least.

My head whips side to side, paranoid thoughts convincing me there's a Watchman—a Prime—waiting for me to take the bait. Waiting for me to stick my hand in so they can tackle me to the ground, pin my arms behind my back, and tighten the zip ties. What if this location is compromised? Didn't Jerald's journal warn of that? What sort of Test is this asking us to be runners. I can't *physically* run, but they expect me to *mentally* run?

I take a deep breath, centering myself. There's no reward without risk. How can I keep complaining about Foxtrot and never *do* anything about it.

Keeping my head straight, my peripherals scan the area, watching for movement. There's nobody left in the alley, and the doors to the textile shop are far enough to my right that everyone entering it has their backs to me.

There aren't any Watchmen here with me, and there weren't any on the walk here. Everything is fine. But shouldn't there have been at least one Watchman *somewhere*? Yes—they must have been there, and I didn't see any. Which means they didn't see me. No one saw me.

I lean harder against the wall, willing myself to be camouflaged, to become one with it. The smooth metal presses back on me, its chill leeching my warmth. I rub my back against it, swaying side to side, tilting my head while I think. Someone had to have seen me. But I'm one person. What's there to see?

My body vibrates with electricity, butterflies swarming in my gut. My eyelids are balmy, my heart galloping, and my ears blazing hot. I pop my knuckles and wince. It's too quiet back here, the popping might as well have been a fizzy can exploding. I should paint a bullseye on my chest with that red nail polish I made months back. Better yet, I'll make a color that resembles—no. I'm not going to keep making nail polish to get by. I'm not going to keep waking up to fall asleep and do it all over again. This movement has a purpose.

I don't need to be a relay or a recruit, but I need to prove my worth. To the Cicadas, to Jerald, to myself.

Closest to my height with the least bit of tiptoes, I step for the center vent. Carefully opening the hinge, I reach my hand in. There's a piece of paper—and something else. Something handheld, some type of clay. I grab both and shove them into my tote, not chancing a peek. Briskly walking down the alley, I slow my pace once back on the street and merge with the casual flow of the Sec-Four crowd, heading for the threshold.

The sight of Olivia waiting for me is an oasis. I return her downward nod, exhilaration consuming my anxiety.

"I almost threw up," she whispers, patting her tote. "How did you do?"

"It was the easiest thing I've ever done."

"You're lying." She nudges me.

"I was a case of nerves, but it only took me one try. Didn't have to search through more than one vent." I flash her a proud smile.

"Me too! I was overthinking which one to choose from and finally picked one. I was so relieved when I felt that paper because I'm not sure I would have been brave enough to try again. There was something else in there. I didn't know what it was, but I took it. Haven't checked it out yet. I wanted to get out of there."

Suspicion tingles my spine. I keep my voice hushed, leaning closer to her as we walk. "Was there a journal in there, or a piece of paper with the mystery item?"

"A single piece of paper and a mystery item. Did yours have something else in there? A pointy blob of clay or something?"

"Something like that." Did we take something we weren't supposed to? There should have been a journal in there, not a piece of paper—we failed the Test. I press my nails into my palm. This isn't something to spiral about. Flint and Sandstone will have more information on how to fix this, and they'll know what to do. Passing through the main corridor, I change the subject. "Speaking of mysteries, what have you heard of Prime Watchman Gideon?"

The Wraith.

"All of nothing. I know it's a male, and I know his last name, but that's it. No one knows what he looks like. I'm not sure how to avoid someone without a face." She sighs, and I quietly share that weight with her. "He's a silent killer, an assassin. We have tech folks in the movement, but no one can find out anything about him. If I see a nametag with 'Gideon' written on it, I'll assume it's the Prime. You better do the same."

I nod my head in agreement, too aware of the secrets burning in my tote. I fall a few strides back, and Olivia heads behind the commissary. I count to one hundred, then follow her.

———— ⦿ ————

We're the last of the nymphs to arrive, Magnolia and Poppy harnessing their usual irritation, Squid and Sandstone not in attendance. Anglerfish grins wide, motioning for me to stand beside him, Olivia, and Flint.

"Well done, all of you," the veteran whispers. "Open your totes." None of us makes a move. Is this still part of the Test? Open our totes *here*—where someone could see us? "Go on."

Making the first move, I open the tote, push aside the herbs and bag of rice, and remove the paper and mystery item, holding out both for everyone to see. On top of the paper, a small clay sculpture of a starfish—of Foxtrot—sits in my palm.

"Read the paper," Flint encourages.

Taking the sculpture in my left hand, I read the page aloud. "Foxtrot is a haven under the sea. Its five sectors keep us safe. The Warden is honorable, and his Watchmen are admirable. We must all give our thanks to—what the fuck is this?" I crinkle the paper.

Olivia digs into her tote, pulling out the same figurine, mumbling identical words under her breath while reading from her paper. Magnolia, Poppy, and Anglerfish mimic the same. Though none of them crumple the paper or step on the clay, we all stare at Flint with silent demands.

"*This* means you all passed the first Test," Flint says. "None of you were in danger of retrieving a true journal. All the vents and ducts in those locations have the same items. No matter which one you chose, you would have collected the same things. If a Prime found these items in the vent, they'd think nothing of it. What *this* means is you're ready for the next phase, but the group won't be as large. It has to be split amongst you in shifts. Normally, we have an even number of nymphs to partner up, but with Squid being assigned elsewhere, one of you will be solo. Apricus, since you were the first to retrieve your items, you have the first pick. Would you like to partner with someone here, or move alone?"

This turn of events is enough to light a flame inside, but I smother it. Somehow, it feels like I'm a child who was afraid to go down the slide at the playground because it seemed to be a thousand feet tall—but it was chest level with adults standing next to me and holding my hand.

Be humble. This was a safe experiment. It was questionable at first, but it makes sense now. Even if the initiation was devised, I'm here for the experience, for a purpose. To test myself and learn how to trust myself.

As far as if I'd rather partner or move alone to the next Test, the answer is simple—alone.

"I'll partner with Olivia," I answer. She beams, nodding her head in agreement. Being alone is easy. I can't evolve as a person if I always choose the same path.

"Very well," Flint says. "Your next Test has a few phases, but I'm not your veteran for that. Both of you head to the tech hub in Sec-Three. A Cicada who goes by Roanoke will meet you there, and you can't miss him. He'll tell you he's over seven feet tall, but that's because he rounds up. Don't let his size intimidate you, and don't stare too long at the scar down his lips." He winks, then shoos us away.

22

Sec-Three. Another section I hardly visit. Why can't all of this Cicada stuff be in Sec-Five so I don't have to walk miles and miles and sweat so much doing it. I'll have to ask a veteran what sort of assignments there are besides recruits, relays, and techs—all things I'm not familiar with. But I can learn. I can bend. I can synergize.

"What are you thinking about?" Olivia asks.

"Do you know a lot about the inner workings of the movement?"

"Odds and ends. What are you wondering?"

"I'm wondering if I'll have to work on my endurance. I've never walked so much before. I know all of this is deceiving." I flex the nonexistent muscles in my arms and point out my weak calves. "But I am severely out of shape. The furthest I ever go is the commissary, and that's once a week, if that. School is around the corner, my mom is close by, and I live with Mason. That's my whole life in Sector Five." My depressing, redundant life. I should make a banner to hang in my room that reads *Twenty-Six, Miserably Dismal Existence!*

But it won't be for long. Foxtrot is the constant; Cicadas the anomaly.

"From what I understand, once you're assigned, you don't have to venture too far. You'll keep working where you work and live where you live, but on the low, you're a Cicada. Besides, we can't put in a change of address request until we're thirty. Even if we weren't in the movement, we're stuck in the sector we're in. That's one Warden rule that works out for the movement, if you ask me. It's harder to track Cicada involvement if we aren't doing anything out of the ordinary. We're like everyone else."

"Or it makes us easier for him to find," I spout. Her head whips in my direction. Another thought I should have kept to myself, but I'm not naïve enough to believe being *normal* but *unpredictable*—by being predictable—isn't cause for concern.

"Can I ask you something?" she asks, tapping her fingers.

Entering Sec-Three, I hold back the hitch in my voice. "Of course."

"Why do you seem so mad all the time?"

I chew on my sour words, grinding them to a powder. "I'm mad at everything and at nothing at all," I admit. Have been my whole life. "Being angry means no one wants to be close to me, and no one can hurt me. If I expect the worst in people, then I can never be surprised. Having a reservoir of rage means—"

My back hits the floor. Hard. The taste of blood fills

my mouth from biting the inside of my cheek from the tackle. Why is my airway closing off? Why does it feel as if weights are pressing on my sternum? Panicked, shallow breaths escape the hands around my throat. I can't make sense of what's happening.

A curtain of dark hair covers my eyes. I struggle beneath the unknown force, unable to hear anything except the white noise coursing through my ears. Until she speaks. "There are blinking eyes all over you!" the woman above me screams. "All-seeing eyes across your skin—hundreds and thousands—millions of eyes that can see. Your flesh is on display, it is *mine* to take! More needs to be done." Saliva drips from her mouth, landing on my forehead. "I can see it all. I can see and hear everything!"

This woman is so much larger than me, so unbelievably heavy. I buck my hips to lift her off, my hands gripping the tops of her wrists to twist and relieve the pressure from my throat. My eyesight is blurring, my head filling with dizziness. My hands flail above as her hair cascades over me. Taking a handful of her hair in my frenzied palms, I form a fist and yank her head to the side with everything I have and meet the paralyzed gaze of Olivia, who seems too far away and stuck in quicksand.

I rock my body to roll the woman off me, but she's an immovable force. "Your skin crawls with despair!" she shrieks. "I can see it. I can smell it. I can feel your life between my fingers. Everyone will watch as I steal it."

I've been on the ground for either ten years or ten

seconds, there's no way to tell. The reality of what's happening is slipping past, unconsciousness delicately kissing me. Her hands around my throat suffocate me. Her knees on my chest smother me. The strands of her hair falling into my mouth choke me. Her wild eyes pierce me. Her modified ears ...

Nearly out of breath, three of my fingers find their way through the hole of her jewelry. With fleeting strength, I pull the thin, pendulous skin on her left earlobe down in quick, violent succession. Wet, coppery tang splatters across the bridge of my nose, and her primal scream of pain vibrates through my body. She tightens her grip around my throat, fingernails digging into the muscles on each side of my neck. She lifts my upper body off the ground, slamming my back into the floor again and again, as if I'm a buoy against a savage ocean storm, blood rain dripping across my face.

My eyes burn—a mixture of tears and sweat, broken vessels, saliva, and blood that's not my own. My legs abandon their futile bucking, my arms deadweights, too heavy to lift. My oxygen-deprived brain refuses to send signals to defend myself any longer. An increasingly numb sensation sweeps over my body, and acceptance washes over me. This is it. This is how I die. The absolute panic subsides, and the stranger above me becomes a bright, glowing light. Warmth fills my chest cavity.

Sunshine, have we finally met? I've waited so long. You're radiant. Breathtaking. Powerful. You should have told me it was you, I wouldn't have fought. I would've gone with you, willingly. Silly sunshine, don't you know we're meant to be together? If you've come to take me home, I'm ready. I'm—

I inhale greedily. A pair of hands roll me to my side, aggressively hitting the space between my shoulder blades, over and over and over. "Give her a minute," someone says, their voice a booming whisper echoing all around.

Constant noise and movement surround me, yet everything is dead silent and still. Someone is patting my back, the hollow thuds reverberating through my skeleton like a distant thrum of war drums enticing me to fight. But I don't know if I have anything left.

Someone sits me up, leans me forward, and lifts me. My knees firmly press together, my ankles bobbing up and down in sync with the trot. My eyes are open, alert, and focused, but everything is a silent blur. The man carrying me through the crowd is a stranger. Past a brutal scar, his mouth moves quickly. Barking commands to whoever is listening, I'd imagine. To my side, Olivia appears and breaks off into a sprint wearing my backpack, then is out of sight.

Voices from the crowd swirl all around in mumbles and grumbles. None of it makes sense individually, but as a whole, it's somehow cohesive. "Is she all right?" a woman asks from somewhere to my side. "Who was that mad woman?" a man calls out from behind me. Or from the front? "She was dead for nearly two minutes!" someone cries out. "Find the Indicator and toss her in the Vat!" multiple people shout at once. A witch hunt.

"Put me down," I try to say. The phantom pressure still gripping my larynx causes the words to fall short. *Dead*, someone said. Who died? With my voice failing, I wriggle. His grip on me tightens, locking in my movement so as not to become unbalanced as he continues his jog to wherever it is he's taking me.

"You're all right. We're almost there," the strange man says powerfully, my sense of hearing more clear. He looks down at me, smiling deeply with his eyes.

"Please, put me down," I plead again, the words raw and raspy.

"Can't do that, kid. Rest for a minute. We're almost there, I promise."

Rest, he says. The odds of a lion's mane jellyfish swallowing me whole are far better than the odds of me resting—but I'll close my eyes if only to stave off the motion sickness.

As soon as I do, shooting stars soar through the blackness behind my eyelids.

23

"What if she doesn't wake up?" a woman asks.

It sounds like Olivia, but somehow her voice is far away yet close by.

"She'll wake up," a male replies.

A familiar voice, yet foreign all the same. The man who carried me here?

"What if she doesn't? I should have done something, but I couldn't think. I couldn't move I—"

My eyelids are heavy, comfortably heavy.

"—Don't make this about you. No one knows how they'll react to something until they have to. She sure as shit didn't think she was going to die, but she fought damn hard while everyone stood around staring."

I'm the one who died? Where am I?

It's as if I'm everywhere and nowhere.

I'm below. I'm above. I'm between.

"You lifted that woman off her as if she weighed nothing, then saved Samara with those chest compressions. She wouldn't be alive if it weren't for you, Roanoke."

"I help where I can. All we can do is wait. I'll give it

another hour before calling for a medic. She's stable and resting, that's good. She's recovering."

"How long can the brain be without oxygen before it's ... dead?"

The tingling in my body is fading.

The soothing blackness starting to cool.

"About four minutes, give or take."

"She was gone for almost two. She's going to be fine, right? She's been asleep for six hours, but that doesn't mean her brain is dead, right? She's—"

Six hours?

"—Stop. She's going to wake up."

Wake up.

"Please, God. Please let her wake up."

"There are no gods," I quip. The voice coming from me is damaged, delicate, and painfully quiet. I barely heard it myself. Instinct peels my eyelids open. A mural of sea turtles painted on the ceiling above reveals itself to my clearing vision.

"Samara, you're awake. Let me help." Olivia's voice is nurturing, but her warm hands are hot knives against my forearm, jolting me upright.

"Don't touch me." Uneasiness swims in my gut. Everyone needs to stop touching me. Those hands around my throat—Atlantic, I can still feel those hands. Where am I? Am I safe? Roanoke is a stranger, the woman who attacked me is a stranger, and I'm in a strange place. None of this is in my control. And I ... died.

"Kid, let me help," Roanoke says benevolently. His fingertips inadvertently brush the top of my knee.

Gooseflesh swarms my skin. I swat his hand away. "Do not fucking touch me. Nobody gets to touch me, not a single person." My wobbly knees hold my weight. I stand up, taking in my surroundings.

It's clear this unfamiliar place is a Cicada safehouse. It looks abandoned. There's nothing personal belonging to anyone anywhere, and the windows have cardboard taped to them. The appliances are old, the fabric on the limited furniture is worn down, and there are at least three bedrooms. Sliding my backpack off the counter, I shoulder it and head down the creaking hallway.

"Second door on the left, kid. There's a bedroom with a private suite inside. Take your time," the mind-reader says.

"Stop calling me kid," I say with heat, willing myself not to slam the door behind me.

This room is plain. A bed in the middle sharing the empty space, a closet with hangers, and a bathroom attached. I unzip my backpack inside the sink, taking out clothing and medical supplies while avoiding the mirror. That woman's fingernail divots can still be felt. Her invisible outline of palms and fingers. A scent of blood, sweat, tears, and spit lingers, along with a headache made of icicles and salt.

If I dare a glance at my reflection, I know my beast is in the mirror with broken blood vessels in each eye waiting to stare back at me. But I don't want to see myself. Can't look her in the eyes. I'd fall apart if I did. How can I face myself knowing I wasn't strong enough to save her. I ... died.

Head down and both palms on the counter, I contemplate what to do first. What does someone do after they come back from the dead? Do they cry? Scream? Eat human flesh?

That woman was another abuser. Another attacker I couldn't fight off. Struggling to stay alive was humiliating. It was chaotic and *wrong*. I didn't matter. Why does defending myself lead to pain. Why does everything in this facility circle back to hurt, suffering, and death. I am *sick of it*.

Evacuate below or burn above, and this is humanity's great second chance. Reduced to living underwater to escape the sun, only to suffer in more creative ways. If I had been given the choice, I would've laughed under the dying sun and said *fuck it,* then toasted the apocalypse with a cold lemonade. I didn't ask for this inherited existence.

Why couldn't I have stayed in that soothing darkness before I was brought back? Accepting death was simple—it answered everything. I've always craved that release, haven't I? An end to the struggle of survival. In the void, there's no hunger, no light regulations, no fear of the Vat. No anger, no grief, no loss. If I'm lost, I can't lose anyone else. I don't have to cope with reality. It'll just ... stop.

Pulling myself away from the darkness of my thoughts, I set the pocketknife down and sigh. My impulsive, self-loathing beast is starving in the depths for a reason, but I withhold the mental spoonful. I will not feed it—I will not entertain it. I have a purpose. The surface is up there, and it's my reason to live.

Engaging in autopilot, I absentmindedly form my hair into two tight braids. The clothes I died in become a neat pile on the floor, and a dry hand towel from the drawer turns damp and soapy. I blot the cuts on my neck, rinsing the rag clean as I go. Wincing at the stinging from the antibacterial ointment on my neck, I chew two painkillers dry. The blood on my hands, the blood from that woman's ear, washes away in the sink. Fresh, clean clothing drapes over my skin, and the memory of the attack pierces the back of my skull.

I stare at myself in the mirror, at the other stranger I've never seen. It's not the blood-speckled faux freckles that raise any alarms—blood can be washed off. It's not the bright red patches sharing the whites of each eye because those will heal in time. It's not the redness or fingernail cuts around my neck because the inflammation will subside, and the cuts will scab and most likely scar. No—none of those things make me question my reflection. It's the tingling relaxation pulsating throughout my body and my soulless stare that's cause for concern.

24

Aside from the beating of my reincarnated heart, I can't feel anything. Not even as I lay on what I can only assume is a comfortable mattress, pricking the tips of each finger with my pocketknife until scarlet beads form. Have I gone mad? No, that would come with a feeling. I think.

"Virginia? That's on the West Coast, right?" Olivia's voice is close, approaching the room I'm in. The hallway creaks from her footsteps. She must be unhinged if she's even considering entering this room. But to answer your question, *Oncilla,* Virginia was on the—

"East Coast," Roanoke says from somewhere in the living room, and he's correct. If memory serves, Roanoke was the name of a city in the state of Virginia. If I were a high roller, I'd bet his family line originated from there, sparking the alias.

Olivia sighs, her voice closer. "I should have paid more attention to the geography lessons."

Or maybe you should have paid more attention to public safety and combat training from the academy. Serves her right to have been discharged. She would have made a terrible Watchman. Her flight triggered and she stood there, in quicksand, watching me die. She's a lousy partner.

The door across the hall abruptly closes, the creaking in the hallway fading. I crack open the door, listening to their conversation.

"My mom says we come from somewhere in Canada. Have you heard of it?"

"I have. It used to be the second-largest country in the world."

"Used to be? What do you mean used to be? Wouldn't it still be?"

"I doubt that. Don't you remember what happened to the surface?"

"I know from school that it was nearly destroyed."

"It's more complicated than that," he says patiently. "It didn't happen all at once. It was gradual and crept over time, but the simple way to put it is that the sun got too hot. Then a global plague of malignant melanoma. Nastiest stuff you can imagine. It was a pandemic. That was the first hard truth. Then wildfires inherited the surface, acid rain, electric storms, earthquakes, and volcanic eruptions. Hell, even some of the oceans boiled. Three *billion* people died before some bigwig announced it was time to evacuate the survivors. There's some conspiracy behind what took so long to descend. Some say the U.N. wanted to wait it out and let it pass, but it didn't. Others think they waited so long because someone miscalculated how many people these outposts could hold, and they needed more people to die before evacuating to Alpha through Zulu. Guess they didn't want to be overcrowded." He pauses, his vacant stare perfectly finding mine through the crack of the door. "To put it lightly Livs, my answer is no. I don't think Canada is still the second-largest country. I don't think there's a Canada left anymore."

"If it was all destroyed, what are we fighting for?"

Empathy builds inside of me. Jerald answered all my questions about the surface, but not everyone was as privileged. I understand now why he risked everything to share the information from the book of the surface. Unfiltered knowledge of the surface is rare. I forget not everyone is familiar with it. Cicada or not, not everyone has read that book. Or studied it. Or obsessed over it.

"Because it's been damn near two hundred years since the calamity of the surface. If the sun truly evolved into a red giant, we wouldn't be here. Our entire planet would've been consumed. Cicadas believe the sun didn't fully evolve. That it was a warning. Without humans doing everything we did to ruin the planet, we gave the surface of the earth a break. There's a chance it reset itself. There's something up there for us, for all of us." He nods to her, then discreetly to me.

Olivia's voice is unsteady. "We're risking everything for a chance?"

"Everyone needs hope," I interject, stepping out from behind the door and joining them in the living room. Neither of them acknowledges my response. They're both staring at me as if I'm being held together by nothing but tape and glue.

"How are you feeling?" Olivia asks.

I look between the two, deciding whether to fan the growing flames inside or synergize. Why not both? "I'll be fine. I want to move forward with the next Test and put all this behind me. But I swear to whatever god Olivia was praying to earlier that if you both keep staring at me like I'm some broken thing, I'll rip out your eyes. I don't need to be coddled."

Roanoke gives two thumbs-ups and a big smile, his scar spreading wide. "You got it, Revenant."

A hot twinge pinches my neck. I tilt my head to the side, studying him through knitted brows. "What's that now?"

"You know, Revenant. Because you died and all." He smirks. This man is odd, but an inner voice is telling me he's my kind of person.

"If you're going to call me anything of the sort, call me Zombie." I give him a bow. "It's another word for Revenant. A synonym." A harmless lie, one nobody can prove or disprove. But it's my special word. A word I'd never imagined would be so ... fitting. Eighty-six the flesh-eating part, I'm the living dead.

"No soft voices or sad eyes if I want to keep them," Olivia says. "Done and done. Let me ask you something ... you don't believe there's a god?"

What a strange question. I muffle a scoff. "I believe in the surface."

She tilts her head. "That doesn't answer my question."

"No, I don't believe there's a god."

"Why not?"

"Because gods are beings who live on an unreachable plane of existence," I explain in my scratchy, second-grade teacher's voice. "Mythological gods live on Mount Olympus. Traditional gods live past the sky or far below us in the underworld. There are even gods who rule over the cosmic body. But they're only shared with us through stories. No one has seen or touched them—how can they be real? But the surface?" A smile slips past my teeth. "The surface is real."

Cavalier laces her tone. "That would make the surface your god, wouldn't it?"

Brashness laces mine. "How's that?"

"You've never touched the surface, yet you believe in it. You've only seen the surface through illustrations, and it's only been shared through stories. You have your god, and I have mine." She crosses her arms with a cocky grin.

I motion for the door. "Then what are we waiting for? Let's meet my god."

"We aren't meeting anyone's god yet," Roanoke interrupts, his stormy gray eyes flashing between us in mild frustration. "There's a plan, and the plan doesn't include the two of you making your own goddamn plans. We wait until lights-out, then we move. That's the plan. Not all this shit about meeting gods. Does anyone have a problem with that?"

Olivia lies vertically across the only couch in the living

room, her forearms covering her eyes. "Nope."

I retreat to the bedroom. "Let me know when it's time to leave."

25

Either my *partner* or Roanoke has left the hallway light on. The glow seeps through the crack beneath the door, but the motivation to remove myself from this bed to turn it off has yet to be found. I'm mentally and physically exhausted.

The voice of my attacker still echoes in my ears, the memory of her hands on my throat pressing on my skin, my bones. My eyes are as blurry as my head is foggy. Through the ringing in my ears, a faint dripping from the bathroom entertains my curiosity.

Did I leave the water running after cleaning up?

A pool of bloody water fills the basin, so rich and dark, my hand is lost in merlot swirls as I reach for the rag clogging it. I pull it free, but the water doesn't drain. Twisting the knob to stop the dripping, water barrels from the faucet, overflowing the sink and splashing crimson-stained water at my feet.

Shoving a towel under the door, I reach for the cabinet for more to soak up the mess, but it seems the drawers are glued shut to the vanity. Desperate for ideas, I rip the shower curtain from the rods and drop it onto the floor to absorb the water, but it floats past me.

Somehow, the water is above my hips, and an anatomical heart-shaped padlock is in place of the door handle, the door itself a spiraling blackhole.

The bathroom tilts.

The water shifts, the vanity rotating to the ceiling, but I stay in place, standing on solid water beneath my feet and holding my weight. A splintered, upside-down mirror materializes, and I step forward, crossing the water's surface.

Facing my reflection, I open my mouth, and hundreds of silent cicadas flurry from it. The swarm flutters to the walls behind me, perching above the waterline, and transforming into keys through the fractured glass. Carefully studying each key, I reach into the mirror and choose one—a vibrantly yellow key that feels *right*. I turn to the padlocked, spiraling door.

With a steady hand, I insert the key, and it clicks. A perfect fit. The spiraling stops, and the blackhole becomes a solid door. It swings open, revealing pitch-black nothingness inside. A tickling sensation spreads over me, and I step forward.

My skin disintegrates, drifting into the void like smoke.

———◆———

Cushioned fabric lands on my face. "It's time to leave, Zombie."

I sit up, wiping the sleep from my eyes. "Did you throw

a pillow at me?"

"Yes. Yes, I did. You said no one can look at you all sad, but you didn't say we can't throw things at you. Pack up, we're leaving in thirty."

26

Finishing inventory of the contents from my backpack dumped onto the bed, Ruth's voice sings in my ears, *You're a survivor.* And what is it that I've survived—abuse? That's nothing special. My murder? Someone's always killing someone else at least six times a month, give or take. Malnutrition? Sure, a handful of times—but who hasn't. And what do I have to show for it? A sour attitude and simmering disdain. I want control. I want to live on my own terms. I want to do what I want, when I want—no rations, no Watchmen, no endless rules about every goddamn thing. That's not too much to ask. It can't be.

"You're too heavy," Roanoke accuses from behind.

"And you're too tall."

"I mean your pack. You're carrying too much. You need to pack light."

"If you're so well-versed on how to pack, humor me." The quickness of my sarcasm spins me around. He's leaning against the open doorframe, palming the length of his beard. My shoulder blades are surprisingly relaxed. There's no tension on top of my skin, no urge to upheave electric butterflies. I think some of my anxiety died alongside me.

"For starters, take all that food out. We can stock the kitchen here with whatever you have. Take these." He tosses a handful of vacuum-sealed packages in my direction. I don't try to catch them in the air. I watch them land on the mattress beside the canned soup. "Soup and a can-opener? Are you working on your full body strength with all that weight?"

I take a deep breath, reeling in my attitude and swallowing down the spitfire response. He's a veteran. Between the two of us, if anyone knows what they're doing, it's him. I couldn't pack strategically the first time, what makes me think I can salvage this pile on the bed? Besides, he's my ally, not my enemy. And he saved me. "Can you help me?"

"Wear something comfortable. Something you can run in if you have to. Not too loose so it snags, but not too tight either. You want to be flexible. Keep the rest of your clothes here, it makes your backpack bulky. You're supposed to blend in, not look like you're running away."

I *am* running away, but I don't want it to look obvious. While he speaks, I sort through my clothes, gradually realizing he may be right, and I might have packed too many. Without overthinking it, I pick out a black long-sleeved turtleneck that's form-fitting to cover my bruised neck, and black denim jeans. I set those aside to put them on once I'm alone, and hurtle the remaining clothes through the air into the open closet where they land in a pile on the floor. The clothes I died in can stay here, too. In the bathroom. I don't want those, either. "What else?"

"Leave the flashlights. I'll give you one that's pocket-sized on the way out. Keep all the first-aid stuff but leave everything else—including the Cicada journals. I'll have someone come by once we're gone and clean up here."

Nodding my head in agreement, I make two piles on the bed. A pile to keep, a pile to leave behind. Taking out my lucky nail polish, a giggle bubbles through me. It jitters from my hand, dropping at my feet. Staring at the bottle, another giggle escapes. I pick it up and impulsively toss it over my shoulder, laughing a bit harder. Clicking the flashlight on and off, off and on, I put it under my chin and widen my eyes at the veteran, then double over, laughing hysterically. I have definitely gone mad.

Roanoke joins me in the room, clearing his throat. His tight smile is more of a wince, the scar slanting with it. "You all right, Samara? Anything you want to talk about?"

Befuddled laughter jostles out of me. "I have no idea what I'm doing! I brought nail polish, enough food for an army, and Cicada journals. *Cicada journals*!" I hold my aching side. "Why did I pack those? What if I lost the pack? What if someone stole it from me? Fuck the Atlantic, how naïve can I be?"

"You brought comfort items. Can't be too hard on yourself." He chuckles, gauging the conversation. "Anyone could have done it."

"No." Full stop. "No one else would have done it, but I

did. I risked those journals and packed a backpack fit for an elephant to carry because I have no idea what I'm doing. I'm a schoolteacher, I'm not a clever, secret agent. I'm a regular person." There it is again, the doubt.

"It doesn't matter if you're a schoolteacher or a regular person. What matters is what your heart is telling you. What matters is that you care enough to try. What matters is reaching for the surface, even if you have no idea what you're doing."

"But—"

"—You've been a Cicada for what, all of a week? You don't have to know everything. You have to know when to ask for help, and you did. You can do this. Finish up here, we'll be waiting in the living room, then we leave for the first phase of the next Test. Trust yourself, Zombie. You're a badass." His voice is as calm as my nerves are from his reassurances.

"Roanoke?" I call out before the door closes behind him. He turns back with a look of patience and understanding, a look Jerald used to give me. "Thank you."

Olivia is sitting on the kitchen counter, doing her best not to give me sad eyes, but I can see through the forced toughness. I reach out my hand, hoping for a handshake. "Still partners?" I ask. She opens her arms, inviting me for a hug. "Not going to happen." I laugh lightly to hide the hurt aching in my chest.

I don't want to be touched, even if it's a gesture of friendship. My past trauma has always sat on my skin. I've done my best to pluck its thorns, but the attack in Sec-Three has regenerated new ones. I'm a cholla cactus pretending to be lamb's ear.

She gives me a playful pout, then reaches for my hand. Tapping the back of my hand twice with the back of hers, she grasps my palm, the padding of our thumbs pressing together. "Being partners is special. We should have a special handshake." She lets go of her grip, her smile melting. "I'm sorry, Samara. I should have done something—anything when—"

"—Olivia, I don't blame you for not helping me with the attack. At first I did, but it must have been terrifying for you. I understand that now. I'm not sure what I would have done if that woman latched onto you instead. Self-preservation and all. I get it. We're all doing our best. Good thing this titan was there in time." I point my thumb to Roanoke. "How tall are you anyway?"

"Seven feet," he answers. It almost sounded like a question. My jaw hinges to the side, my left cheek rising in a grimace. He crosses his arms and laughs. "Six foot six, but don't tell anyone else. Seven feet sounds better."

"Roanoke, the *giant*." I flash him my palms, standing on the tips of my toes, measuring our height difference. "What's your real name, Roanoke? You know mine and Olivia's, it seems only fair. We didn't get much one-on-one time with the other veterans. They were very … business-like. You seem different." He shakes his head, that scarred grin endearing. "We could always ask other Cicadas and figure it out if we *really* wanted to." I wink at Olivia.

"Scott," he mutters. "But stick to Roanoke. To me, y'all are Livs and Zombie. I like the nicknames. Doesn't have to be more complicated than that."

Playfully bullying someone who is at least twenty years my senior—I'll add that to my list of achievements.

Olivia hops off the counter, shouldering her embarrassingly smaller pack. She knows how to pack strategic. "Now that it's lights-out, where are we headed?"

Roanoke's smile fades, his tone increasing with importance. "We're going to the tech hub. You both need to stay quiet and stay close. Lights-out means it'll be dark, but it won't be pitch-black. Sec-Three is the center of technology and the hub has an ambient glow and surveillance, so we need to cut down residentials until we're close enough to slip in through the back. A Cicada works in the building. She's going to let us in. Any more questions before we leave?" His eyes shift between us.

Yes, actually. About a billion things—a trillion things—but he might not have any answers to the absurd number of questions I have. But I do have one question I know he has the answer to. "How did you get that scar?"

Maybe it's not what he meant by *any more questions before we leave.* But I've been wondering about the scar since I met him. The way it starts under his left nostril, over the tops of both lips, past his chin, and ending underneath his jaw. It's magnificently brutal.

He laughs, heartily. "You're the first to ask me that since I've had it. Guess people don't want to come across as rude. Most pretend like they can't even see it. I know they can see it, and I can always tell when they're purposely not looking. You speak your mind there, Zombie. I respect that." His fingers move across the outline of the scar. "Too long of a story short, the person who did this has a bullshit mindset. He doesn't like to be questioned about anything. I learned that the bloody way."

It's as if stitches were not enough. Whatever medical care he received, the wound was stapled shut, too. Little dots, like freckles, sit above most of the scarring. The blade, or knife, or damn machete—whatever it was—it was damning. Some of the peaks are crooked, as if the cutting started, then stopped, and started again. I shatter the spell cast by the scar. "I'm sorry that happened to you."

He shrugs as if he's accepted his past, his shoulders singing, *it is what it is*. If given the choice of meeting the person who made someone as large as Roanoke feel so small or being tied to a boulder at the bottom of the Atlantic, I'd ask if rags could accompany the chains around my ankles so I wouldn't chafe.

"Anything else?" His hands frame his face as if he's some sideshow attraction, then wave the length of his body. "My height, my scar, my name—would you like to know how often I brush my teeth? Or what I had to eat earlier?

Maybe you'd like to know my mother's maiden name, or what my favorite color is." He tosses another vacuum-sealed package my way from his bag. I catch it this time, and he hands one to Olivia. Feeling like I've overstayed my questions, I shake my head and tear open the bag with my teeth, taking a bite of the chocolate-covered graham cracker with vanilla swirls. "I'm messing with you, Zombie. You have a curious mind. Good news is, the Cicadas don't sink people if they have one. You're in good company. Last call for any more questions. Once we leave this place, we move silently until I say."

"Why are we going to the tech hub?" Olivia asks through a mouthful of her treat.

Excitement swells behind his eyes. "It's where we need to be for the first phase before the next Test. I'm going to reprogram your badges to gain access to the Arboretum, then you're going to learn how to swim."

27

"The Cicada who works here set the cameras to idle for maintenance," Roanoke says once we're inside the tech hub.

It was easier than I thought it would be to maneuver through Sec-Three. My heart pounded in my ears. We crept around buildings and crouched behind bins to avoid the Watchmen who patrolled, but Roanoke took the lead and moved effortlessly. A natural leader. We followed quietly and matched his every move.

Olivia and I glance around the empty lobby. "Where's the Cicada who let us in?" she asks.

Roanoke sets his pack on a ledge near the door. "She'd rather be heard than seen. It's only the three of us, but the doors are programmed to seal after twenty minutes. We need to be done well before then. Don't touch anything. Remember, we were never here."

We follow him down the hallway, passing dozens of cubicles and computers along the way. "Care to fill us in on how we're gaining access to the Arboretum?" I ask.

He chuckles over his shoulder. "Do you want the complicated answer or the short one?"

"Would the complicated answer take less than twenty minutes?" Olivia muses.

Approaching a sealed door at the end of the hallway, Roanoke enters a code onto the keypad, and it opens, revealing a shallow entryway with a central control panel. "The short answer is we're borrowing software from anyone who has the authorization."

Olivia's face is as confused as mine. "How are we using software if someone already has it?" she asks.

Roanoke's fingers swipe across the touch screen, entering too many codes to keep track of. "High-ranking Watchmen have authorization to the Arboretum. The short but complicated answer is that I'm tricking the software. Duplicating existing authorization and uploading it to your badges. When you swipe your badge at the card reader outside the Arboretum, it'll recognize the piggy-backed software and approve the entry." He manually overrides the control panel, an irritated grunt escaping his nostrils. "Damnit. Left the script in my pack. Thought I could get by without it. Wanted y'all to think I was badass for doing all this on the fly." He winks, his fingers still busy at work.

"I'll get it," Olivia says, skipping down the hallway back to the ledge with the packs.

"She's spirited." Roanoke grins, entering patterns and codes from memory. Olivia retrieves the pack, quietly singing into it with closed eyes, pretending the straps are a microphone.

"Fill me in here Roanoke, because I want to keep

up. You have the gift of resurrection, you're an actual bodyguard, you're somehow stealthy for a tall person, and now you're proving to be a hacker. What's your secret? Are you a real person, or are you some kind of robot?" I tease, kicking the back of his shoe.

He gives Olivia a nod in thanks as she hands him the pack. "If I'm a robot, then it's news to me. I'm a real person who happens to have a real curious mind."

"How did you figure out how to do all of this?" Olivia asks.

"I'm in tech support, both inside and outside the movement." He digs through his pack for the script and sets it on the counter. "I like to know how things work. Why they work, what happens when they don't work, what happens if they stop working. What happens if they *start* working. Just a prying mind." He motions for our badges and inserts them into the control panel.

For a moment, flashing amber lights bounce from the terminal, reflecting off our badges as if fireflies were hovering above. The amber lights turn green, and a soft, internal click releases our badges. He hands them to us.

A bit of suspicion dances around my lips. I place my upgraded badge around my neck, tucking it underneath my shirt. "That makes two prying minds in this group. Who's the high-ranking Watchman we stole the authorization from?"

He shakes his head, a silver strand breaking free from behind his ear. "Now that is an answer I can't give you."

Sneaking into the Arboretum was as straightforward as it was to enter the tech hub. The card reader outside the dome accepted our upgraded badges with no fuss, and Roanoke assured us we were out of sight lines for surveillance. Is my predisposition to being suspicious of everything slowly fading, or is being involved with the Cicadas this simple? Either way, I feel unstoppable.

As our bodies become lost in the foliage, Roanoke makes a static sound from his mouth. I've heard that sound before when I was near the Vat—when Olivia signaled me to exit the Watchman hallway. "Why is he making that sound?" I whisper to her.

"It's the sound real Cicadas make," she whispers back. "Well, the closest we can recreate. All you have to do is push air through your front teeth. Like this." She demonstrates and I mimic the sound with her until another hissing, static sound is heard. It's not from either of us or Roanoke.

Joining us in the cornfield, another person bumps elbows with Roanoke. "Sal, this is Oncilla and Apricus, your new students. You two, this is Sal," Roanoke says.

Sal extends both calloused hands to us, his arms outstretched and crossed at the elbows. Olivia takes his right hand, and I take his left, my voice jumping around a bit from his enthusiastic double shake. "Sal, huh? That's a regular name. I thought Cicadas were supposed to have an alias."

"Sal *is* the alias! It's short for Salamander." He lets go of our hands, flashing us a smile. He's similar in age to Roanoke, early to mid-forties. Not as tall, of course. But Sal is athletic, that much is obvious. Lithe.

"A double alias. Clever, clever. If I had picked my own, I would have gone with—"

"—Can you really teach us how to swim?" Excitement bubbles out of Olivia.

Sal offers me a look of encouragement to finish what I was saying, but the interruption didn't bother me. *I have a twin*, I want to say to Sal, *I hardly finish sentences*. I give him a smile and a subtle wave, approving the change of topic. He must have siblings because he understands the signal.

"I can teach a hippopotamus how to swim," Sal says, confidence in his tone. "Before you say anything, hippos didn't know how to swim. They sank. But if you listen to me, you'll swim." His fingers move through the russet-brown mess on his head.

"How do *you* know how to swim?" I ask. I should have known my skepticism would creep back around.

Another flash of a smile. "Because outside the movement, I'm assigned to maintain the outer walls of Foxtrot. There are only a few dozen of us who have been approved to swim. The overlord believes it's a niche trade, top secret, no one can know. You ask me? Everyone should know how to swim. What if there's a breach? It's the reason I became a Cicada. I want to help save lives."

Of all the time I've spent thinking about the inner

workings of this prison we call Foxtrot, I've never once considered how detrimental the ability to swim would be for our safety. What if there *was* a breach? What if these two-hundred-year-old windows gave out? Cracked? Leaked? We couldn't swim to the surface, but sections could be sealed off to prevent flooding the whole facility.

What if someone was trapped inside a sealed sector, not knowing how to swim or at least stay afloat awaiting rescue? They get a ... good luck? For the love, hate, and to the absolute depths of the Atlantic with Warden Calum Gryme and all the Gryme's before him. For almost two hundred years, not one of them thought it was important enough for any of us to learn to swim in case there was an emergency. It took a dreamer, a Cicada, someone from outside the political game, to take a step away and realize the fault in this system.

"Samara, are you coming?" Olivia's voice swims through my ears. I break free from the paralyzing disassociation to see Sal and Roanoke ahead, heading deeper into the enclosure. She gently takes a husk of corn from my white-knuckled hands. "Where do you go when your mind wanders?"

Everywhere. Nowhere. All around. Above and below. Between. I give her a toothy smile. "Usually somewhere dark and full of hatred."

"Can you be somewhere dark and full of hatred as you move your legs? Specifically, as we follow Sal and Roanoke since they're leaving us behind?"

"Listen here Olivia, *I* can multitask."

She tilts her head, smiling a flirtatious smile. "Then keep up, doom and gloom."

Leaves crunch beneath my steps, and their sound is euphoric. My fingers trace each tree trunk we pass, and they're exactly how I'd imagined they'd feel. Sturdy, rough, ancient. The creek sounds as Jerald had described, casual yet hurried, going exactly nowhere and everywhere. Thorns from blackberry bushes snag on my jeans, and my eyes well with joy. This is where I'm supposed to be, except, in less of a manufactured environment. The reality of it all is within my reach, all I have to do is learn to swim, but the thought of swimming is terrifying.

As a child, I dreaded bath time. I was sure the water was an angry, clear creature made of liquid, hoping to find its way inside my mouth so it could control me as if I were a puppet. I'd flail whenever I was waist-deep in tub water to make myself larger than it. Being submerged in the clear liquid scared me to death. The water moved wherever it pleased, never where I wanted it to go, completely out of my control. I despised it. But a shower is like rainfall. A light, reliable, predictable flow.

Approaching the pond, I understand the body of water ahead is not a clear creature. With the only source of light being the recessed lighting from the catwalk above the dome and reflecting off the dreadful water, I realize the dark liquid is a distant, dying galaxy of a creature, daring me to enter. This is how I get to the surface. This is my trial by water.

28

"Don't worry, the Test isn't a sink or swim. I promise," Sal tells Olivia, both heading for the pond. I sit patiently on the bank with Roanoke, a stone's throw away, waiting for my turn. Sal said the lessons should be individual, and our group of four becomes a set of duos.

Olivia glances back at us. "Sink or swim?"

Roanoke gives a laugh and a wave. "He means he's not going to toss you in the deep end and say *good luck*!"

"Lovely." Her sarcasm slips through before they're out of earshot.

"Nervous?" Roanoke asks me, both of us watching the silhouettes of Sal moving his arms in circular rotations at his side, Olivia copying.

"A little," I confess, vacantly staring ahead, watching them perform the next set of moves. My fingers dig into the mud. "I never thanked you for pulling that woman off of me."

"You don't need to thank me. My assignment in the movement is technical. Upgrade badges, get Cicadas into the Arboretum, and introduce them to Sal. It's an easy gig, but no Cicada has ever died on their way to meet me. That woman must be suffering from a terrible Indicator. Some type of schizophrenia or hallucinations. Your paths crossing was a horrible coincidence. I should have been there sooner." He turns his body to me. "I'm sorry."

"I'm thankful you were there at all. You don't need to apologize for anything. If you hadn't—"

"—I do need to apologize. I promised your pops I'd keep an eye out for you."

A pain sparks in my chest. "Are you saying you knew Jerald?"

Roanoke's voice cracks. "He was the closest thing I had to a brother."

Jerald was personable and likable, he made friends with everyone, but too many questions flurry through my mind to take hold of. There's one I need the answer to, one I'm sure Roanoke doesn't know. But if there's a chance he does, I have to ask, otherwise, I'll keep breaking. A tear falls down the side of my cheek. I stare ahead, watching Olivia and Sal enter the water. "Did Jerald know he was going to die?"

A heartbeat of a pause, as if contemplating whether to tell me a lie or offer the truth. "He did."

My ribcage knocks against my knees. "Do you know how he ..." I search for the strength to finish the sentence.

Roanoke sighs, adjusting his posture. "It was his partner, Watchman Marlow. He figured out he was a Cicada."

That's Ruth's suspicion, too. Jerald learned his identity

had been exposed—he wrote it in his journal, the one I read at Ruth's. It said Maeve and many others reported seeing his true name in journals, and I'd imagine Cicadas are informed when a member is caught. But what I don't know is how Watchman Marlow fits into all of it. All I have is the aftermath.

Of Jerald's lifeless body lying on the medical examiner's table, horribly bruised and cut. His uniform torn in seven places—I counted. His shattered left wrist and fingers on his right twisted back. Bald patches marred his scalp where his hair used to be, and his skin was cold, infinitely cold. My warmth couldn't reach him. I'll never forget it. That memory clings to my skin like a scar.

"Do you know *how* he died?" I finally get out, the desperate question falling from my mouth.

"Gryme brought him into a confidential interrogation room, one that's not on the blueprints." His strange comment sparks another question in my racing mind, but I remain silent, letting him continue. "Jerald didn't deny being a Cicada. He knew they had his name. Marlow questioned and beat him for two shifts, but Jerald never answered their questions. They dumped his battered body outside the Arboretum and injected him with enough toxins so he didn't wake up." Streams of tears vanish into his beard.

This is more information than I can process, more information than I've ever been told. If Warden Gryme had Marlow bring Jerald in, then his death wasn't random. It was planned. Staged. A bullshit coverup. And somehow, knowing that feels worse than living in denial. There's a pain in my chest, one impossible to explain. It's deep and hollow. It's darkness and hatred. It's riddled with suspicion.

Vehement thoughts rattle in my skull, inviting a dull sense of paranoia that Roanoke is hiding something. "You're the first person to give me any answers about his death. Watchmen have brushed me off, and Warden Gryme has refused to meet with me or investigate the incident. Atlantic, even Ruth doesn't know how Jerald died. How is it that you know all of this?"

Another heartbeat of a pause, then another. And another. Reading body language is a silent art. His right hand palms the length of his beard, his left tracing lazy half-circles on his knee. He's thinking. He's thinking too long, filtering through some intricate mental web to sew back together. "I have a connection," he says at last, lacing his hands together.

His stormy grays find my mahoganies. I hold his stare. "That's all you're going to give me? That you have a connection?"

"Some things are better left unsaid. I've said too much already."

He holds my gaze, but it's my eyes that are full of storms. I turn my body to him. "Roanoke."

"Zombie, it's not that easy. Leave it alone. It's safer if you don't know what I ..." He stops, as if afraid to say more.

Like hell I'll leave it alone. "Scott." His name is foreign on my tongue.

"For lack of a better word, I have a canary. A canary the Cicadas don't know about. It's risky to use the information from it because eventually the canary will be caught and will be made an example of. To protect the Cicadas, I need to protect the canary. I've told you too much already, I'm trusting this stays between us."

I break our gaze to contemplate, absorbing the information. My focus is drawn to the pond ahead, to the dying galaxy. "It's a Watchman, then?"

"You know I can't tell you that."

"Let's say it's a Watchman, hypothetically. You could ask the canary for the location where Desmond is, and we can get him out before he goes into the Vat. He's a Cicada, Roanoke. Indicating age or not, he's part of the movement. He deserves to see the surface. If no one was able to save Jerald, maybe we can help Desmond. We can—"

"—Desmond is already dead. Sucked from the Vat while everyone slept." A small piece of whatever is left of my heart breaks for Sonia.

My suspicious nature rears its wonderful head. "And you don't think that's valuable information to share with the Cicadas? How can you stand upright as if your shoulders aren't topped with the guilt of knowing things others don't? Protecting your canary is more important than being honest with the movement?"

"Goddamnit, Samara. Enough. We cannot save everyone. It'll do nothing to bring Desmond back if everyone knew he was caught for being a Cicada. You're new to this, so let me fill you in. When we lose a member, the movement turns slack. They panic. For all anyone needs to know, Desmond was Indicating age and given the standard senior-age sinking. Gryme will explain to anyone wondering that Desmond requested the Vat during a sleep shift because he didn't want anyone to watch him die. No one knows he was interrogated, and no one needs to know. Do you understand?"

There it is. He knows more than he's saying, more than he's pretending not to know. Roanoke is deflecting, hiding something. Mason accuses me of not leaving well enough alone, but it allows me to gauge situations better. It allows me to poke and prod until someone slips up. Roanoke is a spider trapped in his very own web, crafted by my persistence. "I understand," I say evenly. "I won't tell anyone about Desmond or about your mysterious canary." *For now.*

"*Samara!*" Olivia shouts, her silhouette thrashing in the galaxy. She's yanked under.

"Olivia?" I call out, already running. Where is Sal?

"Zombie, wait."

Ankles deep in the chilly water, I scan for movement from anywhere in the water. Aside from Roanoke's footsteps from somewhere behind me, there's nothing. No splashing, no ripples. The invisible creature must have taken her. No—that's irrational. There is no creature. "Liv?"

The water laps at my knees as I wade farther until it covers my waist. On the bank, Roanoke waves for me to come back, but the fire ants crawling in my ears are too loud to hear what he's saying.

My splashing settles, and a blanket of stillness spreads across the galaxy—a sinister, terrifying stillness. Someone should be somewhere in this water, dead or alive, and something should be moving. "Do you see anyone?" My voice shakes as I call over my shoulder to Roanoke.

In response, the galaxy stirs, rippling with anger. The creature has taken Olivia and Sal, and after all these years, has come to claim me.

Before I can process, the creature yanks me down. The sensation of swallowing light floods my mouth, burning my lungs, my nose, my throat. I flail, sinking like a goddamn hippopotamus. In their desperate black swan, my fingers slice through the water until they meet something smooth and squishy—the belly of the beast.

As if I'm weightless, the creature pulls me from the abyss. I break through the surface, water spewing from my mouth and nostrils. My ears ring violently. "Put your arms above your head," the creature commands, its distorted voice echoing all around. It moves the wet hair off my face with a clawed hand, and I oblige.

"I told you not to do that," someone who sounds like Sal snaps at the creature.

"I thought she'd hold her breath!" the creature protests. The chutzpah of this abomination. Blaming me for its failed attempt at turning me into a puppet. "I'm so sorry, Samara. I didn't mean to scare you."

My lips form a tight line. All at once my irrational fear

drips from my skin back into the pond. I accept my humility. "You're not a creature," I mutter to Olivia.

She wrings her hair out, face twisted in confusion. "Are you okay? I didn't think you'd stay underwater, we're only waist deep. I thought you'd stand up."

I tilt my head side to side, clearing water from my ears. I point at her with a steady finger. "Don't you ever do something as childish as that ever again."

I gather my emotions, taking the prank for what it was. To my embarrassment, we're in a shallow part of the galaxy. Sal cups his mouth, unsure what to say. I mentally take hold of my irrational fear and boil it until it turns to steam.

"Let's all take a rest for a bit," Roanoke says from the bank. "There's no hurry. We got six more hours before the sleep shift ends and we have to leave. There's plenty of time to practice not sinking."

My stomach grumbles as I take a steadying breath. I glance around the Arboretum, letting its stillness anchor me. "Can we pick some fruit first?"

Like death, water is not something to fear—it's something to respect. Water will not kill me. It is not a creature. I am in control of it. I will not fail this Test.

29

Never did I think my toes could be tired. Or my armpits, for that matter. I stood in the muddy sediment for hours, legs bent, arms forward, diving over and over until I felt comfortable enough to go deeper. Until my tiptoes no longer had to support my fears, and I let the water move beneath my arms. Controlled, weightless. I can still feel the water on my skin, though there's not a drop of evidence left as Olivia, Roanoke, and I maneuver through the boisterous crowd forming in the main corridor outside of Sec-Three.

A shrill voice amplifies through the speakers on the floor, freezing me in place. "Sector Three, please give your warmest welcome to Warden Calum Gryme!"

"What do you think this is?" Olivia asks.

I shake my head, breaking away from her and Roanoke in search of a higher vantage point. Taking a folded chair leaning against a building, I press it to my sternum and move against the sea of people, back to the center of the crowd. Unfolding the chair, I plant it on the floor and stand on top of it.

I couldn't see it before over the herd, but now, above

all the tops of heads and sitting outside of Sec-Three, a temporary stage has been built. A banner hanging from it reads, "The Tri-Annual Sector Appreciation!"

I look down at Olivia and Roanoke, mouthing the words from the banner, but my group has once again become a set of duos. I scan the surrounding area, searching ahead, to my sides, behind me—until I find him. Toward the back and away from the stage, Roanoke moves stealthily through the crowd. He veers in and out of congested spaces, his back slightly hunched until he's out of sight.

I step off the chair, joining Olivia in the crowd. "Did he say anything to you?"

"He said he had to leave to meet up with the next applicants outside the tech hub." She dips her chin down to finish the rest of the silent conversation, then trades places with me on the chair. "A rally for Sector Appreciation, and these people eat it up," she says coldly, earning harsh stares from whoever heard. Who, in return, all earn her venom-laced smile.

Their eyes roll to the back of their heads and forward again, landing on me. Impulsively, I display both middle fingers with a wry smile. Olivia laughs a hearty laugh, jumping down from the chair and joining me in the crowd. She clasps my fingers shut in hers.

An ostentatious voice resounds from a microphone, transforming my blood to blue fire. "Thank you all for coming to see me."

Calum Gryme. He gave the order to kill Jerald. Wren,

Desmond. He's hunting Cicadas. Hunting Indicators. Murdering us all, lying to stay in control.

"You're squeezing too hard," Olivia says. At least, I think it's Olivia. I barely heard it, barely processed it.

"I cannot imagine a better sector to celebrate Sector Appreciation in than right here in Sec-Three!" The crowd animates from his rehearsed praises. Cheering, clapping, high-fiving one another, hugging those closest.

"You're hurting my hand," Olivia says again. Somehow, she's so far away.

This community is nothing but a hive mind. Drawn to shiny, fake promises because it makes them feel important for a sliver of a moment. It makes them feel seen. It makes them feel heard and appreciated. And if they're seen, heard, and appreciated, then they're not questioning why we still live on the seafloor. They're not questioning what's above us. They aren't speaking up or talking back because they're appreciated in the most calculated way.

"Let go," Olivia yelps, prying her hand free from mine and breaking my disassociation.

I face the confusion in her eyes. "Olivia, I didn't mean to—"

Warden Gryme's deep, conniving voice drowns me out. "I appreciate you, Sector Three. I appreciate all that you do, of *everything* you do. Foxtrot thanks you all. Please continue to do all that you do and know that I am proud to be your Warden!" The crowd surges with excitement, deaf to the shallowness of his words.

A vague, cut-and-paste speech he repeats three times a year is what I heard, but the crowd heard something different. They didn't hear the politician's words spilling from his serpent mouth, dripping down past his clean-shaven face, and beading over his shirt that's hiding the decay in his heart. It's splashing at their feet, and they're bathing in it. They heard genuine appreciation and feel genuinely appreciated.

I feel nothing but genuine rancor.

"You're abhorrent." The accusation roars from my seething mouth, loud enough for the crowd to turn deathly silent. Loud enough for the Warden to hear me before they did.

"Who said that?" Gryme's anger vibrates through the speakers on the ground, touching the toes of the crowd. They quickly part around me, clearing a path and centering me against the Warden. Our eyes lock, both of us sharing a painted smile with each other. "What's your name, miss?"

All these years, he's been nothing to me except an enemy on paper because of how poorly he leads. He comes from a history of controlling, suffocating, menacing leaders, with so much power he can wipe anyone from existence with barely a blink and no regard because he wanted to.

He lives in his inherited glasshouse, ignoring all the splintered shards on the ground. He sits on a throne held up from the cut and bruised backs of this gutless society who turn a blind eye to his gruesome abuse of power. And he revels in it. I've never had the opportunity to speak to him directly, nor has he ever spoken to me. As many things as I'd like to say, this isn't the time or place. I'm nobody in particular, simply a person amongst people. I am everyone, and he is? Vile. Abhorrent. He doesn't deserve to know my name. He doesn't deserve my time.

"He lives on through me," I say defiantly, folding the chair. Tucking it under my arm and turning my back to the Warden, the crowd parts around me as if I'm infected.

A hand grips the top of my shoulder, pausing my movement. "Ma'am, remain where you are until Warden Gryme releases you," a Watchman orders.

"Take your hand off of me, or I'll break it." I pray to Olivia's god that this Watchman tries her luck. It's not difficult to snap someone's arm, I've done it countless times when men were too handsy. With enough pressure and quick enough movement, the vitamin-deficient Foxtrot bones we all seem to have can easily break.

"Thank you, Watchman Walker, but she may leave," Warden Gryme says endearingly for the sake of the crowd. His tone is perky as he finishes his command, but his watchdog's grip is firm.

"Didn't you hear your master? I'm free to leave. Let go of me."

Her grip tightens, squeezing the muscles closest to my collarbone. "Put your hands behind your back," she orders me.

I remain motionless, an ungodly smile wrapping across my face. My voice is taut, spiteful. "Make me."

Try me.

"Watchman Walker," Warden Gryme warns diplomatically. "It's not a crime to speak one's piece. Release her. Now."

Watchman Walker's grip is rigid. She reaches in her side pocket with a free hand, searching for zip ties, no doubt.

Try. Me.

"Now," Warden Gryme repeats. He must be more concerned that his murder-machine is publicly disobeying a direct order than the safety of a citizen and an unwarranted arrest. The Watchman releases her grip with a deep sigh, stands upright at attention, and spits at my feet.

"Good girl," I applaud, whirling around with a military salute made from my middle finger.

30

I didn't know if Mason would unlock the front door for me, but I knocked anyway. The last time we saw each other was at the Vat, and a hundred million things have happened since then. I didn't expect a warm welcome. But when he opened the front door and saw my battle wounds—after he saw the altered me who no longer resembled his twin—he hugged me. Deeply. And I sobbed. Uncontrollably. And he cried. Angrily.

I told him everything. About what's happened, about the Cicadas. I couldn't keep lying to him when it's too easy to die. And he listened while we sat on the kitchen floor, backs to the wall, eating from a jar of peaches. We laughed about the moves Sal taught me at the Arboretum until we couldn't laugh anymore—until reality crept back in.

"I don't know if anyone has told you this, but you look like shit," Mason half-assed insults, handing me a fizzy drink and joining me on the couch.

I highlight my still-red eyes with a flutter of eyelashes. "Eat your heart out."

Worry gently rests on his brows. "Can I get you

anything else?"

"Not unless you have any sanity to spare." I tap the top of the can. He shakes his head.

"I'm—" we both say. I keep quiet, silently encouraging him to finish his sentence. I'm not sure what to apologize for first.

"I'm sorry," he says, resting his head in his hands, elbows bent at the knees. "I know I've been difficult. I said those awful things to you at the Vat, and when I was discharged, I … hated you. I hated you for taking that away from me."

I've put him through too much by being selfish, yet here he is apologizing to me for how he reacted to my impulsiveness. I should have never lied to him. To the depths with my heart and brain being in a death match. I should've trusted him more. I softly rest my hand on his shoulder, readying myself to apologize, but it's as if he's in a suspended animation, not registering anything besides the stridence in his head.

"I worked hard to be strong and disciplined." His eyes glaze over, staring ahead. "Living in the system nearly destroyed me. I craved structure, routine, and stability. All the families I was placed with were so … bothered by me. I wasn't worthy of anyone's attention. I needed someone to love me enough to not punish me for being a child." Tears fall into his open palms, my heart splintering. "I wasn't sure I was going to grow up. I thought I was rotten. That's why no one cared enough to try. I thought it was my fault that no one gave a damn about me."

I swallow the anguish caught in my throat. "I've always given a damn about you."

"But we were separated for so long, Sam. It felt *wrong* that we weren't placed together. It was fuck-all wrong, and nobody gave a damn!" he snaps. I know with my heart the anger isn't directed at me. Mason has been bottled up most of his life. It's time for a release. "I didn't even know if you were alive. Every family I was placed with, I always ran away so I could find you. My last placement, they caught me but didn't take me back to the agency. They hit me until my bones ached and used a heated rod. I never tried it again." He tilts his head up, showing me a burn scar under his chin I've never noticed. "But then we were saved—we were adopted—together!" His surge of excitement makes me jump. "Someone gave a damn about both of us. I wanted to *be* Jerald. After I lost my position, all I had left to do was think. I realized it wasn't your fault I was discharged, it's mine. I'm not supposed to be a Watchman."

"Why would you say that? You've always wanted to become a Watchman."

"At the Vat, I had options. I could have stopped you from going down the Watchman hallway." My eyebrows raise, challenging his statement. "Let's be honest, Sam. I could've. But I didn't. Because I knew I would've had to detain you. You would've had a shockwave you didn't need, one I didn't want to give you. It was my choice to let you go into that hallway to get the information you needed. Hell, I was wondering why a child was in there, too. I figured after

I apologized for being an ass, you'd tell me about it once we were home, but there were consequences. I was discharged and angry and blamed you for it, but don't you see? It's not your fault."

He's making me question if his sanity is lying on the seafloor alongside mine. "Look who's being cryptic now? Remind me again how it's not my fault?"

"I'm not supposed to be a Watchman. I wanted the structure of it, sure. But in a strange way, you interrupting my first patrol shift was a test. I failed it, but I still passed. I'm not cut out to blindly follow orders because the Warden said. I know that about myself now." He stands, placing his hands on the top of his head at the revelation. "I'm not rotten. Foxtrot is rotten, and it's because of the Gryme family line. They dictate who sinks, they allow children to be abused, and they hunt for Indicators instead of helping them. I know I was hesitant before, but I'm all in. With you, with the Cicadas. I need to protect you. We have a common enemy. Warden Gryme needs to be taken out. This controlling cycle needs to end."

"Hang on a second, we're trying to get to the surface, not kill anyone."

"And you think he's going to let that happen? If he doesn't die, we all will eventually."

"Listen, the Cicadas are coordinated. Besides, you can't *join*. Weren't you listening when I was telling you about the Tests? There's an initiation you have to do, Mason. This organization is massive. Let me change my clothes and I'll take you to Sonia. She'll know how to get you ..." I cross my arms, testing him with a smile. "Tell me shithead, did this epiphany of yours come before or after you demolished my room? Because I'm waiting for an apology on that, too."

"I'd apologize for doing it if I had done it. I came home and it was like that. Figured you trashed it yourself."

"What do you mean you came home and it was like that?"

"I don't know how else to say it. When I came home after being discharged, your room was already a mess."

I look around the living room, unsure if we're alone. "Someone else was in the apartment?" Charging down the hallway, I swing open the door to my room, taking in the sight of disarray. My thoughts circulate around the confined space inside my head, a vague memory kickstarting an unsettling awareness. "Mason, can you come in here, please?"

"You need help cleaning all that up?" he asks through a mouthful of something from within the kitchen.

Standing in the center of my room, anger and confusion fog my vision. "Come here."

"Yes, milord?" he muses, joining me in the mess and obnoxiously eating a handful of grapes.

My heart throbs in my throat. "How well did you know Watchman Parker Locke?"

"The Prime? I told you, he was an overseer at the academy."

"But did he talk to you?"

"No more than the other overseers did. I was a greenhorn. Our paths didn't cross on a personal level. Why?"

Pacing around the room, I pick up broken glass from the floor, placing it in a neat pile on the dresser to regain some type of control from the untidiness. "It was him."

"That doesn't make sense. No offense, but why would Watchman Locke care so much about you specifically that he'd breach protocol by breaking into the apartment?" he asks, still eating. I can almost hear the eye roll.

"Are you going to help me clean this up, or are you going to keep shoveling food in your mouth?"

He pops the last grape in his mouth and mounts my closet door back on the hinges. "Yes, ma'am. Are you going to tell me why you think Watchman Locke was in here to ransack your room?"

I know teachers live close to the school for an easy commute, maybe that's where I've seen you. How can you be sure we've never met? Who are your parents? Locke had asked me. Interrogated me. Tried to solicit from me. My answers weren't evasive enough. He was the Watchman who detained Desmond, the one wearing black gloves. The one who violently slammed the shuttle doors after claiming his Cicada prize. He could have watched us enter the building.

"He said I looked familiar. Our adoption papers are missing so he knows I'm connected to Jerald. And Marlow knew Jerald was a Cicada, which means Locke knows too, right? Maybe Locke thinks I'm a Cicada and needs to connect me to the movement." I pace around my room. "Or maybe he *knows* I'm a Cicada and was looking for proof. I didn't have anything here for him to find, though. Why did he take Ruth's earrings? To be difficult? To make it seem like you did it?"

"Samara, slow down. You're getting yourself worked up over something you can't prove." His logic slightly calms me down, but too many dots scatter in every direction and they're not connecting. "Look," he says confidently. Brotherly. "He and I were in the same general area for six months. If you tilt your head and squint hard through semi-painted glass, you and I kind of sort of look alike. It's a simple answer to why you look familiar to him, because I'm familiar to him. But there's no reason for him to have been in our apartment." The infamous *heads* side of him subdues my speculation, but barely. It makes sense, but it doesn't. Damnit, I hate when he's right.

A loud triple knock on the front door turns both of our heads. "Are you expecting someone?" I ask.

Through the peephole, three Watchmen stand in the hallway outside our front door. I open the door, and a fourth Watchman, who must've been off to the side and out of sight, steps in front of them, directly in front of me.

He reads from a laminated index card, his head down and service cap hiding his face. "If you are Samara Johanna Quinn, please acknowledge."

"Yes, I'm Samara."

"Acknowledgement received." He flips the index card over with a black-gloved hand, his other waving side to side, signaling I'm in the way. I don't move. Not until Mason yanks me back by my shirt, stepping in front of me. "If you are Mason Jackson Quinn, please acknowledge."

Mason tightens his fists, his chest high. "I am."

Watchman Locke lifts his gaze from the index card, a devilish gleam flashing in his eyes. "Acknowledgement received," he says dully. "Warden Gryme is asking for both of you. Now come with us."

31

"I'm feeling claustrophobic," Mason whispers to me in the backseat of the shuttle.

Our thighs and forearms press together, sandwiched between two Watchmen. "Don't say a word," I warn. "Not here, and not with Warden Gryme."

"Do not speak to each other," Locke says with biting aggression from the front passenger seat.

It's as if I'm tiptoeing on a tightrope above an acidic bog. If I don't maintain my awkward balance, I'll slip and sink into the unknown. If I'm not allowed to speak to Mason, I'll test my luck with Locke. Even if this man's aura whispers death, and even if he's a Prime, a kindling made of damage control is growing inside of me, and it's rapacious to light.

"We've met before, haven't we?" I sweetly ask The Death Whisperer. My peripherals pick up on Mason's whiplash. He turns his head to me, his eyes burning through my side profile, silently begging me to make eye contact so he can signal me to back off. I stare at the back of Locke's head.

The tone in The Death Whisperer's voice is tranquil yet

savage. "We have. You're the teacher who claimed to be lost in Sec-One. An only child, I believe you said."

"I did say that," I answer, searching for a reason why I did. "But I'm a private person, and you're a stranger. Surely you can understand."

Ridicule oozes in his tone. "Surely."

At a stalemate, I change the topic. "Are you going to tell us why we are being summoned by the Warden?"

He half-turns in his seat, staring a burning heat into my core with his haunting eyes. "No, I'm not. I don't owe you an explanation for anything because I don't owe you shit. You're not going to ask me any more questions, and you're not going to whisper to your brother. You're going to sit there and shut the fuck up."

"It only took twenty-six years," I say with scorn to Mason as we sit alone together in a waiting area inside the Sec-Op building.

"For what?"

I adjust my sitting position sideways in the uncomfortable chair to relieve the pressure on my tailbone. I cross my arms. "To be detained."

I don't know how long we've been in this holding area, but given the white noise sensation in my thighs, it's been too long. Someone's probably watching us through a surveillance camera hidden somewhere in this room, waiting to see how long it takes until madness overcomes us.

"I'm one ahead of you. This is my second time," Mason reminds me, sitting one chair over with unfaltering posture. "What did you do to get us in this situation?"

I stop panning around the room and tilt my head in his direction. So much for being *all in* with me. The first sight of trouble, and he's defaulting to his *can't break any rules* mindset. "Because this is somehow my fault?"

"You're the most impulsive person I know. Hell, you're the most frustrating person I know! You don't give a second thought to any consequences because you react to everything. What did you do, Sam? What did you do to get us here?"

I turn my body to face him, my arms crossed, spitfire on my tongue. He winks at me. "I'm the impulsive one?" I force the attitude, understanding the signal. We can't be a united front. They need to think we're willing to work against each other. Of course Mason would come up with such a clever idea instead of sitting in rage. He is the *heads*. "Am I the one who vandalized homes in Sec-One after I was fired instead of taking it on the chin?" I telepathically apologize through my bone-chilling stare. "I must've forgotten that I was the one who couldn't do a simple fucking job of keeping a member of the public from entering unauthorized zones. An *infant* could have done your job, Mason. How hard is it to stand still and do nothing? And another thing ..."

This is all I have. He hardly makes mistakes.

He picks up the slack. "At least I didn't punch someone

in the face at the Husk."

If I had to guess, he's aware I don't have much to go on as far as safe insults. I admire his quick thinking. I can be deceptive, but so can he. "That's not reason enough to be here you shithead. Do you know how many people punch others in the face without being detained?" I shout.

"That makes you immune to punishment?" he yells back. "You think you can assault people and no one is going to complain? This is all because of you and your selfishness."

Of all the questionable things I've done recently that he knows of, and having been prior to all the Cicada involvement, that incident is the least bit damning. As impulsive as it was, it was well deserved.

I stand up, rolling my sleeves. "Care to know what it feels like to be punched in the face?"

He stands, taking a step toward me. "Try it, and you'll be on the ground faster than you can call out for help."

Damnit, I know he's right. I've never been able to win a playful wrestling match against him. After puberty, he's always been at least eight inches taller than me and with a high center of gravity, making it impossible to take him down. I successfully beat him one time, but only because I turned into a rabid ball of fury and bit his arms. He laughed so hard he fell to the ground, but technically, I won.

I grab hold of his shirt, winding my arm back. "Put your ration cards where your mouth is."

"Enough," an unfamiliar voice shouts over mine, echoing throughout the space. My grip on Mason's shirt loosens, the fabric turning slack. "Both of you face the wall and put your arms behind your back."

I'm unfamiliar with who the stranger speaking behind me is, but I'm familiar with the tone. It's the same tone where a god-complex meets the belly starving for authority. The same tone hoping for a reason to murder someone. The same tone following orders from a parasite.

It's a Watchman.

Searching Mason's face for a signal, he nods at the Watchman who's in his line of sight then looks to me, his eyes painting a warning to follow the instruction. We both face the wall and put our hands behind our backs. With zip ties secured around Mason's wrists, I steal a glance at the Watchman, snapping a mental picture.

The baritone in his voice is larger than the man himself. His chin barely reaches Mason's shoulder, making him hardly an inch or two taller than me. Ages ago, he might've had a full head of ashy-brown hair, but now it's sparse and graying at the temples. He's stocky and well-built, but that's a given, considering he's a soulless murder-machine. My gaze drifts over the Watchman's thick mustache, the freckles dotting his nose, and the static wrinkles etched across his face. Until his near-black eyes find mine. I quickly look away, staring at the wall, wondering why Mason's look was so dire.

Too many seconds pass. My curiosity outweighs rationale. I risk another glance, giving the regular-looking Watchman another once-over. The electric butterflies in my stomach stir at the sight of his nametag: N. Marlow. The

Trapdoor Spider.

———◆◇◆———

"Take that cloth off his face, he can't breathe!" I scream, writhing against the arms pushing me forward. Mason hyperventilates ahead of me, his footsteps shuffled. I can't see him through the cloth over my face, but I can feel his panic. Unfiltered rage shudders through me. Fighting harder against the hands shoving me forward, I push my weight against them, turning and kicking, my hands tugging to slip free from the zip ties. "I know you bastards heard me! Take your hands off me or I'll—"

A jolting pain slams against the side of my skull. Shooting stars soar through the blackness behind my eyelids.

———◆◇◆———

A voice dances around me. "Miss Quinn, are you with me?" I blink. My head, heavy as boulders, lifts from my collarbone. Mason's shape sharpens on my right, and I twist my neck to the left, following the voice. A large, blurry outline of a wooden desk comes into focus, as does the figure behind it. Warden Calum Gryme, with a smile as sweet as poison. "Ah, there she is. I must apologize for authorizing forceful restraint. Resisting arrest is quite a crime, Miss Quinn. You left me no choice."

My tone is sharp, matching the headache made of

barbed wire creeping across my forehead. "You're saying not all your victims are escorted to you in this manner?"

His hollow eyes swoop over me. He chuckles lifelessly. "There are no victims here, sweetheart. Only guests."

I could vomit. *Sweetheart*, he says.

I part my lips, preparing for a beastly response, but Mason is the first to speak. "Warden Gryme, I think this has all been a misunderstanding."

The abhorrent man waves lazily at Mason, his gaze fixing me in place. "Nothing more from you, Mr. Quinn. I've heard enough from you. It's your sister's turn to speak."

A soft knock comes from the door behind me. I straighten up in the chair. "What is it that you'd like to know?"

Warden Gryme motions to the doorway. Entering the room, Watchman Marlow hands the Warden a lighter and a cigar. He stands at attention, facing us from behind the desk.

Warden Gryme inhales the rare tobacco, plumes of smoke billowing past his lips. "That, Miss Quinn, is a wonderful question. I'd like to know everything."

32

"You're a popular young lady, aren't you?" Warden Gryme barbs, combing a fly-away from his coppery-brown hair.

I slide my hands under my thighs, fingers absently picking the fabric beneath, and force my stubborn shoulders to relax. "And what makes you say that?"

His venomous eyes devour mine. I meet his gaze with a polite smile, drowning out his calculated tension. "Because of your mounting reputation, of course."

The sweet taste of spitfire lingers on my tongue. "If I didn't know any better, Warden, I'd say you have something on your mind. As much as I enjoy being your guest of honor, why don't you spare us both the time and get to the point already?"

"Sam, let's be calm." Mason's words are steady, but his restless fingers give away his nerves.

Atlantic, he's right. I clear my throat, mentally flipping my *tails* back to *heads*. "All I'm saying, is if the Warden has something to say, he should say it. It's not difficult. I'm sure he's busy"—being useless—"and has far more important things to do than ... whatever all this is about." I wave a hand around the room. I've never been to Warden Gryme's office, but I know this isn't it. He's a narcissist. A man like him wouldn't tolerate an empty room with just a table and a handful of chairs—no. This room is different. "We still don't know why we're here, but I'm sure he does." My gaze sharpens, my smile so goddamn sweet it hurts my teeth. "And I'd like to know why."

"She's a feisty one," Warden Gryme muses, inclining his head to Watchman Marlow. Both of them nod, sharing the silent agreement. "She must've taken after Watchman Jerald Quinn. Speaking of whom." His attention snaps back to me, his expression oily. "You must believe me when I tell you that Jerald's passing was a true loss for us all. My deepest sympathy for the pain your family endured."

You're deeply sorry for torturing and executing my father? To the deepest, hell-ridden depths with—put out the fire. Put. It. Out.

"Thank you for the condolences."

The Warden's head cocks, as if my comment wasn't what he was expecting. "As far as why I've brought you here, I'll be honest with you if you pay me the same respect. I'd like to discuss the information you may have about some alarming reports that have come across my desk. Are you willing to share it with me?"

Willing, he says. As if I have a choice. The subtle reminders of his control over this situation gnaw at my mind. I dig my fingers deeper into the fabric, puncturing a small hole. He doesn't get a single flame. I'd sooner bathe in bromine than allow him to be gasoline. "I'm afraid I don't have any information for you, Warden. I'm a regular person. I've done nothing wrong."

That lazy smile again. "Well, now I know you're lying. Care if I list all your wrongdoings?"

He's bluffing. He has nothing on me. If he did, I'd be in the Vat already. He's testing me. Waiting for me to slip. Using my own tactics against me. Pity. "Please, do."

Opening a drawer, he removes a sheet of paper and inhales another mouthful of cigar. "It says here the first incident occurred at the Husk. A concerned citizen reported that you punched a merchant in the nose."

"He—"

"—No, no, Miss Quinn. I'm speaking. After the assault, we tracked your movement to the foster agency in Sec-Five. The receptionist verified your presence after Watchman Marlow here showed her a photograph. She said the interaction with you was interesting. After some crafted questioning, she admitted you were acting suspicious but thought nothing of it. Now, suspicious behavior is not a crime, per se. But I watched the surveillance feed myself. The information you gathered from reading a confidential record led you to the Vat."

Shit.

"After arriving at the Vat, a gift shop worker reported a noise complaint, stating she heard screaming in the hallway. Hysteria indicates a diseased mind, Miss Quinn. Reports of an Indicator are taken quite seriously." He pauses for my reaction, but my expression stays granite. "Watchman Locke was dispatched to the location where he had an interaction with you about a medical issue. After you were cleared by Watchman Locke, instead of leaving, you were seen on surveillance entering an unauthorized zone where you bypassed your brother here and used Watchman resources to speak with the individual being held in the Vat."

I figured he already knew about the last bit, but double shit.

"It's my understanding it was a student of yours in the Vat. Now, I can forgive all these acts as a simple misunderstanding. Perhaps you wanted to say goodbye?" He puts out the cigar. "A few shifts went by with no incident, but then you assaulted yet another merchant. With a knife, no less. Did you say you were going to sew his lips shut?"

Shit, shit, shit.

"Your movement was a little trickier to track after your last visit to the Husk, but I couldn't help but notice you ended up in an alley behind Sec-Four. You were there for approximately ten minutes, then went to the commissary. What were you doing in the alley?"

Fuck, shit, fuck.

"Miss Quinn, I can tell from your face that you're shocked to hear I know of your manic behavior. Being impulsive is not illegal, but crimes don't go unnoticed around here. Though we can both admit you've gotten yourself into quite a mess, I'd like to know how you're doing."

"What does that mean?"

"I heard you were attacked in Sec-Three!" Sarcastic pity dissolves in his tone. "I must say, though it is uncommon, paranoid schizophrenia is an unfortunate Indicator to suffer. We're still searching for the woman, but I assure you she will be dealt with. Now, Miss Quinn, this is the part where honesty comes into play. Where did you go after the attack?"

A Cicada safehouse. The tech hub. Arboretum.

"Shouldn't you know that?"

"You see, this is where it gets interesting. As luck would have it, the entire surveillance system throughout all of Sec-Three and the main corridor malfunctioned for twenty-four hours right when you were attacked. I find that a bit odd, don't you? It's as if someone had access to disabling the cameras. Because the next time we see you, you're calling me, what was the word? Abhorrent?"

I don't know why I hadn't considered any of my actions leading to this. Mason's right. I'm not immune to punishment. I stand by all of what I did, and I'll sink with it, too. "Do we leave for the Vat now, or do you have another list to read off to me?"

His eyes shift between Mason and me. "Miss Quinn, no one in this room is being taken to the Vat."

"Then why are we here?"

Warden Gryme puts the paper in the drawer and leans back in his chair. "Do you know how to run a society?"

I can't hold back the spite any longer. "Nepotism."

Watchman Marlow advances a step, his demon-eyes

promising death. The Warden extends an arm, blocking his path. With a flick of his wrist, the watchdog stands down. "Watch your tone with me," the Warden seethes. "To lead means sacrifices must be made to ensure Foxtrot's safety, even if they're small. Why do you think I allow the Husk? It's to prevent riots. If people want to trade their scraps for more scraps, so be it."

Scraps, he says. He's never had to trade for anything in his life. He's never been down to his last ration card, desperate to eat and unable to wait for the commissary to open. He was born in an ivory tower with servants who wiped endless food from his power-hungry, spoon-fed mouth, with an ego larger than my entire apartment.

"You may believe apprehending an Indicator is cruel and meaningless, but it's not. It's the most humane solution. It would be crueler to keep them here." His grin is appalling. Abhorrent.

Fire sweeps across my skin faster than I can control it. "Thank you for clearing up all the confusion. I now see how keeping your Watchmen from tearing down a trading section and ordering them to sink *human beings* are detrimental sacrifices you make to keep Foxtrot safe. Tell me, Warden, how is it that I rack up two alleged assault charges and blip on your radar? How is it that my father is *murdered,* and there's no investigation? But when I'm attacked by a random woman, I'm in an office being interrogated? How can I ever thank you for running the faulty, controlling, absolutely worthless excuse for a society that's Foxtrot? How can I—"

"—Cicadas are a cancer," the Warden says, his voice cool and unnervingly smooth.

I remain unbothered by the comment. Dumbfounded, even, as if I'm supposed to know what he's talking about. "And what's that? Some new strain of the disease?"

He leans back in the chair, the movement slow and deliberate. His lips curl into a sickening smile. "Something like that. It's my understanding that the idealists have reemerged, still thriving off the false hope that the surface is livable. My father silenced the faction during his term, but I've been anticipating a resurgence since I took office."

Another soft knock sounds from the door behind me. The Warden motions to the door, inviting another Watchman to join us in the room and stand beside Marlow. My heart sinks to the deepest depths of my stomach. He's here—S. Gideon. The final Prime. The Wraith.

"Let me be very clear, Miss Quinn, and pay close attention because I will only say this once," Warden Gryme continues.

I stare at the magnificently brutal scar on Watchman Gideon's lips, then at his familiar stormy gray eyes. The only emotion on The Wraith's face is contempt.

The Warden snaps his fingers, bringing my attention back to him. "You will serve as my voice and warn everyone in the movement that if whispers of the surface continue, or if anyone remains a Cicada, they will be considered enemies of Foxtrot. Not only will they be sunk, but everyone they care for will join them in the Vat. You have two shifts, Miss Quinn, to warn everyone. Otherwise, it will be you in the Vat, along with your brother. And he will go first, of course, so you can watch. Cicadas are poisoning Foxtrot. I will not allow people like you to live here and taint this community. Your morbid curiosity about the surface will mean the extinction of this entire facility should too many follow. Don't be a dodo bird, there is nothing up there. If you take anything away from this meeting, let it be this warning. It will be your only one. Two shifts, Miss Quinn. Two."

I stand up, not waiting for permission to leave. I'm going to be sick. I need to get out of this room, away from these Primes and this madman. Away from Watchman Gideon. "Let's go, Mason."

"Sit down," Gryme barks, his voice commanding. Mason lowers himself into the chair, but the defiance burning in my veins keeps my feet planted. The Warden laughs. "Ah, there's the fire Jerald wrote about."

The last ounce of conscious effort to keep the flames down drains from my body. My palms slam onto his desk, reverberating through the room. I lean in, my voice low and steady. "Say his name again, and I'll rip your fucking tongue from your mouth."

Swiveling in his chair, Gryme dismisses me and relights the cigar. "Watchman Marlow, put the cloths and ties back on them. If she resists, rip out her brother's tongue. Watchman Gideon, ensure they're escorted out of the building."

Both Primes nod without hesitation. Watchman Marlow steps forward, placing a cloth over Mason's face. My gaze shifts to Watchman Gideon, burning with disgust. He walks past me, his expression cold and detached. Zip ties tighten around Mason's wrists. Marlow stands him up, guiding him to the door.

A cloth covers my face. An angry tear trickles down my cheek, absorbing into the fabric.

"I've got it from here," Watchman Gideon says from behind me while we walk, his comment directed to Watchman Marlow.

I'm not certain if we're even in Sec-Op anymore. The path they've guided us down is a maze, too many turns to keep track of. I don't remember walking for this long before, but then again, I was struck unconscious. Someone likely carried me to the office we were at with Gryme—the confidential interrogation room that's not on the blueprints. The same room Jerald, Desmond, and countless other Cicadas were last alive in.

Marlow laughs—no—cackles in front of me. "What if I need to rip his tongue out?"

Gideon's palm on my shoulder propels me forward. "I can handle it."

My movement is stopped, my chest pressing against the

wall. Then, Mason is beside me, our elbows touching. He makes a small, welcome rotation against me. *I'm here*, it seems to say.

Powerful footsteps behind us. More hands on me, confirming the ties are secure enough with a tug. A double-check before we're left alone with a single Watchman. As if Mason and I stand any chance of taking down The Wraith if we try to flee.

Confident with our restraints, Marlow whispers something inaudible to Gideon, then his receding footsteps fade.

We're moving again, hands on my shoulders, shoving me forward. "I know how this looks, and I know what you're thinking," The Wraith whispers to me.

My voice is dangerously calm. "If you think I'm thinking you're a traitorous bastard, you're correct."

We take a corner, then another. "You're wrong. I can explain, but not here. Pick the spot, wherever you're most comfortable, and I'll have the cameras switched off again and meet you there during lights-out."

Are my eyes open? Closed? I can't tell. It could be lights-out as we speak, and I wouldn't know the difference. We could be walking through a pitch-black, never-ending void, and I'd take another step. And another. Until I step off the abyssal plain. I choke down the anger. "What makes you think I care about anything you have to say?"

The Wraith's tone shifts, forcefully aggressive. "Stand still and don't move." The front of my body blindly collides with the back of Mason's. "Once released from the ties, enter through the door in front of you. It's the lobby of the detention facility in Sec-Op. Exit the building and return to your sector."

The zip ties snap off. I remove the cloth from my face and turn around, staring a burning heat into the familiar eyes of The Wraith, who seems uneasy behind his facade. "Tell me where to meet you," he repeats.

I have no intention of meeting him. I lightly push Mason forward, malevolence on my lips. "Go sink yourself, Roanoke."

If I had known Warden Gryme had an insider hiding in the movement, I would've been more strategic. I'd have feigned submission and played the part of someone terrified of consequences. I'd have begged at his feet for another chance, promised to warn the Cicadas to give up because it's what's best. I'd have told him exactly what he wanted to hear, with no intention of keeping that promise, and made a mental note to be more careful. Instead, I let the flames engulf me, feeding into his calculated comments.

I should've pressed Roanoke harder at the Arboretum. All that information he had about Jerald and Desmond—it was too much. Too precise. Of course he knew. He's a Prime. The Wraith. The Canary.

33

The triple knock on the door wouldn't have woken me up, even if I'd been asleep and not sitting in the darkness of my living room waiting for it. The knock was almost pitiful as it softly thudded against the front door, full of shame and cowardice. It was a knock not made to be heard. It was a thought of a knock, a depleted effort.

His voice is quiet, defeated, yet somehow louder than the knock itself. "Zombie, please."

"You should hear him out," Mason whispers beside me.

I forgot he was next to me. I've been stewing on the floor of my living room since we got back, even before the lights-out sirens chirped. Mason switched all the electricity off in our apartment without my help and sat beside me silently. Close enough to be a presence, far enough away to not be a burden, allowing me to disappear into myself as I make sense of what's happened. With Warden Gryme, with Roanoke, with the fate of the Cicadas. Too much developed too soon. My ability to process is shutting down. I can't form a thought. I've been sitting here, absently.

"Let him in," I say.

LYNZEE SCHOTT

Mason opens the door, a flashlight beam projecting my shadow in front of me. "She's in the living room. Do you want me to stay here with you, Sam?" I nod.

The Wraith's presence takes over the apartment. He steps into the living room, trickling with hesitation. "Have a seat, Prime Watchman Gideon," I say with detachment, pushing past the two-ton weights anchoring me to the floor. I sit on the chair across from the couch, away from The Wraith.

He angles his flashlight down. "I'm not Prime Watchman Gideon."

Anger vibrates through my body. "Your nametag said S. Gideon. Am I supposed to believe you were wearing someone else's uniform?"

He sighs, his shoulders sagging slightly. "That's not what I mean. Yes, I'm Scott Gideon. I'm a Prime. But in my heart? I'm Roanoke. I'm not working against the Cicadas, I'm working against Gryme."

Mason sits on the arm of the chair beside me. "That sounds an awful lot like something someone would say when they've been caught."

"I won't waste your time with fillers," Prime Watchman Gideon, The Wraith, Roanoke, The Canary says, directed to me. "I know you're suspicious, but I also know you speak your mind. Ask me everything you need to ask me. I have nothing left to hide."

He's either entirely guilty, or he's someone trying to earn back my trust. I can't read this situation, my thoughts

246

have yet to form. Regardless, whether he's a snake or a canary—a traitorous bastard or an ally—I'm curious about what he has to say. Whether I trust what he has to say or if I'll use it against him is still up for debate.

"Where did you go during the Sector Appreciation?" I ask. It's the only question I can come up with.

"I wasn't expecting the Warden to be there. Couldn't let him see me. Told Olivia I had to meet up with the others and got out as fast as I could."

"You're a Prime and didn't know the Warden's whereabouts? That's a lazy excuse. Isn't it your whole job to know what's happening?"

"No, Zombie. It's not. Standard Watchmen stay close to the Warden, and Primes stay out of sight. No one except Gryme, Locke, Marlow, and me know about the Primes—aside from the Cicadas. The other Watchmen don't know there's a split in the ranks. They know we're high-ranking, but that's it. I don't patrol with other Watchmen, and I don't keep tabs on the Warden."

"No, you're keeping tabs on the Cicadas for him," I spout with bated breath. Atlantic, is he lying? But Olivia said the same thing—Roanoke left to meet up with the other nymphs. I let that thought simmer, feeding the conversation another morsel. "Who all knows you're a Cicada and a Prime?"

"The two of you." His tone is firm, unwavering.

"You told me you knew Jerald. Was that a lie?" I ask as soon as his answer fades, my thoughts stretching out instead of staying crumpled in a ball.

"No. He truly was like my brother."

"And he knew you're a Watchman but didn't know you're a Cicada?"

"That's right. I knew him the same as he knew me."

"How? How did your paths never cross as Cicadas?" I demand.

"Zombie, I didn't know he was involved in the movement in any way. There are so many damn Cicadas, all of them going by an alias. We stay undetected for a reason, even amongst ourselves. We don't have meet-and-greets."

Atlantic, all of what he's said makes sense. It's difficult catching a lie when the truth is so clear. "Claiming someone to be as close as a brother is a bold statement. How did that friendship come about?"

"We met through work. He was a standard Watchman and I—well, I'm high-ranking. Different assignments, different beats, different everything. But we were close. The shift before Marlow brought him into that room with the other Primes, Jerald seemed cagey. On edge. He pulled me aside and asked me to keep an eye on the both of you. Figured he meant keeping an ear to the ground if y'all started to earn a rap sheet since I have more authority. But now I know what he meant by it. He was a Cicada asking his high-ranking friend to check on his kids."

"Wait—you were there? You were there as he was being killed and did nothing to stop it?" I stand up, fists forming into tight balls. Mason takes hold of my elbow, gently guiding me back to the seat.

The Wraith's head sinks between his knees, his voice cracking under the weight of shame. "Yes." He looks like a slumbering grizzly, his hunched posture moving up and down with each silent sob.

That memory will sit on Roanoke's shoulders for the rest of his life. He'll never forget watching his friend's murder without stepping in. That punishment is enough. I don't need to sharpen the executioner's blade.

This is bigger than me, beyond any reach for personal vindication. No one could know that Roanoke is a Prime, someone in the movement would have mentioned it. It's too crucial, too powerful of an advantage not to use.

Accepting that he and Jerald found friendship and shared the same secret, I ask, "Were you a Prime before or after you were a Cicada?"

"I was a Prime first."

For some strange reason, relief washes over me. It doubles down on us being the only ones who know. He can't be lying. It would've been too many webs to sort through that quickly. "Why did you become a Cicada?"

"I have a family. A wife and two girls. One of my girls is sick, but not the normal kind of sickness. It's her body. We manage with home remedies, but she's always in pain. It started when she was two, and I forged a death certificate for her. I couldn't stand the thought of her in the Vat. No one knows about her, but even if they did, no one would care. An Indicator is an Indicator to them." His face is painted with disgust, full of want for change. "Primes weren't formed until a few years back. That's the first time I heard about the Cicadas. Sal was the first one I met. I was out of uniform on my way home, and he came up and asked if I knew how to swim. The rest is history. I became a Cicada to save my family. If the surface is livable, I'm getting them up there. She can be a kid without fear of the Vat. I know how controlling Foxtrot is. I'm not going to let my family stay here."

My history is repeating itself. I'm too quick to be defensive and feel betrayed when I lose minor control. It happened with Mason at the Vat, and now with Roanoke in the interrogation room with Gryme. If he were a cynical Prime hoping to turn in a Cicada, he'd have outed himself once we were all in that room. Gryme would've revealed Roanoke was undercover and working for him to infiltrate the movement to send a deeper warning. A warning that proves he has eyes on the inside working against us.

"What are the rewards for turning in a Cicada?" Mason asks, startling me. I forgot he was next to me again. I was too busy looking at the pain on Roanoke's face.

"It depends. Typically, it's dedicated time off to spend with family. No interruptions. It's a bit odd though because it seems I'm the only one with a family. I mean, I'm not close with any of the Primes, but they never mention their families. Hell, I never see them out of uniform. Their addresses on file default to Sec-Op. But who am I to accuse of secrecy when I'm hiding my own girl?"

I stifle a gasp, swallowing it down. *Their addresses on file default to Sec-Op.* I unknowingly traded nail polish for the name of a Prime and a dead-end address.

"How many Cicadas have you turned in?" Mason asks, my head nodding in agreement.

"Since I became one, zero."

I'm trying to make sense of this because I think what he's been saying adds up, but I'm still suspicious. "How have you not turned over a Cicada for five years? Wouldn't Gryme or any of the Primes be suspicious if you're the only one not doing your job?"

He smiles that magnificently scarred smile. "Because it's difficult to find Cicadas. I told you a half-truth back at the tech hub. I don't work in tech support outside the movement, but I do within it. I know a shit more than the average person. I know how to manipulate the surveillance in Foxtrot. I know how to make it a little wacky sometimes when it's convenient. Watchman Gideon listens to radio communication and possible dispatch locations for Cicadas, and Roanoke warns the movement."

I like to know how things work. Why they work, what happens when they don't work, what happens if they stop working. What happens if they start working. Just a prying mind.

"Desmond was the latest detainment, but I didn't hear it in time. Before that, it was Jerald. There's been two in the last month, but sometimes it's the way shit lands. It's more common not to find a Cicada. There was a time when the movement wasn't careful, and Marlow, Locke, and Sampson were turning them in by the bushel. The faction tightened up, and I think that's why Gryme let you off with a warning to give everyone. Mental politics. Hoping that after you tell everyone he's breathing down their necks, they scatter to the wind for easy pickings."

"Why haven't you told anyone else you're a Prime?" I ask, it being my final question before rendering his verdict.

"It's safer for me, for my family. Could you imagine if the movement knew I was a Prime? They'd want to take immediate action, storm the castle. They'd think because there's a high-ranking Watchman in the mix that we're invincible. I may have the authorization, the badge, and credentials, but I'm one guy."

He's put himself at risk too many times to be untrustworthy. He saved my life, reassured me at the safehouse, got Olivia and me into the tech hub and Arboretum, introduced us to Sal, and made sure all the cameras were idle so he wasn't seen working with the Cicadas. Gryme seemed surprised to hear the cameras malfunctioned when I was attacked, moments before I met Roanoke for the first time. He's fighting for his family, for the injustice that's Foxtrot, all from the inside while being a key player on the outside. He's a perfect canary.

"We won't tell anyone about you being a Prime or about your family. You're Roanoke, that's it," I say, Mason nodding to my side. "That's as long as you don't lie to me again."

Roanoke leans back on the couch, hands behind his

head. "If I didn't know any better, I'd say that sounds like blackmail, Zombie."

"No," I say confidently, standing up. Because it's not. I'm securing an alliance. I guess that's blackmail—accidental blackmail. "I'm saying I will trust you if you trust me. That's all."

Roanoke stands up, moving toward me, his massive height towering. I hold my ground. Mason steps between us, his arm outstretched to close the gap. "Sir, back up. Let's talk through this. Sometimes Sam says things without hearing how they sound." The daggers in Mason's eyes gut me. "She gets a little ahead of herself."

Roanoke swats Mason's arm away, deadly storms swirling in his eyes—I'm going to die again. Grabbing the back of my shirt, he scrunches it in his large fist and does the same to Mason's, spinning him toward me. We collide, and everything goes quiet.

"You can trust me," Roanoke whispers through the heavy embrace.

My swaddled words barely make it past the fabric. "Roanoke, I can't breathe," I wheeze. His arms tighten, pulling me in closer. "You're going to pop my head off!" I shout, breaking into a laugh. He loosens his grip. I tilt my head, finding an opening of air past the thick cotton of his shirt, between his elbow and rib cage, and breathe in deeply.

"Sorry, Zombie. Sometimes I forget how big I am. You can trust me, and I know I can trust you."

"Does the same go for me?" Mason asks, making me

aware they haven't formally met.

"That promise extends to you too, bud." Roanoke reaches a fist out for a bump that Mason meets.

Interrupting Mason and Roanoke's blossoming amity, I ask, "What the hell am I supposed to do now? Pretend that Gryme's threats were empty? Do I go about my shift-to-shift life as if none of that happened? He has to have eyes on me. If I contact any of the Cicadas, it's a death sentence for them and the ones they love. Do I hide? Warn the Cicadas?"

"That's a lot of questions there," Roanoke says as I spiral. "I've put a vague word out to Sonia asking if she can tell the Cicadas to be silent for the time being. I haven't heard anything about keeping active eyes on you, but the Primes are authorized to intercept should a situation arise. It's up to you whether you back off or not."

A choice. A heavy one. One that will damn me to the depths if I choose wrong. If I back off and hide—if I sever myself from the movement and take the secrets with me—how long until I'm caught? Warden Gryme gave me *two shifts* to warn the Cicadas before he doesn't need me in his scheming book of plays. Before his bloodhounds find me. He promised to sink me and to sink Mason first so I could watch.

I'm at a crossroads.

One path is lit with buzzing, fluorescent lights. Mandated, programmed lights. It's a path of food rations and executions. A path with no sympathy. A path that screams, *do as I say because I said it.*

The other path is bathed in torches made of sunlight. Bright, glowing sunlight. It's a path of growth and freedom. A path made of truth. A path that screams, *this is where you belong.*

"I'm not going to risk a Cicada, and I'm not going to hide. I'll find a way to get myself to the surface within two shifts," I confess. I don't know how, but damnit am I going to try. If I fail, at least I'll die doing something meaningful and worthwhile, not another notch in the Vat's tally.

"Sam, why are you saying that?" Mason's tone is somewhat shocked that I didn't say I was going to hide.

"I have to. The Warden gave me two shifts to scream his warning from the rooftops. The longer I wait without doing anything, the more suspicious he'll be. I need to get out of Foxtrot. I can be careful. I *will* be careful."

"He is waiting for you to make a mistake! He is expecting you to do something. He has every reason to sink you. If he doesn't have active eyes on us, we need to hide in another sector." Mason's hoping his logic will break my impulse, but my mind is made up.

"No. His Primes can't find Cicadas, and I'm not going to lead them to the movement. Gryme can't put out an announcement to the public without breeding curious minds, which means he needs me. If he wants me to be his puppet, I'll be the catalyst instead. If Roanoke says there are no eyes on me, then there are no eyes. It's worth the risk."

"But that can change, Sam! What if Gryme changes his mind and orders someone to follow you? Either in person or in surveillance? What then?" Mason demands, still trying to force reason down my throat.

"Here." Roanoke hands me a radio. "It's a Prime's. Used to be Watchman Sampson's. I might've stolen it off her uniform before she was put in the Vat." His grimace makes me laugh, and the strain on Mason's face relaxes. A little.

"Fine," Mason breathes, his tone kind of sort of satisfied with having a small piece answering parts of the unknown in my hands. "Where do we go from here?"

"What's been in the works for some time now is getting into the wing of escape capsules," Roanoke says, reminding me of an entry.

"I read from a journal that said most of the capsules were damaged but that Cicadas were hoping to fix them and find the wing with breathing equipment. What happened with all of that?"

"I don't know what year those journals were from," Roanoke chuckles, "but the escape capsules have been fixed by Cicadas with respirators hidden in most. Have been for a while. It's that no one has been wanting to be the first to hit eject."

"I'll do it," Mason and I say simultaneously. We turn our heads to each other in sync. It may be selfish, but it's a relief to hear he's still in this with me. I half expected him to keep pushing back, but he's as stubborn as I am with the same bounty on his head. It's poetic enough that since we were born into this submerged world together, we're destined to leave it the same way.

A tone of thankfulness lingers on Roanoke's lips. "You two are admirable. I'll get you both into the wing and override the commands to send you off, but I won't be able to stay. Messing with the controls will sound an alarm. Hopefully, you'll be in the open blue before anyone responds. Once you guys are out, I'll tell the movement about Gryme's threats and we can start working on something behind the scenes. I don't trust that his warning of 'two shifts' applies only to the two of you. I'll—"

An unexpected knock comes from the front door. The three of us turn into statues. Why are so many people knocking on my damn door?

Mentally processing a plan, I take Roanoke's flashlight and point it at Mason, then to the couch. He lies on it, pretending to be asleep. I do the same for Roanoke, except point the light at the kitchen, behind the small island in the middle. He crouches behind it. I walk backward to the front door, double-checking if I can see him as another knock sounds.

I'd much rather have Roanoke somewhere else, but it's the closest hiding spot. With the impatience behind the person's continuous knocking, there's not enough time to hide him somewhere strategic. It's dark enough in the apartment that he's practically invisible unless the person behind the door has floodlights, but if I don't open it now, my neighbors will turn nosey.

Giving a final glance around the room, noting this thrown-together smokescreen is the best we can manage, I look through the peephole to prepare myself for whoever is on the other side of the door. My sudden visitor is blocking the view.

34

"Are you trying to get rid of me?" Olivia seethes.

I pull her into the apartment by her shirt. "What the hell are you doing?" I whisper, shutting the door quietly.

"What the hell am I doing? What the hell are *you* doing? You left me in the crowd during the Sector Appreciation. I've been looking everywhere for you. Then I get word from my mom that the Cicadas need to be silent? What is going on?"

Damnit. I forgot about Olivia. I've been an object in motion, oblivious to the waves created in the sudden wake. I don't know what to tell her, haven't given it any thought. How do I explain to her, without specifically saying, that Gryme practically abducted me, knows about the Cicadas, and threatened to sink us all?

Roanoke steps out from behind the kitchen island, joining us in the doorway. "Been a minute, Livs."

Olivia's tone is laced with criticism. "Roanoke? What are you doing here?"

"I heard about the say-so to be silent too," he says. "After I got here, we all started talking about it, but her brother fell asleep over there." He points to Mason on the couch.

Guilt ripples through me from the tips of my toes to the top of my head. It's safer for Olivia if we lie to her. I poke my twin's arm.

Mason, awake on the couch with his eyes closed but pretending to be asleep, puts on a show of waking up. He stirs around a bit, mumbling under his breath. He sits upright and exhales an obnoxious yawn, his arms stretching far and wide. "Aubert, when did you get here?" he asks in a weird way—a way I'm hoping is only weird to me.

Olivia exhales, the suspiciousness in her tone taming. "Hey, Quinn."

If everyone is busy eating, it'll avoid too many questions. "Anyone hungry?" I ask.

I've been thriving off my silver tongue and one point, made a conscious, albeit weak, effort to stop lying. But now, after being in a position where I have to lie, a position I put myself in, I wish I didn't have to. It's mentally exhausting being my own worst enemy.

"I could grab a bite," Roanoke answers, making the first move. Olivia follows.

The four of us sit at stools around the kitchen island, snacking on nuts and fruit. This setting is entirely awkward. Olivia's tapping the counter, Mason's fidgeting with his fingers between bites, and Roanoke's palming his beard—safe to say we're all uneasy. Olivia can't come with us to the escape capsules, but I don't know how to get rid of her.

Roanoke is admirably the first to break the silence. "So Livs, how has everything been since the last we were all together? Are your arms still sore from swimming?"

"Don't bullshit me, Roanoke. What's going on?" The heat coming off her is searing.

"It's not that easy, Livs. We got ourselves into a bit of a pickle." For a moment, I think he's about to tell her everything that's happened, but he's slyer than I've given him credit for. "The escape capsules are ready to launch. Came here to fill Zombie in. But whoever got into that wing tripped an alarm because then the say-so to be silent came out. The problem is that Zombie here has this nonsensical, completely irrational, and childish idea to go check out the wing."

I roll my eyes to set the stage. I don't know where he's going with this, but if Roanoke is the one lying to her, my conscience will be somewhat clear. I may be an accomplice in the lie, but I'm not the one hammering home a fabrication. Besides, I'm hanging on to his every word as if it happened. "Mason here was saying we shouldn't make any moves until we're given the green light from the movement because there's going to be Watchmen patrolling, no doubt about it." Mason opens his palms, nodding. "The argument got a little heated, so I took a walk. I have to agree with your brother, Zombie. We can't go into that wing yet." He looks at me, the disappointment in his eyes swallowing me whole. His gaze shifts back to Olivia, stern yet irritated. "Why don't you remind her why we should wait it out? Maybe she'll listen to you."

Roanoke's deterring her. Trying to convince her of a pseudo-setback but giving her hope we're still in this together and will regroup another time. As she thinks, Olivia pulls apart an orange, gently setting the peels in a pile, not bothering to eat. Once she agrees it's best to lay low and heads back to her sector, Mason and I will sneak into the wing. She'll be safe, and if we're successful, she'll follow suit with the rest of the Cicadas.

Her almond eyes find mine. "When do you want to leave?"

"Olivia, you're not coming with me," I say firmly, meeting Roanoke's confusion.

She shakes her head, not accepting my answer. "I told you that I have your back." Whether she's trying to convince me of that promise or herself, I'm not certain.

"I know, but this is different. I'm going alone, then I'll report what I find to the movement. I'll be in and out." I swallow past the pocket of lies stuck in my throat. With Gryme's death threats, this task is too dangerous for extra bodies.

"I need to come with you. I need to do something because my mom ... my mom, she ..." Olivia's voice breaks, her head dropping between her arms.

"What is it?" I ask after a moment.

Her head lifts. "My mom has an Indicator. Cicadas at the hospital found lumps in her breasts. If Gryme finds out, he'll put her in the Vat." My breath tightens with the confession.

Olivia's voice strengthens as she continues. "My mom has been a Cicada longer than I've been alive. She's told me the stories about the Cicadas who were caught and the examples they were meant to serve. Do you know what Calum Gryme's father did decades ago to silence them?" She looks between the three of us, her palm massaging her collarbone, all of us shaking our heads.

She takes a deep, shaking breath. "There used to be a Cicada leader, Eloise Wright. My mom says she was a powerhouse. She memorized the schematics, learned all the Watchmen shift changes, and knew which alleys had blind spots. She inspired people without using fear as power. She listened and she was patient. She was everything the Cicadas needed—everything Foxtrot needed. Calum Gryme's father learned about her." She crosses her arms, staring vacantly at the table. "He had his Watchmen bring her and fourteen other Cicadas into the recycling center. They strapped thirteen down to the compactor conveyor belts and made her watch as it crushed them one by one. He had his Watchmen leave, then took her to the top level, gagged and tied, and pushed her into the steel turning shredder." She puts a hand to her mouth.

Bile rises in my throat, a hot shiver running up my body. I look to the two at my side, to Roanoke's eyes filling with tears and Mason's face stripped of color. "What happened to the last Cicada?" I whisper.

Olivia clears her throat, wiping away a tear. "The Warden let him live so he could warn the movement. That Cicada was young, almost thirty, and had been a recruit for many years before the incident. But he left the movement afterward. Gave all his journals to Sonia to keep, then he lost himself. My mom believes Calum Gryme and his father let Desmond live, even after knowing he used to be a Cicada, because his presence was a silent reminder. The way he broke was his punishment. They ... *made* him live."

"Did you know about this?" I snap at Roanoke. I didn't mean for it to come out so harsh, not when Olivia doesn't know he's a Prime. Foolish, foolish tone. The incident happened decades ago, the Primes formed a few years back under Calum Gryme, not his father. Roanoke didn't have a hand in the fourteen deaths. He didn't strap those innocent people to machines. I gather myself, swallowing down the wildfire building inside. "I mean, do the veterans—"

"—I didn't know," Roanoke says. "Not the details, at least. I knew the last Warden did *something* to silence the movement, but no one talks about it. No one." His stormy grays hold steady, the double emphasis telling me that *no one* includes the Primes.

"That's ... atrocious," Mason says. "It's ... it's—"

"—Unspeakable," Olivia adds. "It guaranteed no one would rebel. It's been too long since anyone has made a move. Our generation has been brought up with the hopes and dreams of our parents but held back by fear of not being brave enough to make it happen. We're the change."

The passion she's feeling is contagious. Jerald raised me with innocent tales of the surface, and Maeve raised her with tales of battles between Cicadas and the Gryme government. Calum Gryme's threat to sink me was less imaginative than his father's, but his "solution" is a purge. He won't murder fourteen people to send a message—no—he'll sink every last Cicada, including the ones they love, to rid us all from the bunker at once. No more warnings, no more cat and mouse. It'll be a mass sinking.

Clasping his palms beneath his chin, Roanoke's fingers form into prayer hands around his scarred mouth. He stares at Olivia hypnotized. "I'll be the first to admit I might've had some doubts about you, Livs. You strike me as someone hesitant to make a move even though you know what you want. But that? Goddamn. Let's get into that wing."

"Roanoke," I warn politely, trying to remind him that we can't bring Olivia with us.

"No, Aubert's right," Mason says.

My head swivels to him. I telepathically scream at him that we can't bring Olivia with us. At the very least, I know he can hear it. There's an unfounded scientific explanation for twins on that somewhere.

I try to regain control of the web. "Olivia, let's—"

"—No. I'm coming with you." She takes a bite of the orange. "We all are. We'll scope it out together and relay what we need to the Cicadas, then I'm getting my mom into one of those capsules. That's the end of it."

35

I can't keep pace with Roanoke to speak with him. He's too quick leading us down the hallway full of peeling wallpaper, down the stairs, to the front of the building, through the lobby, and taking odd turns while hugging walls. And we're busy following him, Olivia on his heels, unaware that a Prime is ahead and doing all the strange moves we're copying to stay in the blind spots of cameras.

Behind the empty reception desk and off to the side, hidden behind a faux Ficus, Roanoke steps in front of a door, the sign reading *electrical*. He enters an incorrect set of numbers on the keypad, clearing his throat when it buzzes the denial, then swipes his badge as Olivia looks around the lobby. To her, he's 'hacking' the card reader since he's in tech support. To me, he's using sleight of hand with his firewalled Prime badge.

The card reader approves the entry. Waving for us to follow, Roanoke's voice is hushed. "Come on."

The door shuts behind us, my skin feeling prickly. Is it lawful evil to keep Olivia out of the know, or is it selfish? Roanoke being a Prime is not my secret to tell.

Roanoke sidesteps between us, toward the back of the small room, and moves aside a half-empty shelf. Another card reader is hiding back there, but there's no door in sight. He swipes his badge, the four of us watching the amber lights flickering until it turns into a steady green. The metal wall beside me hums and lifts into the ceiling, revealing a hidden hallway lit with red bulbs.

"Let's roll," Roanoke says with a cheeky smile, entering the hallway.

Moving between Mason and me, Olivia grips our shoulders and joins Roanoke. "Right behind you."

Mason takes a few steps into the hallway, an unusual eagerness in his gait. The looming darkness swallows his shadow, the crimson glow of the lights reflecting off his skin.

The three of them stand there, side by side, staring at me while I stay in the safety of the room, the whites of their eyes making me nearly surrender. A wave of existential dread crashes over me, doubt and fear seeping into every crevice of my being. I stare into the complete unknown, past my twin and friends, my body screaming at me to turn around. To turn around and hide. To not step into this hallway because if I do, then it's real. If I step into this hallway, into that River Styx, I know I won't be coming back.

A familiar palm rests on the top of my head. "We got this, Sam."

My voice is painfully quiet. "What if we're all wrong? What if there's nothing up there?"

"Don't overthink it. Of course there's something up

there, everything is going to be fine."

He can't know that. No one can know that. If we breach the surface only to find it to be a complete wasteland, will I be able to live with myself with whatever time I have left and be proud? Proud to say, *at least I tried*. When all of this was simply a thought, a dream of a chance, a journal entry—it all seemed within reach. But now, after everything unfolding the way it has, am I naïve enough to follow through with it? To the depths with my soul, that was shattered long ago. Am I willing to risk Mason's life as he follows me on a suicide pact?

A calm voice breaks through my residual panic, his large frame stepping in front of me. "Are you doing all right, Zombie?"

Am I unstoppable?

"Samara, is your mind wandering?"

What if this is all a fairy tale?

"Give her a minute to think, Aubert."

Can I go live up there, Jerry?

"Sam, maybe you should sit down."

Of course you can, my little bug. But not yet. You need to be able to fly first.

"Zombie, what do you need?"

What do I need? I need ... I need safety. I need to know all of this isn't for nothing. I need someone to tell me I'm not batshit-fucking-mental for doing this. I need evidence.

"How do we know if anything is up there?" I ask someone. Any of them. All of them. Myself.

Olivia's voice is velvet. "You told me it was hope. You're lucky because your god is real."

What if my god is angry and we die in vain? What if my god is rotten, even after two hundred years?

"How does anyone *know*?" I repeat, hoping to starve the beast burrowed in my head that's feeding on second thoughts.

Nothing about the surface has been proven. Everything is a whisper of what someone heard from someone else who heard it from someone. How can anyone be sure? How can I be sure there's something up there. Do I need to be sure? Am I brave enough to be the first to make a move? Should we hide? Atlantic, what am I fighting for. Olivia is fighting for her mom, Roanoke his family. But me? Because I fell in love with Grand Stories, am I willing to write myself into the chapters on this unbound ride? This all made perfect sense before, but now that I'm *here*—staring into this hallway, faced with the reality of escape—it doesn't.

"Listen to me, all of you," Roanoke says, snapping me out of my disassociation. "Hardly anyone knows what I'm about to tell you. I was planning on updating the Cicadas when we got back, but if it'll help give you back your confidence, I'm going to tell you now." I wonder if by *hardly anyone,* he means no one because he's about to tell us something only Prime Watchman Gideon knows. "There was radio traffic from someone named Henry Cassidy. It was on a loop, but it kept saying, 'Aybee has a message for Foxtrot'. Now, I don't know who the hell this Henry Cassidy guy is. I ran him through the system and nothing came up. And I sure as fuck don't know what Aybee is, but we've had zero communication from any station for over fifty years. So where did that transmission come from?"

Without questioning him in a way that could make Olivia suspicious of *how* he knows this, I ask, "Are you sure it said 'Aybee'? Because he could have been saying Whiskey. And that would make sense if it were from another station. Whiskey was the twenty-third outpost. If it was on a loop and Whiskey kept saying it had a message for Foxtrot, that transmission could've been from fifty years ago. It could've been from before the descent for all you know."

"I know what I heard, Zombie. And it sure as hell wasn't Whiskey—it was Aybee. Now, I don't know what Aybee is or was, but there was another thing this Henry Cassidy guy said on the loop that made me question damn near all of this. He sent regards for the loss of Prime Watchman Sampson."

A tornado made of knives thrashes against my mind. That doesn't make sense. Watchman Lilly Sampson died in the last week or so—when Wren carved double M's into her cheeks. How could anyone from another station send their regards? How would they *know* to send any regards if the Primes are only known to Gryme, Locke, Marlow, Roanoke, and the Cicadas? I take a step back, digesting what he's saying, trying to mentally grab hold of any of the endless questions to say aloud.

"What does that have to do with the surface?" Mason

asks.

Roanoke smiles widely. "It means there's more out there than Foxtrot. For half a century, we've been told that all the other stations have gone offline. But this? This is telling me there's more out there, and someone is lying about it."

"Even more of a reason to get into that wing and out of Foxtrot," Mason says, Olivia nodding.

"I'm still in," she agrees. "I don't need any of that to make sense right now to check out the escape capsules. I'd like to be there when you tell my mom about the transmission." She directs her comment to Roanoke, his head nodding in a dizzying way. Has he always been this tall and blurry? "I'm ready when you are," Olivia says to me, her voice stretching across the room.

Mason's smile is fuzzy, his arms stretching out in slow motion, beckoning me to enter the hallway with him. "Come on Sam, waiting on you."

Rubbing my temples, I turn my back to the group and take a few steps away, filtering through my thoughts. "Roanoke, can I talk to you?" Mason tries to follow, but I wave him down.

"What's turning in that head of yours? Do you want to wait it out a bit? We can head back, get some rest, and recharge. This doesn't have to happen right now," he whispers to me.

My reach for validation falls from my mouth. "Do you think I'm a good person?"

I don't know why I'm asking, but somehow it feels

important. Good people aren't molded from excuses of anger and hurt. Good people learn from their hurt and break the cycle, they don't project it. Mason is the *heads* of our relationship, and if anything should still be trying to convince us all to listen to his reason. I might listen this time. But I don't know why anyone is following me.

"With everything I've seen in my lifetime, I don't think anyone is a good person," Roanoke says, a bit of hurt spreading across my skin. I suppose I shouldn't ask questions I don't want the answers to. But he promised me no sad eyes or soft voices. I respect his answer. "But I think you've been through enough bad to know what bad is, and what good needs to be."

I cradle my self-doubt. "Am I leading them to their deaths?"

He chuckles. "We're all adults, Zombie. No one is leading, and no one is following. We're taking the reins. This ain't the blind leading the blind. You should be proud of yourself, of all three of you. No Cicada has been this far before. Livs is right, y'all are the change. I'm here to help any way I can."

His power to calm my nerves is a heavy presence. He reminds me of Jerald in a way I can't entirely explain. It must be why I'm comfortable telling him my fears and how he always knows what to say. I'm sure he's a wonderful father.

To the depths with these doubts. I'm a Cicada. I knew the price may be my soul. If I fail, at least I'll serve as a purpose for what not to do. I can be the guinea pig if it projects hope.

36

Roanoke leads us through the hidden hallway until we stop outside a door near its end. He swipes his badge, and we funnel inside. Wires line the floor in neat rows, connecting to monitors mounted on the wall. A surveillance feed displays on each, purple taped lines separating groups of screens and categorized with handwritten labels: Sec-One, Sec-Two, Sec-Three, Sec-Four, Sec-Five.

"How's it looking, Andromeda?" Roanoke asks the woman across the room.

With her back to us, an impressively long ponytail is our initial greeting. She half-stands, right knee bent on a sad-looking bean bag chair, nearly face-first into a monitor. "This schmuck is proposing." Popcorn crunches between her teeth. She points to a monitor in the Sec-Four group. "See? Right here, look right here. Tell me he's not proposing."

Roanoke steps to her, and we follow. Sure as anything, there's a man on one knee in front of a woman flailing her arms around. "I'll be damned," he says. "Anything else happening that's worth mentioning?"

"I saw you coming here," she says casually, watching the screen. The woman on the monitor tackles the so-called schmuck to the ground with a hug. Andromeda pops a handful of candied nuts into her mouth. "I take it she said yes."

"Where's Orion and Betelgeuse?" Roanoke asks.

A memory shifts to my temporal lobe. *Many family units share commonalities between names,* Sonia had said. Andromeda, Orion, and Betelgeuse must be a family of stargazers who watch surveillance. My guess? Cicada surveillance.

"They went to the commissary. Betelgeuse wanted to see if any coffee was left to get us through until we're relieved from our surveillance shift. And you know Orion, he doesn't trust Betelgeuse alone. Beets would've come back with a wheelbarrow filled with snacks if he thought he could get away with it." Andromeda smiles.

Roanoke steals a potato crisp from her desk, popping it into his mouth. "What's that saying about casting stones?"

"Ha-ha." Andromeda offers the tray of goodies to the rest of us. With my stomach feeling queasy, I silently decline with a polite smile and a wave. Olivia picks out a piece of pink taffy, and Mason snags a handful of candied dates.

Roanoke clears his throat. "Andy, did you remember to—"

"—Yes," she says impatiently. "Yes. I remembered to make you all blurry. Will a shift ever come when you don't ask if I've remembered to do that? Because I'll build a machine and teleport myself there so I can live in that timeline. You know I can find the parts to do it, too."

"I know you can," Roanoke chuckles, "don't mean to pester, Andy. It makes me feel better to ask, is all. You saw us coming here, but you don't know why we're here. I need three favors." He grimaces, holding up his fingers.

She crosses her arms, pinning the three of us with a playful gaze. "A favor for each of these Cicadas you haven't introduced me to?"

"This is Apricus, Oncilla, and ..." Roanoke's finger stops at Mason. "What's your alias, bud?"

"I haven't thought about it," Mason admits, and neither have I.

Is he even a Cicada? He didn't take any of the Tests, he's sort of ... accidentally here. What's the stage of a Cicada before a nymph?

"His name is Egg," I say, a wicked laugh escaping my chest. Mason shares a shit-eating grin with me, and I pat him on the shoulder.

"Nice to meet you all," Andromeda bows. "Tell me, Noke. What are the three *death-defying* favors you need from me?"

A split-second pause for Roanoke to build his web. Too fast a second for anyone to notice the delay, but I read it. "We're heading to the wing of escape capsules to scope it out. Can you put out a word for Ocelot to meet us here? We should be finished by the time she gets here." Andromeda writes in a journal as he speaks. "The second thing is, I'm wondering if you can keep an eye on us?" She looks up from the pad, almost annoyed, not bothering to write that part down. *Obviously*, her face says. "But I mean really keep an eye out. Watch only the screens we're on and signal me if there's anything that looks odd. Make sure we're blurry so that ..." The air in the room turns sharp. I glance at Andromeda. Her facial expression is daring him to finish the sentence. Roanoke clears his throat. "The third request is ..." He looks between the three of us. "Can you give us a minute?"

"What do you think he asked her?" Mason whispers to me while we walk through another hallway, Roanoke and Olivia ahead.

"I'm not sure. Can you distract Olivia? I'll ask him." Mason nods, lightly jogging to catch up with them. Briskly walking past Olivia and Mason stopped in the hallway, him tying his shoes and asking about her time as a Cicada, I casually catch up to Roanoke. "What was the third request?" I whisper.

"I knew you'd be asking me," he whispers back. "I couldn't say it in front of Livs, but I asked Andromeda to reprogram the capsule alarm so it doesn't trip. Told her I was going to play around with the controls as a test. It hasn't been done before, but she's been messing with the wiring for some time. She says she'll try, and I think that's better than nothing. We'll get into the wing and find a capsule closest to the window. I'll override the programming and give you a quick lesson on how to use it so that whenever you're ready, it'll be ready."

All of this makes sense in a way that it doesn't. Preparing myself for escape, I shake off the tickling sensation in my fingertips, trying to imagine what these capsules look like. Metal? No—too heavy. I take a deep breath, reminding myself that I don't need to know until I have to. If I know now, I'll spiral about it. I don't need the distraction.

Loosening the tightness in my shoulders with small rotations, I try imagining the feeling of ejecting into the ocean and letting it swallow my fears instead. It'll be weightless. Cleansing. It's going to be fine, everything will be fine.

If Andromeda can tease about building a time machine, she can kill an alarm. If she can—wait. "If she can make Cicadas blurry on the screen, how do you get by as Watchman Gideon without being seen by anyone in the movement watching the cameras? How can you keep the double alias a secret?"

He turns to his left, pressing the button for an elevator, Olivia and Mason catching up. "Once you know where all the cameras are, it's easy to avoid them."

<hr />

We descend in the elevator, moving deeper into Foxtrot. Deeper into the belly of the beast—closer to the seafloor.

"We're almost there. If anyone wants to wait, now is your time to speak up," Roanoke says.

"My nerves are steel." Mason flexes, earning my playful swat.

Olivia taps her thighs. "Remind me of the plan again."

Second thoughts are devilish, but it means there won't be any meandering in the wing. In her worrying mind, this is a quick recon to relay information back to the Cicadas, not knowing our true intentions. My mental *tails* spins and spins, landing on lawful evil.

"Andromeda is watching the cameras for Watchmen," I remind her, hoping it'll center her and me. At the very least, that's the truth. My silver tongue gains traction, the disguised plan forming in my mind. "We'll get into the wing and go for the capsules closest to the elevator to avoid going through the center. Roanoke will see if he can hack an interface, and we'll head back and make another plan with more Cicadas. Easy." By the time she's back in her sector, Mason and I would've circled back and already hit eject—but she doesn't need to know that.

Her fingertips cease their dancing. "In and out."

Roanoke looks between us as the elevator comes to a gentle halt. "Y'all are badass. Follow me."

Keeping to our usual routine of being on his heels, Roanoke leads us through a narrow hallway until we're standing in the entryway of the wing. And it's much larger than I was expecting. In perfectly placed rows, escape capsules perch on mechanical rails in front of windows as tall as the Arboretum, facing the obsidian ocean.

Closest to the windows, a water-tight door sits in front of each capsule first in line, leading to a small chamber outside of Foxtrot—a secondary checkpoint for the capsule so the wing doesn't flood.

Nauseatingly enough, this whole setup is essentially the Vat. Whoever designed the layout of this facility to have clear, interlocking chambers facing the ominous ocean must be a madman. Even the capsules themselves are in the shape of bubbles, clear acrylic plastic showcasing an assortment of controls. If I'm possibly meeting an endless sleep, I'd rather it come in complete darkness, not surrounded by the impenetrable ocean from see-through caskets. But dreamers can't be choosers.

37

On the level above, the same layout is visible through metal catwalks and railings, as is the level above that, and the one above that by way of stairs. Six stories high, hundreds of rows of at least forty capsules deep and more than that wide surround us. If all of this has been here, why is no one making a break for the surface?

Olivia's chilling tale of the recycling center suddenly comes to mind, as does Saturn's journal entry about a rumor of a detonation switch—*No one can prove it or disprove it. It could be a scare tactic.*

"Roanoke," I call out, stealing a moment to speak with him privately while Olivia and Mason look around the wing as if the ceiling is dripping with gold coins. The same look I pulled myself away from. "Are there kill switches in these capsules?" I ask once he's beside me. "If Gryme finds out we launched, can he hit a button and make us go poof?"

"Do you want me to lie to you, or would you rather know the truth?"

My two personal coins suspend mid-flip between needing to know the truth or begging to be lied to. If I don't know the truth, my well-polished lucky *tails* coin will stay comfortably in my pocket, reliably unpredictable and ready to change course. But whatever is left of my withered *heads* coin reminds me there's no running from the truth, no matter how hard it might be. "The truth."

"I have no idea if there's a detonation switch or not. I know there's an alarm, and I know if it goes off, the Primes will respond by any means necessary to prevent a launch. But I don't know if anyone will go poof." His hands mimic a small explosion.

I commit to the challenge—accept it. "Guess if we go poof, it'll be a faster death than our lungs collapsing."

He pats my shoulder with a light laugh. "That's a funny way to look at it."

I'm hyper-aware that Roanoke and I are alone in the hallway. Scanning the area, I step further into the wing. "Mason? Olivia?"

Mutterings of whispering lead me into the wing and to the left, away from the stairs and catwalks. They're crouching at the side of a capsule.

"How do we know which ones work?" Mason asks Olivia.

"There has to be a button or something," she whispers back.

"There should be a sticker under the bellies of the ones that function," I answer from behind. "It'll feel like a raisin. Next time you two want to sneak off, do you mind sharing it with the class first? This needs to be clean."

If they're caught, I'm caught. What was Mason thinking?

In true twin fashion, Mason gives me the *look*. He turns his head slightly to the left, the joints in his jaw moving side to side as he chews on his words. His lips part, the tip of his tongue resting on his incisors, furrowing brows nearly meeting for a handshake.

Roanoke squats down with Olivia to feel for the sticker, their backs to us.

I raise *my* eyebrows in the silent discussion, challenging Mason's facial tone with a derisive handshake, flashing my palms at him. He tilts his head to Olivia, then to Roanoke, his eyes explaining the situation with a pointer finger swirling around the wing. Atlantic—Mason and Olivia heard bits of my *poof* conversation. I knew her tagging along would be prickly.

Roanoke stands, waving the length of the capsules in the back. "You three keep crouched in this row and feel for stickers. I'll make my way to the front and do the same."

"Why would it take three of us to check for stickers in the same row? Why not split up?" Olivia asks. And she's right. I would've asked the same question if I didn't know that Roanoke was sneaking off to a capsule closest to the window to override the programming.

A web forms in my mind. If Olivia leads the unnecessary scavenger hunt for stickers, it'll put the most distance between her and Roanoke. "We'll cover more ground this way. Olivia, you go first and check the ones furthest away.

Mason will focus on the ones in the middle, and the rest will be for me."

The look she gives me is vexed—no—glowered. A bit of both. Within seconds, Olivia takes off, Mason following her same path. Roanoke waits only a second heartbeat, moving the opposite way to the front row. Looking between the three of them, an inescapable cloud of guilt forms over me, pouring droplets of lies as Olivia looks back at me with uncertainty. She's suspicious, has every right to be, and it's all my fault. Even though I may or may not go poof, I can't leave her behind in Foxtrot full of doubts. She deserves whatever truth I can offer.

Moving in her direction, keeping my posture low, I step over Mason lying on his stomach. "It *is* like a raisin," he says to himself.

"Olivia," I whisper as I near her. It's clear she's ignoring me, there's no way she *didn't* hear me. I repeat her name, except this time the way it falls from my mouth is as if it's been cast into an acidic bog. My awkward balance on this tightrope has caught up with me.

She keeps her back to me. "I know you're lying to me."

"You're right. I am." She twirls around, facing my storm cloud of guilt. "Trust me when I say I want to tell you, but also trust me when I say I can't tell you everything. It'll put too much at risk. I'll tell you the real reason we're in this wing if you promise not to ask for more than I can explain." I pause to think through the webs that can connect without tearing the whole thing down. "Gryme and his Primes know that I'm a Cicada. They know what Mason and I look like and where we live. The Warden gave me two shifts to warn the movement, otherwise he'll sink both of us. But I'm not going to risk leading him to any of the Cicadas. I'm not going to keep doing what he says because he said it. I will not give him that power over me. Roanoke will explain to you and everyone else what's happened. He'll make a more detailed plan with the Cicadas, but Mason and I are getting into one of those capsules, and we're doing it while we're in this wing. Now." Her eyes grow wide, jaw flexing, as if she's having trouble processing the detonation of my word-vomit bomb. "Say something."

"I'm thinking." She taps her hips, swaying back and forth. "Self-preservation," she says at last. "If you're damned either way, you might as well damn yourself, right? Doom and gloom and all." She winks. My stunned stare finds her flirty smile. "And Roanoke is here because he's a tech guy to help with programming. I get it." *Roanoke is here because he's a Prime, who's also a Cicada, who promised my father he'd keep an ear to the ground for Mason and me with a scout's honor—Scott's—honor.* I give her a nod. "You should've told me back at your apartment. Did you think I was going to invite myself into one of those capsules with you two? I'm not leaving without my mom. If you had told me the truth, I still would've come. Even if it was only to help out and see you off."

I reach out for our handshake. "I didn't want you getting caught up with this, but I should've trusted you.

You've been—"

The lighting in the wing shuts off, leaving only the glowing tracks beneath the capsules visible like a trail of bioluminescent algae. Red lights flash above, and an ear-piercing alarm in three-pitch intervals echoes.

"Run!" Roanoke yells. Olivia sprints for the hallway with the elevator, but I'm locked in place, watching Mason maneuver from his stomach to stand up. "Zombie, Mason, *now*." Roanoke and Olivia violently wave for us to follow them to the hallway.

Mason faces me from the middle of the row. "I'm with you either way," he shouts.

He's waiting for my *tails* or *heads* to land. Waiting for my flight or fight. Waiting for confirmation if we're launching into the expanse or running away from danger. Shoulders back, chest out, chin high—he's ready to fight for our chance at escaping this prison. We won't get another opportunity to do this.

It's not until I take hold of his hand, and we run for the first capsule in line, that I know I'm ready too.

38

Mason is first to the capsule I can only assume is the one Roanoke was working on, considering it's the only one with an open door. The same capsule I can only assume tripped an alarm that Andromeda wasn't able to kill. The same capsule we might be going poof in.

"Get to the escape wing, now!" Warden Gryme's voice screeches through the Prime radio in Mason's palms. My shaking hands feverishly try to close the door of the capsule.

"Wait," a man says at my side.

On reflex, I punch him in the forehead. Disregarding my accidental assault, Roanoke's face is painted with pure fear. "I'll get Livs out of here. If you're doing this now, listen up. The blue button closes the door, and green makes you move forward. The capsule will stop itself when it's near the window. Enter 6733, and the second door will open. Once it shuts, that's it. The capsule will move itself into position and chime when it's ready for the next phase. The red button fills the chamber, and once it's full, it'll launch. Wait until you're at *least* a hundred feet from the surface before you eject yourselves by pulling the black handle, otherwise, you'll get the bends. Got it?" He blinks between the two of us, searching our faces for an answer from either.

What in the Atlantic kind of instructions are those?

"Blue, green, 6733, chime, red, black," Mason repeats. I mutter the same under my breath.

"So long, Zombie."

Before I can say any of the hundred billion things I want to say to Roanoke, Mason presses blue, and the capsule door closes. It shuts us in, and Roanoke takes off in a sprint. I wanted to thank him for everything, but it's safer if there aren't any heart-to-hearts or long goodbyes. He needs to leave with Olivia, I need to meet my god, and we don't have any time.

"I'm almost there. A couple of minutes," a voice responds to Gryme through the Prime radio—The Trapdoor Spider.

"I'll be there in two," another says—The Death Whisperer.

"I'm coming from Sec-One. I'll be there in ten," the final one answers—The Wraith.

Mason's fingers hover over the green. "Are you ready?"

I press down on top of his hand. "As I'll ever be."

The capsule moves forward on the rails, going exactly *somewhere* and everywhere in a casual yet hurried flow. The palm of my hand finds its way to the top of Mason's head.

"You don't have the same magic as I do," he laughs, "I told you, my nerves are steel."

For reasons I can't explain, it's peaceful sitting here

alongside my twin, alongside the person I'm destined to be beside. It's comfortable sitting in this capsule. As it moves along the rails, I appreciate everything around me, all the possibilities ahead, until a question comes to mind that's crucial to our escape. Mentally doubling back on what Roanoke said and if he mentioned it, I ask, "Do we know if there are respirators in this capsule?"

He turns his body, searching the backseat. "Let's check."

I open random compartments in the front in search of the equipment, tossing aside odds and ends. What am I even looking for? I've never seen a respirator before. I guess it'll look like something that doesn't belong here—a squid hugging your face—if I remember Saturn's entry correctly. Whatever that means.

"Samara." Mason's voice cracks with panic, and an icy grip locks my limbs.

Slowly, I turn to face the back. Staring through the window of the bubble-like design, Locke charges toward us, unstoppable and fierce. With too-quick feline movement, The Death Whisperer is beside me, banging his baton against the side of the capsule. He's yelling something that looks like, *you're both fucking dead,* if my lip-reading skills are still finely tuned, but his words are muffled, nearly muted.

If the thickness of the acrylic plastic we're encased in is strong enough to withstand the pressure of the ocean, then Locke's threatening words and flimsy baton hits will have no damage. With a sidelong glance, Mason and I keep searching for the respirators while Locke tries to break in.

"Here, they're here," Mason says, closing the hidden compartment underneath the backseat. We both sigh in relief. "There are four of them here and even flotation belts. Which is neat because, well, I don't know how to swim."

My jaw drops to the bottom of the seafloor. Why didn't I think of this—why didn't he mention this sooner? Why did he agree to come with me, knowing he can't swim? The foul taste of medicine returns to my lips. I was convinced Mason would weaponize his love for me as a deterrent from following through with any of this, but here I sit, alongside my other half, responsible for being the one who weaponized love to get my way.

I reach for the blue button to open the capsule door. "We aren't doing this right now. We'll open the door, fight off Locke, and head for the elevators. We'll hide in another sector and wait to do this another time."

Mason swats my hand away from the touchpad. "No, Sam. There's no coming back. It's either this or the Vat. You showed me what Sal taught you, the moves you practiced for hours. You said so yourself, once you figured it out, it was easier than breathing. I know I can do this. I'm not afraid."

Deep down, I know he's right. Between the two of us, Mason is the most graceful. Every move he makes is calculated and composed as if he's a royal Bengal. He once convinced Ruth and Jerald to enroll him in ballet in fourth grade because he said he could *see* the music. He was the only boy in class with no prior training, but by the time the semester ended, he was the star pupil.

I accept his decision. Accept the trust I have in him and the trust he has in himself. "Put on the flotation belt and stay close to me after we eject. Watch and copy, breathe slowly, and stay calm."

"Who is it?" Gryme's voice barks through the radio lying between us.

Locke takes a moment from swinging the baton to catch his breath. "Both of the Quinn's sir. They're in a capsule."

A drawl from the Warden. "Watchman Marlow, bring the hatchet."

Marlow materializes beside Locke, a bloodthirsty glint in his eyes. Before I can process it, the hatchet is already slicing through the stale air, striking the windshield. To my utter astonishment, the glass remains intact. Not a hairline crack—not a scratch.

My voice erupts into a stream of absurdities until Gryme's master plan comes through the radio he doesn't know we have. "Tech support is assuring me they can shut off the electricity in the capsule in a few minutes. Delay the Quinn's, I don't care how you do it. Tear the rail from the floors, take the hatchet to the wheels, or lay on the fucking tracks to stop it."

His two Primes share menacing glances. Forming an unheard plan, they point to this, that, and the other, their lips moving too fast to understand, sidestepping alongside our capsule as the final Prime appears.

Roanoke looks between Marlow and Locke, his scarred lips adding to the unheard discussion. He glances at the main window we're approaching and back at us. I wish he could tell me what he's thinking, but if I had to guess, it's something like, *I'll delay these two as long as I can. Be ready with the code to open that door, Zombie.*

39

Desperately sifting through the cracks and crevices of my mind about what Roanoke said during his confusing instructions, we near the obscenely large window. "Mason, what was that code again?"

Confidently, he types *6377* on the interface. An error code displays, and he scrunches his face. "3677?" he asks himself, inputting the second set of numbers. The interface rejects that code.

At the front of the capsule, Marlow hacks away at the underbelly of it with the hatchet. I don't know what the bottom of this is made of, but judging by the base of the capsule, it's not the same material throughout. It's made of some type of textured polyvinyl, the same as the dashboard housing the controls. Marlow can't be doing any real damage, can he?

A small, concave dent forms at my shins.

"Mason, what the fuck was that code?" I shout, frantically pressing buttons on the keypad in all the transposed variations I can come up with. Another dent forms at the belly. Like a bolt of electricity, the correct set of numbers comes to mind. I enter them on the interface, and the door to the anteroom opens.

I pray to whatever god is listening that the capsule picks up speed on these tracks. This thing needs to move as if it's aware that two Primes are trying to break in. So long as Marlow doesn't make a hole with the hatchet, we'll make it. I may not be an engineer, but I know an escape capsule can't ascend if it's taking in water, and we're too deep to free swim.

I'm not sure what's worse—dying at the hands of a hatchet-wielding Prime, slowly drowning in a bubble, ejecting too soon and getting the bends, going poof, or being vacuumed through the Vat—but I don't want to find out.

Roanoke is at the front of the capsule. Moving aside the hatchet-wielding spider, he pushes against the capsule to rock it side to side, but it's firm in place. Locke joins him, then Marlow, the three of them trying to lift the capsule off the rail with their combined strength. Well, two of them try. Zero effort coming from Roanoke. He's doing enough to make it seem as if he's trying, but he's not. He's delaying them, and for that I'm thankful.

With the door to the anteroom open, we move along the tracks, the threat of the hatchet as discarded as the weapon is on the ground. With failing efforts from three Primes unable to stop the capsule from moving toward the door that doesn't open once closed, I look to Mason. *We're doing it*, his mahogany eyes tell me, each fleck of green in his iris a burst of hope.

This is it. It's happening. We're getting out of—

The capsule halts outside the threshold of the anteroom, swaying my body forward and back. The control panel's interface powers down, emitting a soft, mechanical noise.

Locke steps to my side of the capsule with a rabid smile and blows me a kiss. He presses against my door, clicking it inward, and the door of my safety bubble opens. "Get out of there. Now," he orders us. Without a fight, we exit the capsule.

With his aggressive Watchman Gideon voice, Roanoke points to me, then at the front of the capsule. "Step here, turn around, face the capsule, and put your hands behind your back."

Locke grabs Mason by the back of his neck, guiding him away from me. Shoving him against the back windshield, The Death Whisperer kicks the back of Mason's knees, and he buckles. I step toward him, hellfire blazing through me. "Touch him like that again and I'll—"

"—You'll what?" Locke sneers. "You'll do *what*?" He tightens the zip ties around Mason's wrists, and my twin winces. Locke lifts him to his feet and shoves him forward, glancing back at me with a black-gloved finger dragging across his throat and a god-awful grin.

My legs start moving toward them, beyond my control. No—no, no, no. The Death Whisperer doesn't get to take Mason from me.

"Quinn," Roanoke shouts.

I keep walking, plotting, plotting, plotting. Locke has a

knife in the hilt on his belt loop. I will be *damned* if he takes Mason from me. If any of them take Mason from me, I'll—

"Samara Quinn, step over here and put your hands behind your back," Roanoke repeats. Stern, demanding, fatherly. I halt. "Don't make this worse."

I turn around and face The Wraith—my ally. He points to the front of the capsule. Marlow steps behind him, nodding at Locke to continue taking my twin away. *Heads* or *tails*, *tails* or *heads*. Do as I'm told or chase the impulse. But I can't do ... anything. If I try to fight Locke, Marlow will step in. And where does that leave Roanoke? Forced to choose between blowing his cover by helping me or assisting the Primes? Fuck. *Fuck, fuck, fuck*. With lead in my shoes, I do as I'm told and walk back to the front of the capsule with my hands behind my back.

Roanoke steps behind me and gently grabs my wrists. Bent slightly to reach in his knee pockets for zip ties, he whispers, "Fight me."

He has a plan. I have no idea what it is or if I can even execute the unspoken plan, but a primal urge to fight surges through me. Roanoke subtly allows me to press my back against him, his large frame providing leverage. I plant both feet on the front of the capsule, bend my knees, and push. He stumbles backward. I land on the ground, spinning around to face him. Roanoke nearly falls, but he recovers, balancing on one knee. He slowly stands, the storms in his eyes pleading for a fight.

Marlow's demon-eyes pin me in place, and I hesitate,

clamping down on my teeth. The Trapdoor Spider's gaze shifts over my shoulders, to Locke escorting Mason to the elevator, then locks onto Roanoke. "You're boring me, Scott. Restrain the Quinn girl, or I'll give you another scar to match. I have the hatchet here—you remember it, don't you? End this."

Marlow maimed Roanoke. Marlow murdered Jerald. Marlow the Trapdoor Spider. Marlow the Mutilator.

Rage blazes through me from the bottom of my spine, past my neck, to the crown of my head. I charge at Roanoke. Welcoming my attack in a calculated way, he allows me to throw my shoulder and weight into his collarbone. He staggers toward Marlow, a redwood chopped down.

Marlow repositions himself at the entrance of the open anteroom to avoid the collision, but he's not fast enough. The impact from Roanoke sends Marlow stumbling backward through the open door. He tries to regain his footing, but Roanoke is faster.

Overriding a control panel outside the door, he shuts Marlow inside. Pounding on the see-through door, The Trapdoor Spider's shouts fog the window, but all sound stays with him in his death-sentenced room.

With laser focus, Roanoke enters a flurry of codes, too many to keep track of. "For Jerald."

Whether he's speaking to himself or me for validation, I can't be sure, but I don't question his decision to sentence Watchman Marlow to the deep.

I stood there until the chamber was filled with enough

water. Until the clear ceiling of it opened. Until Marlow's buoyancy carried him out of the chamber and into the endless ocean, his body contorting in an awful manner. I turn my back on him for a visual on Mason. The Trapdoor Spider doesn't deserve my sympathetic eyes to watch as he drowns.

Across the room, Locke shuffles Mason forward, oblivious to his sunken comrade, nearing a different hallway than the one we entered from.

"Parker." Roanoke's voice booms throughout the wing, shaking me to my core. The slumbering grizzly has awoken, and he's full of resentment.

Locke stops moving. He turns around and faces us to say something back to Roanoke, probably something cynical and made of coal, but his eyes lock onto Marlow behind us through the colossal window. Shoving Mason to the ground, he fumbles in his pocket for his radio.

Roanoke darts.

In one swift motion, Roanoke picks up the forgotten hatchet off the ground, and with a decisive throw, launches it before I can process all the movement. Locke collapses to his knees, the hatchet embedded in his chest cavity, the Prime radio dropping from his hand. Roanoke closes the distance, and I follow.

"You're a coward," Locke sputters, blood dripping from his mouth. "All you had to do was follow orders and keep these lunatics from getting out, but you couldn't, could you? Let me guess, you're a Cicada too?" Roanoke nods with pride. "I fucking knew it. I knew you didn't belong with us." A coughing fit takes over, blood splattering to the floor. "You're all going to die down here. You're all going to …" He takes a final breath and lands on his side, blood pooling beneath him.

40

Cutting off his zip ties with the knife I swiped from Locke's body, Mason stumbles to his feet. "Roanoke, what the fuck?" he demands. "We could've fought him off, tied him up, taken him hostage ... something! Now what are we supposed to do? We have no leverage."

Staring at Locke on the floor, Roanoke's eyes glaze over. "They were going to kill you," he says softly. "When you two left the interrogation room, we were all called into Gryme's office for a meeting. Our orders were to kill you both if we caught you sneaking around."

"Why didn't you tell us this at the apartment?" I ask.

"I thought you two were going to hide, lay low. We started talking about this wing, and I thought I could get you into the capsules."

Mason's anger flares. "You were wrong. And now we have no way out. Two Primes are dead, the electricity to the capsules is shut off, and Gryme knows we're here. We need to hide, Sam." He grips my hand, pulling me to the hallway.

I tug against Mason, planting my feet. "What aren't you saying?" I ask Roanoke.

Mason pulls my wrist. "Who cares what else there is? We need to leave, Samara. More Watchmen will come."

I yank my wrist free, biting in his direction. "Roanoke?"

Roanoke shakes his head. "It could be nothing."

I take a step toward my lethal ally. "All we have left is nothing."

His stormy grays break free from Locke's bloody mess on the ground, his voice as effortless as Marlow's body floating behind him. "Gryme had a journal on his desk. I've never seen that journal, but Gryme kept pointing at it. Kept saying it was Jerald's and how it was proof he was mentally unstable. From how I took it, in Gryme's eyes, not only did one of his Watchmen have an Indicator, but he was a Cicada conspiring against him. Then he gave the order to kill both of you. Before leaving the office, I picked up the journal and skimmed through the pages. There was something strange written in it. Didn't look like Jerald's handwriting, but whoever wrote in it had circled this saying over and over, layered thick with ink and exclamation marks."

"What did it say?" Mason and I ask in unison.

Roanoke paces around, his fingers weaving through his hair. "*Go through the Vat.*"

I repeat it under my breath, hoping something somewhere inside of me will make sense of it. Nothing clicks. "What is that supposed to mean?"

"I have no idea." Roanoke squats down and closes his eyes, cracking his neck as if to stave off mental exhaustion. "The journal didn't have any cicadas drawn on the cover.

I don't know who it belongs to. I mean, it could've been a shared journal and didn't have the drawing yet, but I've never seen a Cicada journal with only one person's handwriting in it. I didn't have time to read all of it, guess it could've had entries from other people. I only flipped through it. But *go through the Vat* was written a bunch of times, along with the occasional *Foxtrot is bullshit*, and my personal favorite *Gryme can eat shit*." He tilts his head back and laughs.

As if answering a summons, Gryme's voice comes through the radio lying near Locke. "Watchman Marlow, give me an update."

With a grin still on his face, Roanoke steps over Locke's body and picks up the radio. He points to it and mouths to us *Gryme can eat shit*. He clears his throat and straightens his face. "Sir, this is Watchman Gideon."

"Watchman Gideon, what's the update?"

"The capsule didn't make it into the anteroom," Roanoke says carefully.

"Excellent. Where is Watchman Marlow?" Gryme's tone is laced with suspicion. *Why didn't my right-hand man answer my call*, it seems to warn.

Roanoke looks between Mason and me, speaking in his Watchman Gideon voice. "He's escorting the Quinn's to the sixth floor of the wing with Watchman Locke. They're going to stage an accident to set an example."

A vulture's smile on the other end of the radio. "I'm on my way. Tell them to wait for me. I want to be there when their bodies land."

Roanoke clips the radio to his pocket and drags Locke's upper body away from the crime scene. "This is good."

I help lift the body to avoid smearing the blood and leaving a trail. "How is this good?"

Roanoke walks backward to the capsule we were in. "Gryme is keeping this quiet," he says. Mason joins us, sharing the weight of Locke's legs with me, both of us stepping around the crimson. "He's not dispatching more Watchmen. He's planning on it being only him and the Primes in this wing. Well, and the two of you tossed over the rails." He lifts Locke's body into the capsule with ease, not needing assistance from either of us, then shuts the door. He likely didn't need help in the first place, but we'd been caught with red hands long before we moved the body. What's a little more blood?

"I'm still not following. How is this good?" Mason asks, the three of us hustling to the hallway.

Roanoke looks between the two of us, his finger hovering over the button for the elevator. "Would you believe me if I said that I trust Jerald with my life?"

"I would," I say, understanding what Roanoke is implying. "And I trust Jerald with mine."

Mason fidgets with his fingers. "I trust Jerald enough to trust both of your judgments," he admits, sort of answering the question.

As we ascend in the elevator, Roanoke stands with contagious confidence. "If Gryme is here, that means he's not in his office."

I loosen my crossed arms, channeling his strength, letting the anxiety drip from my fingers, and look at Mason. He's relaxed but rigid, needlepoint sharp yet soft as cotton. He's my inkblot, my kindred spirit.

"Mental plans between the two of you might work for the *two of you*, but feather it in for me," he sneers.

Is that jealousy? He must think I'm twinning with Roanoke. I hide a smirk. "If the Warden is in the wing looking for us, Roanoke can pull the lever from Gryme's office."

Mason swallows, his tone uncertain. "What do you mean Roanoke can pull a lever? A lever for what? What lever is there to pull except the one for—we're going through the Vat?"

I grip his forearm with both hands. "It doesn't make sense to me either, but it makes enough sense to try. It's a matter of time until Gryme learns his Primes are dead and Roanoke is a Cicada. If the answer is going through the Vat to get out of Foxtrot, Roanoke can rally the Cicadas and storm the castle."

"If they're going to be rallied, why can't we join them and storm the castle? Help take all this down now? Why are we still trying to escape Foxtrot if the answer is to stand with the movement?" Mason asks, hoping to form a more logical plan.

All of this feels wildly unorthodox and recklessly neutral. Why didn't Jerald share that journal with the movement? Was he caught before he could? I'll never know.

What I do know is my decision—I'm damned either way.

"You can join the fight, Mason. You have academy training, and you can help take all this down. But if the Cicadas can't overtake Gryme and his Watchmen, I'm dead either way. Gryme won't let me live if we lose. I'd rather go out on my terms than be shoved off the rails or taken to a hidden room where no one can hear my screams."

Mason takes a deep breath as the elevator comes to a stop. "I'm with you."

41

The worried eyes of Maeve, Olivia, and Andromeda wait for us in the surveillance room, having clearly witnessed the double homicide of Watchman Locke and Watchman Marlow from the Cicada cameras.

"Roanoke, what's happening?" Maeve asks, handing us a change of clothes.

I never imagined I'd be covered with enough dried blood to constitute new attire, let alone blood that's not mine, and it's happened twice now. Not bothering with privacy, the three of us lift our shirts and unbutton our pants because seeing the colorful briefs of Roanoke and Mason and having my bra exposed are the least of our worries.

Roanoke pulls a clean shirt over his head. "Gryme is on the Cicada scent." There's no heartbeat of pause for him to think of a lie. "He's planning to rid us all from Foxtrot at once with a mass sinking, but the movement needs to act before this gets out of our hands. The electricity for the capsules is shut off, but we think there's another way out." I tightly braid my hair, and Mason ties his shoes. "These two are going to the Vat, and I'm heading for Gryme's office.

There's no time to explain more, but we're finally taking Foxtrot. Andromeda, signal all the Cicadas. Have everyone surround the Arboretum and be ready for a fight."

Andromeda nods, typing aggressively on multiple keypads. Through the cameras mounted on the walls, Foxtrot's lights flicker. "Sort of like Morse code," she explains through a rod of licorice in her mouth, answering any unspoken questions.

In all five sectors, people emerge from their homes, looking up at the strange lights. More people filter out from the commissary, the museum, schools, and nearly every building to watch the sporadic pattern. Other people, regular people, continue walking to wherever it is they're headed, unfazed by the normalcy of unreliable lighting. How predictable it is for the fluorescent lights to flicker.

But the ones who know the signal, those with curious minds, understand it.

The flickering stops long enough for me to wonder if whatever needed to be signaled was signaled, when all the lights within Foxtrot flash a lavender hue for a second, maybe two, and everyone on the cameras, those who are Cicadas, scramble.

Some go back inside their homes, hopefully to gather what they need before the insurrection. Most sprint toward the main corridor, tearing open caches from the sides of buildings along the way. It's chaos.

My vision darts between the feeds, my face so close to the screens they're pixelated. "Are those hidden weapons?"

These are Cicada warriors, and they're ready. A flip of a switch is all it took, no questions asked.

"I don't think she heard you," Mason says from somewhere at my side. Or behind me. Or both.

There are so many people. Running, walking, laughing, and cheering. Holding weapons above their heads and chanting something. I'd bet all my nail polish that the energy is contagious. That it could shatter the windows if amplified. People of all ages, all pigments, and all levels of society, no matter their sector, join in the camaraderie. We're all people. Hope knows no bounds, no matter how hard the Warden tries to divide us.

"Sam?"

The hand on my shoulder threatens to spike whiplash in my neck. I spin around, identical eyes locking onto mine. "Do you see all this?" I ask him.

Taking in the faces of my group, they watch the feed in astonishment. Even Roanoke, in all his reverence, seems to be awestruck, his stormy grays following the movement of the crowds. "It's happening."

I've been in this bunker for twenty-six years and have never once seen masses gathering such as this, nor heard of any before. The last Warden might've quieted the movement, but he didn't silence them, and neither could Calum Gryme. Cicadas are no longer afraid to stand up for what they believe in. They're no longer afraid to push back against the power of the Gryme government that has controlled this facility for too long. They're no longer afraid to fight.

Olivia tears herself from the cameras, an arm looped through Maeve's. She frowns, her eyes wandering between Mason and me, dripping with a flat gaze. "Why are you going to the Vat?"

I want to tell her everything, but my mind is too busy. There's too much to explain, too much at risk. "A backup plan," I blurt out, not committing to truth or lie.

She reaches her hand out to me, somehow understanding the obscurity behind my words. "This is goodbye, then?" I meet her for our partner's handshake.

Maeve lightly tugs Olivia's other wrist. "Come, Liv. We have our own path."

Olivia swivels her head to Roanoke. "You'll protect them?"

His storms soften to a category-one. "You have my word, Livs. And remember, you're the change."

"There is life! Up, up, and up. We must go up!" Cicadas chant outside the Arboretum.

Mason and I gently maneuver against the flow of them, listening to whispers of readiness, absorbing the electricity of confidence. Atlantic, this is happening.

"What's the last count?" a Cicada whispers to another.

"A little over three hundred," the other responds.

"Three hundred what?" I ask. Their look is dubious. "I

am everyone, and you are?"

The woman holding a hand-carved bat with screws hammered into it gives me a downward nod. "Three hundred-odd active Watchmen."

Mason steps beside me, joining in on the whispering. "And how many of us?" They side-eye him, the woman with the screw-bat tapping the end on her palm. "I am also everyone," he adds.

"Almost a thousand," the woman with a baton wrapped in steel coils answers, her eyes lit with power.

Casually patrolling Sec-One without a care in Foxtrot, Watchmen pass by. Gryme mustn't have figured out we aren't in the wing of escape capsules yet, otherwise they'd be restraining us.

"Roanoke says a Cicada is stationed outside the Vat. A woman with a buzz cut," I remind Mason, his eyes searching for danger as we step into the building housing the Vat.

"And which one would that be?" he whispers, the warm air from his anxious breath bouncing off my neck.

Two women stand guard outside the Vat, their hair identically cut and sharing a look of unfriendliness.

The woman on the left addresses us. "Do you need assistance?"

"I'm looking for someone," I say carefully.

"And who are you looking for?" the woman on the

right fires back.

My odds are split in half. No matter what I say, the Watchman not meant to hear my response will question my answer. I should've asked Roanoke for more of a defining characteristic of who my ally here is before we split up, but we were on limited time. We still are.

I clamp down on my teeth, a sharp twinge in my jaw. "I am looking for ... everyone."

"*We* are everyone," the woman on the right says through a smile, the one on the left dipping her chin.

They swipe their badges on separate card readers in sync, and the door to the Vat swings open. My gaze locks on the empty chamber, those written words coming to life—*go through the Vat.*

"You can still turn back and join the Cicadas in the fight, Mason." It's the safest option for him to join the many, but I can't do that. I'm too stubborn for my own good, isn't that what he told me? I can't join the fight—I won't. This is my fight, the Vat my arena. I'm either meeting the deep, or I'm proving whoever wrote in that journal right. There's no in-between.

He shakes his head, annoyance in his eyes as if he tires of reminding me. "I told you, Sam, I'm with you."

The hatred in Warden Gryme's voice bites through the radios attached to the Cicada Watchmen. "Code Black. Locate and detain Watchman Gideon and the two lawbreakers with him. Their images are being broadcast as I speak. Form a blockade at the entrances of all sectors. No one exits or enters until I say."

Sharing the same thought, Mason and I stride to the entrance door, opening it barely a crack. With this being the training sector, too many Watchmen filter out of Sec-Op, jogging to the entrance of Sec-One. A chokepoint forms.

"My head isn't that big, is it?" Mason smirks, focused on the blown-up image of himself pixelated on the billboard ahead. A description of his name, height, weight, and age snaking across the bottom. A moment later, his photograph flickers away, and my hollow eyes stare back at me.

My image fades away, and the photograph of Watchman Gideon takes its place. Roanoke's identity is no longer a secret. I don't know what this means for him or his family, but he and the Cicadas are standing against oppression. I have to trust that all of this is not in vain. That we will all come out on top. Gently closing the door, I drag a chair from the seating area and bar the handles.

"Mason, it's time to go."

42

The Vat locks behind us.

"Ready, Zombie?" His voice crackles through the speakers above. I glance up, nodding to the camera in the corner connecting me to Roanoke in Gryme's office.

This chamber is a tomb. A tomb that steals last gasping breaths, screams heard by ears made of wax, and tears from forgotten faces. Jerald died because of that entry, because of those four words, and I'm willing to die trying. Willing to die for a purpose rather than be held captive any longer in this starfish-shaped prison.

Red lights circulate above as the buzzer finishes its third call. Piercing cold water pools at our feet, quickly rising past our knees. The chamber fills fast. My hand reaches for the safety of Mason's.

"Start exercising your lungs. Deep breath, in and out. Be ready to hold it." I demonstrate, and he copies, our arms moving in circular rotations.

The water climbs past our sternums, rising, rising, rising. There's hardly any space left to breathe. Our lips and noses press against the clear ceiling. I take a final, deep, desperate breath and look at my twin. My kindred spirit. My ink blot. My *heads* and *tails*.

We're vacuumed from the Vat with a force stronger than my concept to grasp the sensation of it. The water is powerful, moving in a precise flow. Deciding against the effort it would take to fight the current, I allow it to carry me on its path as we shuttle past the Observatory window.

The familiar spotlights outside the half-moon dome reflect off something strange—something I've never noticed in the countless times I've stood in that very spot, watching the sunken meet the deep. Reaching my hand above as I'm swept in the underwater current, my fingertips glide against something transparent in the openness. My lungs aren't collapsing from the immense pressure of the ocean, and my body isn't caving in on itself, unable to withstand the crushing depths. The water is guiding us through some kind of clear tunnel.

A hundred or so yards away, out of sight from the inner windows of Foxtrot, the current hurtles us toward a square platform held in place by two large pipes—one from above it, the other below.

Atlantic, please let my lungs hold out. We've been in this tunnel for centuries. The involuntary need to inhale is becoming impossible to ignore.

Hold your breath. Hold. It.

I try to twist my body to look at Mason behind me, to make sure that he's holding his breath, but the force of the water thwarts my movement, spinning me back around like a dreidel. This channel of water is damn near consuming, too controlling, too precise. Too stubborn. To the depths with my irrational fear of a dying galaxy, this vortex of immovable water hurtling through this tunnel might kill me.

My lungs burn. My chest burns. The fear inside of me is *burning*. I'm on fire from within. So much fire it can't be put out, not even with all the water from all the oceans combined. I close my eyes and let the fire out, unable to hold my breath any longer.

A door to the hidden anteroom opens, and we funnel inside, filling with the same water we were moving through. The door seals shut, and the water quickly drains. Mason and I crash to the floor of the chamber, gasping for air.

While I struggle to grasp what's happening, he stands up and helps me to my feet because of course he does—he's the *heads*. The most logical thing to do is to stand up and not curl into a ball on the floor to process, which is what I want to do. The most logical thing is to let go of the lingering fire and breathe. Deeply. Because that's what I'm doing. Breathing. The most logical thing is to stand up, simply to remind ourselves that we aren't dead. At least, I don't think we are.

A separate door opens. Head to toe in tight-fitting green rubber suits, two individuals enter our chamber. Judging by their framework, one is a man, the other a woman.

A deep voice muffles through the mask on the left. "Please, come with us."

I take a shambled step forward out of instinct, to prove

to myself that I'm not dead. To put myself in front of Mason. To protect him from this unknown and take the brunt of the punishment that's inevitably to come. To remind myself that I'm no longer drifting or going exactly nowhere and everywhere. That we're now *somewhere*. Another section of Foxtrot. A holding facility before we're sentenced to the deep. I take another staggered step, and Mason follows.

The two lead us through the door they entered from and into a small medical unit. Stainless steel everything and a smell of sterility. The woman prepares a tray of needles and jars of clear liquid. "Vaccination is required. Do we have your consent?"

Do we have a choice? Is what I want to ask, but I can't form the words. I nod.

This was all for nothing. Going through the Vat meant nothing. There's no escaping Foxtrot. This prison's layout is endless, full of hidden chambers and meaningless hope. The living and the deceased go through the Vat to come here and be stripped of their clothing and personal items by these two before meeting the deep, I'm sure of it.

The Warden must not want to pollute the ocean, which is oddly honorable, but I can respect it. I don't need any of my clothing to lifelessly float through the endless nothingness that's the Atlantic Ocean. Hopefully, the flashlight in my pocket is salvageable. Maybe it'll find its way back to the Husk to be reused. How many personal items are distributed throughout Foxtrot that once belonged to victims of the Vat? How many items in my apartment are unknowingly repurposed from sacrifices? Who has Wren's knapsack now? Who will wear my *Q* for Quinn earrings next?

Numb. That's how I feel. Numb.

At least until the needles prick into my skin, the unknown liquid absorbing into my bloodstream. Three shots and bandages cover the scarlet beads on my arms, then Mason receives his doses and dressings. Satisfied, the strangers beckon us to follow. Turning their backs on us to lead the way, toward the only other door in the medical unit, I swipe a surgical knife from the tray and tuck it under my sleeve.

A deep, vertical cut on each arm will drain my lifeblood. I've been through enough trials by water now to know I will not be a victim of the ocean. If I'm going to die, it'll be on my terms. I'll bleed out before the Atlantic can fill my lungs from the involuntary gasp. The suicide pact didn't mean I had to watch Mason die, it meant we both did.

Leading us down a shallow hallway, the two stop in front of an elevator. From my count and judging by the size of this square holding area, there are two rooms in total—the anteroom the Vat swept us into, the small medical unit we left, and an elevator with a trapdoor. Once we're stripped of our clothing, they'll weigh us down with makeshift anchors, shove us in like lambs before the slaughter, and laugh as we sink.

The bottom of the ocean is down there somewhere, past the dark, dreadful water.

The elevator chimes and the doors open. The rubber lady takes a step in, waving for us to follow. The rubber man places an arm on the door, keeping it open.

No trapdoor. They aren't demanding we undress.

"You're safe. Please, come in," the rubber lady says.

The wildness in my eyes must've sold me out. I turn and take Mason's hand, and we step into the elevator, the man following behind. There are only two buttons to choose from: one and zero. Considering *one* was pressed and we're moving up, it's safe to assume the chamber we came from, the one now below us, is *zero*.

Mason grips the towel around his chest, his breathing deep, eyes hard as stone. He's in shock. We both are. We're being escorted to our final resting place.

This is my last chance to gift myself the endless sleep I've been craving most of my life. To silence my doubts and meet any god that might be waiting on the other side.

Feeling for the straw I stole off the table, I pull back the fabric from my right sleeve and look at Mason at my side. "I'm sorry," I whisper. Or did I shout it. Did I say anything at all? My mouth is full of jellyfish, their tentacles tickling the inside of my cheeks. I laugh and stumble forward.

Mason sways left and right. "Sam, did you say something? Your eyes are cherries!" he snickers.

I reach into my other sleeve, feeling for the remote. No—a comb. No—a ruler. Whatever it was, it's not there. I thought I took something off the table in the cafeteria we were just in. Something to help end *something*. There's nothing up my sleeve, aside from bandages.

"Listen, rubber-lady." I point to her with a too-long finger, my knees wobbling. "I don't know what sort of ..."

Where did the words go? I clear my throat, steadying myself against the door of the escape capsule. No—the closet?

"You gave me, you poked me with. Listen. How ..."

Atlantic, my thoughts are swirling.

"I don't like that liquid you had my veins drink. Well, you. Whatever you put inside of me and ... well, I don't like any of it. Not one bit."

Why is her skin made of—

"And why are you rubber?"

Mason thuds to his knees. The rubber-man curls my twin into the fetal position, and as my weight becomes too heavy to hold, I collapse on the floor beside him.

43

It's a mystery how we've come to be in this room.

Somehow, we've made it *here*, wherever *here* may be. Wherever and whatever this room is. A large metal door, four white walls, two beds, a table with three chairs in the center, and a covered window in the corner.

I'm not sure how long we've been in this room, or how long it's been since the Vat. I've woken up on this bed too many times to count, not realizing I'd fallen asleep. The first time I awoke, I was alone. The second time, Mason was sleeping on the bed across from me. The third, he was asleep beside me. Now, after the fourth, ninth, or twentieth time I've woken up, my brain is screaming that it's time to *move*.

"Mason, wake up."

A hinge creaks from the metal door. A tray slot in the center falls inward, and two plates of food slide in. Curiosity stirs me from the bed.

A hockey puck of something layered between bread, lettuce, and tomatoes. The commissary has something similar, but the little index card on the plate beside this says *hamburger*, not *Foxtrot Deluxe*. It doesn't look rehydrated or glistening with poison, but the smell is awful.

Hamburger? Doesn't ham come from swine? Sonia said there's a hot meal from an exclusive menu—this must be it. I could've sworn she said it was for senior citizens, but everything is fuzzy. I take the plates from the tray slot, mumbling a *thank you* to whoever is behind the door, and set them on the floor.

"I'll be in after a moment," a voice says from the other side of the heavy door.

"Where are we?" I demand.

"I'll speak with you soon. Please wait a moment."

"I will not speak with someone who hides behind a door and lacks the courtesy of introducing themselves. I want to know where we are, and who you are."

"Will you be eating?"

"No."

Something heavy shifts on the other side of the metal, some sort of lock mechanism moving up or down. The door swings open. A regular-looking man in his late thirties enters the room. Auburn hair, glasses, a gapped smile beneath a walrus mustache, too many freckles to count, and a black bag across his chest. He extends his hand from the threshold of the door. "I'm Henry Cassidy. It's nice to finally meet you, Samara Quinn."

I meet him for the handshake, my skin a ghastly, washed-out contrast against his. "Henry Cassidy? You sent the transmission?"

He nods, motioning for the table. "We have a lot to

catch up on."

I nearly stumble backwards, reaching for Mason, vigilant on Henry Cassidy as if he's a mirage that will vanish if I look away. "Mason." I slap his shin, stomach, collarbone, and face. "Wake up."

"Sam," he mumbles. "Tell the room to stop spinning. I'm going to yak."

Henry Cassidy glides into the room with the composure of a man in charge, pulling out a chair and setting his bag on the table. He sits down. "You should let him rest. If you're comfortable, we can speak without him."

"I'm awake," Mason says. "I can hear you, but stop hitting me and let me lie here. I'm listening."

I'm sitting across from Henry Cassidy before Mason finishes his sentence. "Where are we?"

"As of right now, you're in a quarantine room. Your immune system would crash if brought straight in. I've been quarantining since you entered the Vat in anticipation of meeting you. You two being in this room is temporary, it should be only another day or so before you can make entry. But I'm sure that's not what you meant. Where you are, Samara, is on the surface. On Mount Desert Island, to be specific. It's a research island off the coast of Maine."

I can't think. Can't form any words to speak. Can't find any saliva to help dislodge the sandpaper in my throat. We made it. I have too many questions, I'm not sure what to ask first. How to feel, how to react. Research for what? How much water the oceans lost from being boiled? Document the revival of the surface?

Henry *is* from the Whiskey outpost—Roanoke heard the transmission wrong. It wasn't saying *Aybee has a message for Foxtrot,* it was saying Whiskey. I swallow the sandpaper. "When did the surface reset? How long have you been up here? Are the other stations here, too?"

Removing the glasses from his face, he sets them on the table and pinches the skin between his nose. "In a perfect world, there would be a psychologist here to help debrief you instead of me, but the audience demanded I speak on their behalf. An exception was made. I hope you find comfort in knowing that everyone else in Foxtrot will be eased into all of this. I hope one day you understand that the sacrifices you made, both in Foxtrot and in this room with me now, will be beneficial for generations to come."

This feels wrong. As if I'm somewhere I'm not supposed to be, sitting across from someone I'm not meant to. How can someone from another station have such an evasive, noncommittal answer?

"What the fuck are you talking about?"

"There's no easy way to say this." He tilts his head, studying me from across the table. "The sun never evolved into a red giant. The world didn't end. It's been the same as it's always been, give or take a war here and there over the past two centuries, but Foxtrot is the only station. There was never any Alpha through Zulu, your facility is one of a kind. It's designed to study human behavior and societal development. What does humanity do in isolation? Adapt?

Innovate? Govern itself without outside influence?"

Am I breathing?

"You all surpassed expectations. It took some time, but the community gained its footing. Individual knowledge and skills from the First Generation were passed down. A type of college was formed where all the textbooks provided by Mount Desert Island were stockpiled. Those who wanted to *do more* self-taught. People evolved into honeybees, finding roles to fulfill. Healthcare workers, cleaners, builders, undertakers, and architects. Teachers, engineers, even scientists. I mean, artificial insemination? Are you kidding me?" His hands shoot into the air as if a bolt of electricity passed through him.

"Then, a type of government emerged. Rules were enforced. People reused, recycled, and repurposed everything. A trading hub came to life, the Arboretum reaped and sowed meticulously. Utterly, utterly fascinating." He clicks his tongue. "But not as much as the Cicada movement. That's a fan favorite. We draw in the most views when recruits explore the Arboretum and learn to swim. It's always a treat to see how wildly different the experience is for each person. Some are natural, others reserved, but most all have a fear of water. A fear of that unknown, a fear of one's capabilities to succeed. Each of you perseveres."

"You've ... been watching us?"

"I'm so sorry Samara, I've gotten ahead of myself. I'm usually more prepared for a meeting with a Below, but I've only prepared for this a little over three days ago since you left the Vat. I don't have my notes with me and, ah, I'm doing it again. You don't care about all that. Yes, we've been watching. We've been observing and learning from you all. The entire world has been watching. Every surveillance camera in Foxtrot is a live feed, including secure locations like Sec-Op and Calum Gryme's office. Think of Foxtrot as a stage. Twenty-four-hour feeds for anyone tuning into the program. It hardly focuses on anyone in particular, more of an overall view of the facility, rotating between sectors every few hours. Listening here and there to conversations and the general public milling about. But when Cicadas start whispering, we zoom in and turn the volume up."

"Your friend Scott Gideon is like a beacon for us. We've learned he's only ever signaled to meet a recruit, so we track his movements. We hadn't had a new Cicada join in some time and worried it ran its course. But when you and Olivia Aubert were sent his way, we retraced the steps that led you to the movement. Your journey is unique. We've been following you since you circled back to Sonia Rivera's apartment."

44

My legs barely carry me across the room. I yank the curtains open, and sunlight hits me, encompassing my skin with a heat I could never have imagined. My sweaty hands lift on the windowpane with shaky strength, and I vomit outside. Tears sting my eyes. I spit the stomach acid from my lips and look ahead—across the shore to the blanket of blue.

There's something sinister about the ocean.

Something eternal and lonely. Swallowing tens of thousands of people whole must've been an appetizer. It's starving, now that I look at it, starving for my pain. The Atlantic Ocean, at last we meet.

Waves lap on the shore with lazy motion, retreating then creeping forward with no end to the pull. Repetitive in a predictable way, but somehow ferocious. The susurration of it is soothing yet nauseating.

This isn't how it's supposed to be. This is all wrong. If Foxtrot wasn't real, is this?

I slip off a shoe and let it drop out the window—one, two, nine, seventeen seconds until it thuds between boulders. Solid. I'm not losing my mind. Fear and anxiety warp my mind, convincing me this tower, this ocean, this surface, this reality isn't ... real.

Testing my theory, I take off the other shoe and toss it out. It's a pitiful throw, but it makes it past the rocks, landing on its side on the sand below. It didn't fall through an invisible barrier. It didn't disappear. How can this be real when it's wrong.

"What do you mean you've been following her since Sonia's apartment?" Mason's protective tone warns he's ready to rip out throats. The foot of a chair grates across the floor, toppling over. I don't have to turn around to know he's awoken from his stupor and is looming over Henry Cassidy.

"Mason, I'm so glad to finally meet you. Let me assure both of you that I mean no harm and remind you that our interaction is being broadcast as we speak. The world is fascinated with how far you've both come. You're the first to ever find a way out of Foxtrot. Let's not make any decisions to warrant security. We can speak civilly. I'll explain all of this plainly if given the chance."

Turning around and leaning into the open window, elbows propped against the pane, I face Henry and Mason. "Let him speak." Mason cocks his head, fingers pulsing in his palms. I have no strength left to care. We may be above, but I'm silently drowning in the depths of my despair. "That's all we can do."

He resets Henry's chair, motioning for him to sit, then sits at the edge of the bed. "Right," Henry mumbles, dragging the chair away from Mason. "In the beginning, Mount Desert Island had a strict policy about not interfering with the study. The whole idea was to let you all do what you felt needed to be done. Once the Gryme family took over the role of governing the facility, everything became stagnant. People went to work, woke up, and did it all over again. Hope diminished, and people committed suicide. The United Nations nearly pulled the plug only a few years in, but someone had the idea to televise it. Ask the world to watch, observe, and vote on how and when to help and document the outcomes. I believe the first interference had something to do with mild sabotage. *Give* the people in Foxtrot something to *do*. *Give* them something to build. To rework and invent and watch as they overcome obstacles. My memory eludes me on the specifics of the sabotage, it was before my time, you see. I'm sure someone can answer it for you, but that's not my role here. I'm not qualified for all that. I am the host! I can answer all questions related to the show."

The host. Of a television show.

I've been a puppet all along—a voodoo doll—gutted and sewn back together by sick, demented beings made of radio waves, helping to create a faux fabric of life.

"You said you've been following her since Sonia's. What does that mean?" Mason repeats.

"There's something I'd like to show you." Henry motions for the bag, both palms facing up, requesting silent permission to open it with subtle movements. Mason nods. Henry removes a book and sets it on the table. Ice melts beneath my skin. Hot pinpricks riddle the top of my scalp, and my legs nearly buckle. I clutch the window frame to steady myself. "Do you recognize this?" he asks Mason.

"That's the book of the surface," I blurt out. "How … how do you have that?"

"It's ours," Henry purrs. "Over fifteen years ago, a vote was cast by the public to provide it to Foxtrot. Place it somewhere inconspicuous so Gryme and his Watchmen couldn't find it, but somewhere strategic in a popular Cicada area. It was a type of interference, but a healthy one. Jerald Quinn was the one who found it and showed it to you two, I'd imagine, and shared the contents with the movement. Our relay person reclaimed it and returned it topside."

"A healthy interference?" Mason shouts. "If that book wasn't brought down, none of this would've happened!"

"That's the beauty of the experiment, Mason. None of anything would've happened if it weren't for the research facility or the viewers. How else would we know a community couldn't survive underwater with free rein if we didn't try? Foxtrot *worked* in the way it needed to work. We could argue over the semantics all day."

Day, he says. Not shift—*day*. There aren't restrictions on the sun, no regulations for its ultraviolet rays. Turning my back on Henry and Mason, I face the open blue and look up, searching for Olivia's god. Searching for some kind of sign that proves its invisible existence. For proof that this was for some bigger purpose, that there's meaning behind the obscurity. For proof that my life wasn't on display for all to see, watching me struggle to stay alive in a prison system designed to kill us. To *watch* us.

There is no god, not even my own. The surface may be alive, but it's dead all the same. The surface isn't real. Foxtrot isn't real. Am I? I pinch the skin beneath my wrists. Nothing. No numbness or anger. No safety.

Far below, past the jagged rocks, a crab scuttles by. I reach down to touch it, the weight of my upper body shifting forward. I close my eyes and prepare to free-fall.

Footsteps frantically shuffle behind me. Two hands grasp my calves, yanking me in. "Sam, what the hell? Are you trying to get yourself killed?" He plants my feet on the floor.

"There was a crab," I mumble.

He hasn't even looked out the window yet. He hasn't seen all of what's been hiding from us for the sake of an experiment. His *heads* is ordering him to *get answers now and figure the rest out later*. My *heads* is saying *I don't want answers, I don't want to figure this out. I want to be done with it all.*

Or is that my *tails* speaking? I can't make sense of the two. I've danced with *tails* all my life, a familiar presence—now suddenly it's a stranger. What does it want me to do. How do I respond to this when I don't feel like a person anymore.

"We aren't real, Mason."

"What do you mean? Of course, we're real."

"What if we're asleep?"

What if we need to wake up.

I wipe the warm brain matter from my cheeks, inspecting the clear liquid. Tears—not the aftermath of exploding eyeballs. I scan the room, waiting for the second me to lucidly appear, preparing for my current body to melt into a pile of keys.

There is no other *me*, besides Mason, but he doesn't count. He's never been in this recurring nightmare before. It's always been me and another me. With eyes exploding, my body melting, and a—doorway. What if the window is the spiraling door. What if the onyx spirals are drowned out by the blinding sun. What if I'm the key to waking up. I peek over the edge.

Mason skirts in front of me, blocking my path to the window. He places a firm hand on my collarbone. "What did they inject us with after the Vat?" he shouts at Henry over my shoulder. "She's reacting to whatever was in those vials. This isn't her, something's wrong."

I twist around, tilting my head back with a smile. "Everything is wrong."

Henry says something about vaccinations and immunizations. Electrolytes, potassium, magnesium, vitamins, and something else. I don't pay attention to any of it. The salty breeze is singing to me, like a Siren. It's warm and hypnotic. I close my eyes and listen.

45

I've somehow made it back to the bed, buried beneath blankets with a half-empty water bottle in hand. I'm both freezing and on fire, my body vibrating nauseatingly. Everything moves as I lie still, rocking with a nonexistent earthquake. I don't know how I managed to fall back asleep with all the motion sickness—this surface sickness—this grief. The surface has been an apex predator lying in wait, sharing the sunshine of the reality it thrives in.

This grief is mine and mine alone.

I have no memory of returning to this bed. I assume I fell asleep. For ten years or ten seconds, there's no way to tell. How could I have fallen asleep if I never woke up. How could I have woken up without falling asleep. Unless I never fell asleep or woke up.

I can't make sense of this, it's ... *wrong*.

"The television show is called *As Below*?" Mason asks, sitting at the table across from Henry.

They're both holding water bottles. Where did the water come from? Who brought it in? How many others are here? The table between them is bolted to the floor, a thick metal pillar rising from the center. At the base, links dangle loosely, as if meant to restrain someone. A precaution. For their safety, or ours? I'd sooner leap out the window than end up chained to that thing.

"Yes, the program is called As Below. Or A.B. for short," Henry answers.

Aybee has a message for Foxtrot, Roanoke heard the transmission repeat. But it wasn't from another station. It was a message from As Below—from A.B.

I bury my face in the pillow, trying to process as Mason's voice cuts through the room. "So let me get this straight. Cicadas became a movement because the viewers of this television show got tired of watching people kill themselves on the seafloor, so they voted to sneak in a book and whispers of the surface to see how we'd react?"

Henry clears his throat. "That's correct."

"Tens of thousands of people have been locked in a bunker for two centuries and fed a lie that the surface was destroyed and that there were other survivor outposts, all so Foxtrot could serve as some sickening, reality show experiment so the rest of humanity can learn from our mistakes? Am I hearing this right?"

Plastic crunches and a cap unscrews. Henry gulps down water. "Yes."

"And you're a television host sent here to debrief us?"

"Also, yes."

Mason's laugh is sharp, bitter. "Because all the small fucking minds in the world decided to televise it? Because nothing sounds more humane than trapping *human-fucking-beings* in a seafloor bunker, watching them suffer, and broadcasting it to the world. You are the most disgusting man I've ever met in my life, Henry Cassidy. The Warden is a goddamn dandelion compared to you."

Henry exhales slowly, his tone almost rehearsed. "I may be the villain in your story Mason, but I'm not dense. I knew there'd be pushback and name-calling before I came here. I've prepared for it, I've accepted it. But I sympathize with you. I'm not here to play the hero because I haven't saved you from anything. You've saved yourselves. But if you'd waited a few more days, you would've been met with a psychologist. Foxtrot is set to be evacuated on the day of the Bicentennial Bash. The facility will shut down completely in less than a week. The experiment is over, you've simply joined us before the others. So please, let me do what I've been sent here to do. I'm not here to answer the how's and why's of Foxtrot. I'm here to interview you, to explain how our two worlds collided, and collect your raw, emotional reactions to learning the truth of—"

A chair slides back, grating across the concrete floor. I peek out from the safety of my pillow as Mason launches across the table.

Henry hits the floor, Mason on top of him.

Fist after fist, thud after thud, Mason swings.

Blood splatters here, Henry's glasses fly there.

I close my eyes to the rhythm of it.

None of this is real.

It's as if I'm everywhere and nowhere all at once.
I'm below.
I'm above.
I'm between.

46

Barging into the room, two men lift Mason off Henry, pinning him against the wall. He spits the blood splatter from his lips onto the floor, turning out his palms. "I'm good, I'm good." He looks down at the broken skin over his knuckles and winces.

A woman glides into the room, calm as a lotus, and perches beside Henry, dual auburn braids hanging past her shoulders. "I hate to say it Henry, but I told you not to come in here alone. Let's get you up." She helps him to his feet and sits him at the table, handing him an icepack. Her head snaps in Mason's direction. "Will you behave?"

A shit-eating grin warps his face. He must be feeling proud of himself. I don't think he's ever hit anyone before. Mason nods to the woman, neutralizing his facial tone. She signals the men to exit the room.

"Since Henry is too slow to get to the point, and you lack manners, we're doing this my way." She sits at the table, pulling a chair out for Mason. Henry flinches, scooting away from my twin. "The faster we get this over with, the faster a mental health specialist can see you and your sister to help you come to terms with all this. Here's the first wake-up call: I don't have a small fucking mind. Millions of people around the world hate and refuse to watch that goddamn program, As Below. Not everyone is getting off from your exploits. Henry here has a job. That job happens to align with your life. He's here doing that job. You hit him again, Mason Quinn, and I will end you. Do you understand me?"

I find myself standing in the corner of the room. Their backs are to me, oblivious to my presence.

When did I stand up?

"A psychologist is on their way and should be here within the hour," the woman tells Mason.

He's surrounded by vipers, yet his posture is steady. Confident. He's ready and willing to take it all in. That's the logical thing to do. Absorb it, not be absorbed by it. He'll be okay without me. I've been holding him back this whole time.

"As Henry mentioned, everyone in Foxtrot will be here in a few days, and we can finally put this behind us. I'll only say this once more, from the beginning, and fill in any gaps—so listen up, Quinn. Foxtrot began as a research facility to study people in isolation. A few years in, it became a lawless society, and a government formed under the Gryme name. With that came restrictions, punishments, rations, and so on. For a time, it seemed to shift into a civilized society, but the Gryme family abused their authority. The community reacted. People died at the hands of others and from their own. Wash, rinse, and repeat for decades. Enter the television show, As Below. Clues of the surface trickled down with whispers of hope. More whispers, more curiosity, and Cicadas began moving silently. For years and years, this movement grew. Then a massive silence. What Michael Gryme did to those fourteen Cicadas at the recycling center ..." She shakes off a shiver. "No one should die like that."

They—all of them—watched that happen and did nothing to stop it. And they've done nothing to stop anything from happening since. I've been like a heron standing in the still waters of Foxtrot, and here I am again, motionless in this sickening reality. The curtains rustle in the breeze. I slowly wade toward the window, careful of my steps.

It feels as if I'm going to burst into a million pieces. As if my skin is made of serrated cast iron, my organs a reservoir for explosives, my mind a striker lever. Pull the pin and see where I go. I glance out the window, feeling so small.

"After decades of silence," the woman continues, "we learned that when another member coordinates with Scott Gideon, it means there's a recruit. We tracked him. That's how we found your sister and followed her path leading up to the Vat. We saw everything, Mason. Every moment. I hate that I'm saying this, but someone from up here was sent down to Foxtrot to intercept Samara on her way to meet Scott Gideon. The woman who attacked her was a hired actor. She wasn't supposed to use that much force."

I cup a hand to my mouth, swallowing the laugh. It's never been real. My death *was* staged, after all. I should've stayed asleep on the bed—the damning truth wouldn't hurt this much if I were unconscious.

I swing one leg over the ledge, then the other, watching them over my shoulder.

"After Calum Gryme brought you both into the interrogation room, and before Scott Gideon, Nathan Marlow, and Parker Locke were summoned for a meeting, one of our Foxtrot insiders planted a journal in Gryme's office. The one that said *go through the Vat*. The audience was rooting for you because none of the escape capsules are functional. They're just props. The Vat is the only way out of Foxtrot. The Gryme's may believe they're executing people and sending them into the ocean depths, but that's far from the truth. We recover all those who've gone through it. Everyone who goes through the Vat alive has joined surface society after being assessed, and all the dead bodies have been properly buried."

Wren didn't find her mom in the abyss—she's up here. And Desmond, too. Jerald's still gone, but he's buried somewhere. He made it to the surface. I hope they place me beside him.

"You two risked your lives by choosing to go through the Vat. You reached our Intake Unit, got your vaccinations, and now we're here. That sums it up." She takes hold of Henry's elbow, guiding him to the door. "The Cicadas overpowered the Warden and his Watchmen with little casualties. Calum Gryme couldn't contain the outbreak," she says over her shoulder. "Scott Gideon gave an incredible speech. We sent a transmission down letting him know you both made it to the surface and urging everyone to be patient—that there's a way out." She takes a deep breath, moving a braid off her shoulder. "I'm sorry it had to be this way, but everyone will be up here soon and join surface society."

Everyone.

No—no, no, no.

My *heads* side of the coin can't find the logic in any of this.

"Wait," I whisper, breaking my gaze from the blanket of blue.

Mason is the only one who hears me. His head snaps toward me, the look in his eyes holding a sympathy as deep as the ocean. "Sam?"

"Wait," I say again, propping myself at an angle against the windowpane. I tuck a leg beneath my thigh, curling my toes. It's comfortable up here. Quiet, somehow. Everything suddenly makes sense, in all the ways it shouldn't. Welcome back, *tails.* Henry looks over, the icepack slipping from his hands. "What happens to the Warden?" I ask, a tone as bright as sunshine.

The woman looks at me like I'm some broken thing, her mouth slightly open. "Samara—"

"—Are there any consequences for what he's done in Foxtrot?" Her brows knit, scenarios fluttering through her mind, no doubt. What will my reaction be—what will she risk? Truth or lie? Lie or truth? *Tell me, tell me, tell me.*

Every second she waits adds to my mental fuse. Accept and absorb or explode and suffocate—heads or tails, tails or heads. "What happens to the man responsible for crimes against humanity."

Not a question—a demand. It'd be a fool's errand to try and hold the researchers, viewers, or goddamn government accountable for everything that's happened, but there's a price. And someone owes a debt. Too many generations have suffered under that wicked family name.

The woman sighs. "The United Nations is pardoning all actions taken during the experiment. I know it doesn't feel fair, but the researchers believe that—"

"—I want to speak with him." A breeze blows my hair to the side. I close my eyes and smile.

My inner beast is starving. Craving that impulse. Since I'm going mad, I might as well set out a plate for it.

"Samara, I'm not sure we can accommodate that. I don't think that's something we could—"

"—I've been made a fool of." My voice slices through, sharp and unrelenting. "I've spent my life clawing for meaning, trying to find purpose in all the empty spaces in Foxtrot. And when I finally find hope, you tell me it was for an experiment. That everything in that facility, even my death, was nothing more than entertainment for an audience. And they're watching now, aren't they?" I pageant wave to the camera in the corner, cold and deliberate. "Are they wondering if I've gone mad? Wondering if I'll jump? What a twist that would be. The unpredictable ending they've been craving." I ease off the windowsill, planting my feet on the floor. "I'd like to speak with the Warden."

"I'll make it happen," Henry says, his eyes blazing with an intensity that mirrors my rage. I give him a small, grateful nod.

I'm done feeling broken—feeling wronged and betrayed. This rage will be my fuel, and the fire will be set free.

"I'd like to be alone until everyone has been brought up," I say. Mason steps toward me, confusion and hurt flashing in his eyes. I raise my palms, silently pleading for space. "Henry," I continue, "will you meet me back here the sh—day—before the Warden is approved to join surface society?"

A sly, almost devious glint lights up the host's eyes. "Of course."

I step closer to Mason, arms reaching out. He pulls me in for the embrace. "I'm burning up with hellfire," I whisper to him. His grip tightens around me. "And I need space. I'm sorry that means you'll be alone because of it, but I ..." The words catch in my throat. I swallow hard, closing my eyes. "This anger and grief are mine. I have to figure it out by myself." He nods and nods, his warm tears trailing down my neck. "I'll see you in a few, shithead." He kisses the top of my head.

"If you need anything, just open the door and ask. You're not locked in here," the woman says. "Can I get you something to eat before we go?"

I shake my head at the offer. For a moment, I consider asking her name, but I can't bring myself to care about such trivial things. My mind feels like it's on the verge of splitting open. My starving beast living in there is stirring, desperate to reach the surface of my consciousness. It's always been there, eager for my reality to shatter. It's been patiently waiting for me to give in. To listen to it. To ride that *tails* impulse unapologetically. The control was never mine to begin with.

"Can I have a journal?" I ask.

I need to release my inner beast and let the madness out—if only for a moment—to find some shred of clarity within this awful reality.

47

Welcome, madness.
Our reality is broken.
What does it mean for us?

I write to myself in my journal.

There's an answer somewhere inside me, I can feel its rage. But I don't know how to find it.

"Is it something to embrace, or something to fear?" I respond to myself aloud.

Why not both?
Let's burn it all down.

I tap the pen on my front teeth, slowly pacing around the room. A deep inhale with each step—a heavy exhale before the other foot lands. Breathing. I'm breathing fresh air. It's not circulated. It's not stale. My lungs are working. I'm not drowning in this reality.

I've been alone for three hours, and my inner beast is still begging for release. How can so many thoughts consume me, yet everything is silent. I slap the journal in my palms, willing myself the courage to confront my subconscious. Madness is knocking, thunderous yet delicate. I open the door. Bent slightly, pressing the journal against my knee, my beast scribbles:

Why are you?

"Why am I? Because I'm human," I answer myself.

That's not good enough.

"Why am I? Because I'm a daughter. I'm a sister."

Dig deeper.

"Why am I? Because I'm deceit. I'm fire."

You know the answer.

Why do you pretend you don't?

"Why am I?" I shout. "Why am I? Why am I? I am because of science."

I slam the journal shut and stand, striding to the door. It opens before my knuckles make contact. Of course, it does. Surveillance.

"What can I get you?" the woman asks.

———◦———

'Barbeque chips' taste like caramelized nuts dipped in ketchup. When I asked the woman to surprise me with a flavor, I didn't realize that Above's have more options than plain and garlic.

It's nice in a strange way—if you don't think about it for too long. The ice-cold lemonade helps. So does staring out the window for hours. Until the sun disappears, and true nighttime greets me.

Hello, sweet darkness
Are you here for an embrace
You've hidden so well

Hello, to you, me
Darkness is not in the void
It's the flame inside

Ignite it, you'll see
You are above, yet below
Burn it to the ground

It's late, let us dream
Dream of below, and above
Dream of dancing fires

Midnight haikus or nightmares, and my beast promises dreams.

48

Day.
Day, day.
Day, day, day.

The word is as strange in my mouth as it is in my thoughts. As strange in my thoughts as it is written down.

Burn it.

"What sort of spiraling are we doing today, beast?" I ask my madness journal. "What do I need to do to accept this? To live with this—after everything? Will it ever stop feeling wrong?"

Not waiting for *its* response, I drag the wooden bed frame across the room and prop it in front of the window. Lying on the mattress, I set my feet on the sill and listen to seagulls in the distance. They're flying and free. I once told Mason I needed to fly, not drown, but the pits of my despair are hauntingly deep.

My hand starts moving:

It will always be wrong.
But will you adapt?

"The better question is, do I *want* to adapt?" I answer

aloud. "If adapting means sitting alone in a strange room and talking to myself in writing, then I'll do myself the favor by standing on the windowsill and leaning forward."

He wins if you do.

"Who wins?" I demand.

Atlantic, I am losing my fucking mind. Do they have Indicators above? I'd be the poster child if they did. But maybe something has always been off inside of me. A chemical imbalance I've hidden. One I've adapted to. One I've learned to live with to avoid the Vat. Self-preservation at its finest. How poetic for my ending to always be the same. Go through the Vat—by force or choice—it didn't matter in the end. I wrote myself into these chapters just for it to be televised.

I sit up and look around the empty room, temptation on my lips to ask for Mason to be brought in—my *heads*.

He's my *heads*. My *heads, heads, heads*. And he ... he said something. Back at our apartment. In our apartment under the sea, our apartment below: *Warden Gryme needs to be taken out.* That was Mason's *tails* speaking.

But if Mason is *heads* and I am *tails*—if I am madness—then I'm both sides of the coin at once. I'm irrational logic. Nothing makes sense. Everything is wrong. Foxtrot is wrong, the surface is wrong. My sense of reality, my sense of being, it's all wrong.

"Who wins?" I repeat to myself.

If you sever the rattle,
is it still a snake?

"Yes."

> *What if you pull out its fangs?*

"Without question."

> *How can you be sure?*

"Because snakes are cold-blooded."

> *Even by altering its appearance,*
> *it is still classified as a snake?*

"Yes."

> *What if you sever the*
> *Warden from a bunker.*
> *Is he still the Warden?*

I outline each letter in the question.
"Yes."

> *And if he's pardoned,*
> *is he still the Warden?*

My pen punctures the page.
"Yes."

> *Isn't he just a man?*

"No, he's a snake disguised as a man."

> *Do you want him to win?*

"No."

> *What do you want?*

"The choice to decide."

I stare at the ceiling, rotating my wrists.

Heads or tails.

Pragmatic or enigmatic.

If I'm tail spinning headfirst down a dark path, I might as well make a list:

Pro: Justice
Con: Irreparable
Or is that another pro?

Who am I?

I stare at my beast's words, and at my hand that wrote them. I take a deep breath. "You are the darkest part of me," I say, my voice barely a whisper. "You are my rawest impulse, caged within the confines of my mind. And I can't set you free, because you can't be contained again. You're everything I've longed to be. You're unapologetic. You're the solution I've always feared. You are my beast, and you crave destruction."

If I am you,
then who are you?

"I'm human. I'm a daughter and a sister." The tone in my voice builds, unwavering. "I'm the coin's edge. I'm heads and tails."

More, more, more.

"I'm deceit and fire." I stand up, throwing my journal to the floor. "I'm a Cicada. And I am Apricus."

49

The bruises around his eyes are healing nicely. He can almost fully open his right. Four stitches line his right temple, his nose seems crooked, and his cheek is still swollen, but he'll live.

"Are you sure?" Henry asks, wincing as he pushes his glasses up his bridge.

I swallow the last mouthful of pear and throw the core away in the bin. "What's their verdict?" I ask, my tone cold and neutral.

He leans back, crossing his arms at his chest. "The viewers support whatever decision you make."

I figured as much. The audience loves a good show. But that's not all of who I meant, and Henry knows it. I hold in the sigh building in my chest. "And what of the government, Henry Cassidy. What do they have to say about this? I can't imagine a world where this would be allowed, but then again, I was born in Foxtrot. What do the Above's know about morals."

He doesn't flinch at the spitfire. He takes it in stride, nodding his head with a clever smile. "You have my word,

Samara. Everyone is supporting whatever finale you choose."

"And who are you to promise me as much when your words are full of carrion?"

He blinks hard, shoulders rising. He reaches into his shirt pocket and unfolds a piece of paper, sliding it to me. "That document grants amnesty, signed by the president herself."

I read the paper over and over, every detail, every sentence. Yes, this will do. I hand the document back to Henry and nod. I'd hate for the paper to be ruined. "When does he get here?" I ask.

"In ten minutes."

"And everyone will be watching?"

"Of course."

"Cicadas, too?"

"Yes."

Good. *We* are everyone.

"And you've had the valves shut off like we discussed?" I ask. A conspirator's grin warps his face. I examine my nails, tracing their edges as I play out the decision cemented in my mind. I can live with myself after this. "Repeat my demands."

Henry straightens up in the chair, removing a notepad from his back pocket. He clears his throat. "Calum Gryme will be brought into this room with a cloth over his face. The chains around his ankles will secure him under here." He knocks on the table. "Two cigars and two bottles of the highest proof alcohol with two glasses." He closes the notepad and sets it down, interlacing his fingers.

I shake my head, letting out a deliberate, irritated sigh. I stand up, pushing in the chair. "You're forgetting one thing."

Henry opens the notepad, his fingers brushing over the edges as he skims through it. The pages blur together, filled with his scraggly handwritten transcript of our last conversation—page after page after page. He mumbles under his breath, repeating the list of items. "I'm sorry, Samara. I'm not sure what's missing. What else do you need?"

I cross my right foot over my left, wearing a devilish pout. "A lighter, Henry. I need a lighter."

50

His chains softly clatter with each step, scraping against the ground with a metallic jingle. His arms swing in a casual rhythm at his sides, the fabric covering his face as timeless as the void inside me.

Two guards guide him to the table, sit him down, and lock him underneath. A dainty smile curls up my lips. I give them a delicate wave. "Remember to keep it unlocked," I call out with a wink as the door closes.

"I'm happy to speak with you and address any concerns, but are the chains necessary, Miss Quinn?" the Warden asks, his politician tone slipping out. He removes the cloth from his face and folds it neatly, setting it on the table.

"Quite," I say through a shit-eating grin, filling our glasses to the brim with a deliberate hand. "I rather enjoy having you escorted to me in such a manner, sweetheart." I fling his glass across the table, fast as a striking asp. The clear liquid sloshes over the edge, spilling onto the Warden's chest. He reaches out, catching the glass before it shatters on the floor. "I apologize, Warden. Let me pour you another glass."

"I must insist I pour my own, Miss Quinn." His fingers

355

motion for the bottle.

In a show of good faith, I down my glass, the liquid fire adding to my internal furnace, and pour myself another. I extend the bottle to the Warden. He nods gratefully, a vile, abhorrent, venomous smile curling his face. I release the plastic bottle before his hand closes around it. The liquid spills, cascading off the table's edge and soaking his pants.

He clears his throat and pours himself a glass, setting the bottle on the floor. "I'll keep this over here for now. You're making quite a mess."

"Do you find it interesting?" I ask, fingering the rim of my glass.

"Hard to say. I'm not sure what you mean."

I take a sip of alcohol, watching him mirror my motion. "Twice we've had the chance to talk, and both times you've said the same thing. That I've made a mess. I'm sure you'd—"

"—I suppose that's—"

"—No, no, Warden Gryme. I'm speaking. I'm sure you'd like to know why you've been brought here, and I'll be honest with you if you pay me the same respect. I asked for this meeting because I wanted to hear your side of it all. I have only a few questions, shouldn't take too long, then I'll be on my way. I don't expect we'll see each other again after this. Are you willing to humor me?"

He nods his head with a lazy smile.

I reach into my pocket, pulling out the cigars. Lighting one, I reach across and place it on the table in front of him.

Lighting the other, I take a slow drag, slipping the lighter back into my pocket, and ask, "Do you have any regrets?"

He leans back, taking a careful drag. "I did the best I could under the circumstances."

"That's not an answer."

"I'm sure some could argue I ran Foxtrot with an iron fist, but laws were necessary. Without them, the facility would've descended into chaos. I don't expect you to understand, Miss Quinn. Leadership demands making decisions that others can't. The difficult, unfathomable ones."

I click my tongue. "Still not an answer. Allow me to rephrase my question. Knowing what you know now, do you wish you had done things differently?"

He taps the cigar to his lips, teeth sinking into it. Reaching for his glass, he takes a sip, gravel in his tone. "I've been absolved."

"I understand." I pull off my thick cotton sweatshirt and set it on the table in front of us. "But the question remains. Think of it as morbid curiosity." I flash him my palms. "Would you have done anything differently?"

He leans back in the chair, placing a palm on his thigh. He moves to cross a leg, but the chains around his ankles snag, a wonderful *clang* echoing. He sighs, setting his foot down. "Not in the slightest. I did what had to be done to safeguard the facility. If it's an apology you're seeking, look elsewhere. You'll find none here."

Flicking off the ash, I lean in and set my cigar on the

sweater between us. "Thank you for the candor, Warden. I expected nothing less."

He reaches forward and picks up the lit cigar, snuffing it out on the table. "May I ask you something, Miss Quinn?"

I place a hand to my chest and give him a thankful wave. How *silly* of me to place glowing embers on top of fabric. What a fire hazard.

"Ask me anything."

A predatory hunger warps his features. "How did it feel going through so much trouble for nothing? The hope of reaching the surface was real enough, but was it worth the price? I imagine the reality of it destroyed your little mind. Was it painful when it tore through you? Were you gutted from the inside out? If you had waited, if you hadn't been selfish—had you not ignited a riot—this transition would've been smoother for everyone. So, tell me. Was it worth it?"

Devilish and proud, my inner beast smiles.

Tails, tails, tails.

Do it, do it, do it.

Embrace the madness.

Burn it down.

I rise from my chair, taking careful steps around the table. "It was worth every flip of the coin. You did it for power, I did it for a purpose, and I'd do it all over again. Same as you."

Standing beside him, I pick up the bottle from the floor and pour the rest of the liquor on him. He tugs at his damp shirt and wipes his hands on his pants, searching for a dry patch. But everything is such a mess. His chest, shirt, pants, shoes—covered in liquor. Atlantic, I'd say his skin is glistening.

My voice is steady, unyielding. "Tell me, Warden. Do you believe you're worthy of the surface?"

He sighs, crossing his arms at his chest. "Throw your fits, Miss Quinn, but it changes nothing. The experiment is finished. I was not the mastermind. I was merely a pawn, same as you. The surface belongs to everyone."

Warmth fills my chest cavity.

"Well, now I know you're lying," I whisper in his ear, my hand sliding into my back pocket. "You are a cancer, Warden Calum Gryme. And I will not allow people like you to live here."

A flick of my thumb, and the lighter sparks to life. I press it to his shirt and step back. The fire catches, spreading to his pants. He bats his thighs, his chest, his face, each frantic strike scattering the contagious flames.

I step around the table and lean forward, the heat licking my skin. I tip his glass of alcohol onto my sweater sprawled across the table and light the fabric, sliding it into his lap.

Guttural and raw, his screams amplify. Moving erratically, his hands swat the flames spreading across him like wildfire. He thrashes in his chair, tugging desperately at the chains binding him in place. The acrid, sulfuric stench of burning hair clings to my senses. I breathe it in with a smile, dragging the wooden bed frame across the room and

LYNZEE SCHOTT

propping it at his side.

Opening the second bottle of alcohol hidden under the pillow, I take a swig and dump the rest of it onto the mattress. In an instant, the mattress, blankets, pillows, and madness journal ignite in a hungry blaze.

The flames dance and twirl.

Spreading, spreading, spreading.

"*This* is the fire Jerald wrote about." I give his burning body a bow and pull the door shut behind me.

Acknowledgements

I woke up one day and told my husband, "I want to write a book about a doomsday bunker in the ocean." And he said, "Do it!" And he's reminded me to keep doing it, even when I didn't want to, because writing is hard and getting in my own way is easy. His support is truly endless. I couldn't thank him enough.

Ginormous thanks to my son for saying I'm cool for writing a book. That inspiration carried me to the last chapter.

To my mom and dad, who always made sure I had journals as a kid, thank you for showing me there's an outlet for my thoughts.

Special thanks to my dogs, Pesci and Penelope, for all the snorting and licking sounds during moments of quiet when I was trying to concentrate—that wasn't annoying at all. And to my cats Sullivan and Zucchini for keeping my side of the bed warm when I was tired of writing goblin-hunched on the couch.

To my Developmental Editor, Kourtney Spak, thank you for diving headfirst into Foxtrot (lack of contractions and all in that first edit) and for encouraging me to see it through.

To everyone who heard me ramble and complain these last few years while I explored my writing journey, words can't describe my gratitude. Sometimes saying nonsense out loud with no direction helps my brain not be jumbled—thank you for listening.

www.ingramcontent.com/pod-product-compliance
Lightning Source LLC
Chambersburg PA
CBHW020548120726
47903CB00001B/187